Ralph,

Good Luck & God!
I wish you the best &
enjoy.

R J Denys

MW01592424

RJDenys @ comcast.net

THE HUNTER
CONCEPTION

R.J. Denys

Bloomington, IN  Milton Keynes, UK

authorHOUSE

AuthorHouse™
1663 Liberty Drive, Suite 200
Bloomington, IN 47403
www.authorhouse.com
Phone: 1-800-839-8640

AuthorHouse™ UK Ltd.
500 Avebury Boulevard
Central Milton Keynes, MK9 2BE
www.authorhouse.co.uk
Phone: 08001974150

First published by AuthorHouse 9/19/2006

ISBN: 1-4259-4167-2 (sc)
ISBN: 1-4259-4166-4 (dj)

Library of Congress Control Number: 2006904810

Printed in the United States of America
Bloomington, Indiana

This book is printed on acid-free paper.

CHAPTER 1

AS PART OF THE MASS of teenagers that emptied onto the campus of South Lakes High School at the end of school, Eric walked to the car that was parked in the same space every day. The school parking lot of this affluent Northern Virginia suburb of Washington more resembled a youthful auto show, the position of a vehicle signifying the status of the person who owned it or rode in it.

He leaned against the sparkling black convertible in the front of the lot waiting for his two friends as herds of students slowly stampeded past the front-rowers, many gawking as they rambled by. His shirt lay slung over his shoulder revealing the sleek, athletic body that developed over the past school year while his sandy blond hair fluttered in the gentle breeze. Just the way he leaned against the car exuded confidence and it was that confidence that many mistook as arrogance. Yet, Eric always had been confident in everything he did mainly as a matter of survival

1

at this school where who you were meant more than what you did, but also as compensation for what he perceived to be a lack in size or height when he was younger. Now, at almost six feet tall with a more muscular build, his only shortcoming disappeared while his confidence intensified.

His friend Jimmy, the owner of the car, appeared across the lot, shuffling toward the vehicle with a girl hanging on his arm. He was a larger, nearly mirrored personality of Eric, never lacking for confidence in himself in anything he did either. His taller than six foot frame stood solid and he possessed a natural strength that augmented itself around people he didn't know or like, becoming imposing when his quick temper triggered. Intelligent but undisciplined, Jimmy typified the rich-man's son, having all the opportunities that life could afford well within his reach.

Before he arrived at his car, he kissed the girl hanging on his arm and watched her walk toward another section of the parking lot, then continued. He silently tossed several books into the back seat and joined his friend watching the crowd as it dispersed into the latter rows of lesser vehicles.

Looking beyond the lot, the two spotted the third of the group, Greg, jogging across the lawn from the athletic fields, an equipment bag strapped over his shoulder. As the leader of the three, Greg was an intelligent and logical young man who thought through everything he did with painstaking detail. Physically, he was just as impressive. Though by no means did he present an imposing figure, his strength attained from years of playing sports and lifting weights compensated for any lack of size. His short-styled, light brown hair and model-perfect looks enhanced by clothes chosen to accentuate his chiseled body attracted the ladies in droves.

Greg threw his bag into the back seat and stood next to his friends, waiting for the right time to leave as protocol dictated the three stay until most of the students passed the front-rowers. They watched as row after row of vehicles emptied onto the traffic clogged road that passed in front of the school.

Silently, Jimmy pushed away from the car then turned and climbed in as the other two copied his motion. "Thank God there's only two more weeks of this crap left!" He exclaimed as he started the engine.

"Yeah," Greg agreed. "I'm looking forward to summer. You doin' your usual country club bit?"

"Hell yeah!" Jimmy exclaimed. "I get a good tan, save a gorgeous girl from drowning and get laid in the number seven sand trap. Y'know, the tough things a lifeguard must go through." He bragged as he zipped out of the parking lot into traffic.

"Maybe some other lifeguard." Eric added from the back seat. "All you do is help some old fat lady with her lounge chair and yell at little brats for pissing in the pool."

"Real funny Eric. So what are you doin', playin' chef at the Reston Tavern again?" Jimmy teased.

"You're a little behind the times there Jimbo." Eric replied. "I've been working at Saddlewood."

"Saddlewood?" Jimmy repeated. "What the hell is Saddlewood, a horse farm where you spend hours upon hours shoveling shit?"

"You're real close Einstein." Eric sarcastically answered. "It's a private resort near Middleburg."

"Why do you drive all the way to Middleburg for a job?" Jimmy asked.

"Because they pay me twenty bucks an hour." Eric informed.

"Damn!" Jimmy shouted. "Twenty bucks an hour! What do you have to do for that kind of money?"

"It's not so much what I have to do, it's what I have to know." Eric arrogantly answered.

"And what do you know that's so special?" Jimmy asked, looking at Eric through the rear view mirror.

"Right now I know you're about ready to crash into that car." He calmly replied as Jimmy slammed on the brakes, screeching the car to a halt as the three braced for a collision with the car ahead of them.

Quickly, the car came to a complete stop, narrowly avoiding colliding with the vehicle ahead. Greg forced air out of his mouth in relief, then turned toward Jimmy, his face red with anger. "What the hell are you trying to do, get us killed?" He yelled. "Keep your eyes on the damn road!"

Jimmy leaned his head backward against the seat and exhaled, the color of his skin drained to a pale white. "Yeah, I will." He replied, still in shock by the close call. "Sorry about that."

Eric leaned forward from the back seat, uncharacteristically composed. "That's okay, nobody got hurt." He calmly stated. "Are you okay to drive?"

Jimmy quickly nodded his head. "Yeah, thanks. I really didn't need to have anything more happen this week. I'm already in a load of shit with the old man about the car."

Greg removed his shirt and wiped the sweat from his face and head, the result of the near collision. "What did you do?" He asked.

The traffic light turned green and Jimmy continued. "Yesterday after the game, this girl and I went out and had a little fun. Dad found out and wanted to beat my ass." He explained.

"I take it this girl wasn't Allison." Eric inquired.

Jimmy shook his head. "No. I met this girl last weekend. Allison doesn't know anything about this." He replied.

"Well there's a surprise." Eric sarcastically began. "You going out with a girl other than the one you're dating."

"It's no big deal Eric. She goes to Herndon so Allison will never find out." Jimmy said.

"No, they never do." Eric replied, his sarcasm evident from the tone of his voice. "Have you not learned anything from me?"

Greg interrupted. "Let me get this straight. Your dad got pissed off at you because you went out and got laid. That doesn't sound like Ray, so what sent him over the edge?" He asked.

"He found some evidence." Jimmy answered.

"Evidence." Eric repeated. "What'd he find a couple of opened packages of your favorite brand of condoms and a six pack?"

Jimmy nodded. "You're close. But so you know, I didn't really get laid. We just, you know, fooled around a little." He began to explain. "But what he found was a loose bottle of one of those little Lynchburg Lemonades underneath the seat this morning before he went to work because, like an idiot, I blocked him in the driveway and he had to move my car."

"Damn." Greg sympathetically stated. "I'm sorry to hear that."

"So was I." Jimmy replied. "So Eric, what's up with this job? What knowledge makes you so special that they pay you twenty bucks an hour to do whatever you do?"

"I don't think what I know is all that special." He answered, pausing but hinting there was more to the response. The fact remained that Eric was special and the people at Saddlewood recognized it.

Eric was gifted, possessing the ability to master almost anything he attempted, whether intellectually or athletically. He was fluent in Spanish, a benefit of having a family who traveled frequently. Then, he quickly learned French through language instruction at Saddlewood. He excelled in sports, being one of the names at the top of many college soccer recruiting lists as well as an excellent swimmer at his high school, then he quickly mastered an equestrian course as part of his training for work. And because he was gifted, he was a perfect fit for Saddlewood.

Saddlewood, however, was also a perfect fit for Eric. He was exceptional in athletics and academics as well as in the social skills required for his job as a service specialist. It was the kind of environment Eric would easily excel in and the training he received made him ever more confident when dealing with people, as if he needed more. That extra confidence became an asset, especially with a position that required continuous interaction with heads of state, ambassadors and corporate magnets. Yet with all of the excellence associated with his employment at Saddlewood, there remained an aura of mystery in the purpose of aspects of his duties. And that mystery puzzled him.

He could understand learning new languages, etiquette and briefings related to unusual customs of the many cultures that make up the world. As an extension of the United Nations,

Saddlewood was an embassy financed and administered as an international peace retreat, hosting people from all over the world, so certain classes only made sense. What perplexed him involved the teaching of self-defense, evasive driving and marksmanship. What was the purpose of this kind of instruction in a facility that promoted peace and diplomacy? The answer eluded him and he never finished his response to his friends because of it.

The car slowly turned onto a tree-lined street, easing along the road until it stopped beside the curb in front of a large two-story professionally landscaped house where two men in suits stood in the driveway next to a car. Greg stared at the two wondering why his father and his father's boss stopped home so early in the day. They worked near Washington, Greg's father Daniel as an assistant U.S. Attorney and his superior, Matthew Collins, the United States Attorney for the Eastern District of Virginia. It was unusual for them to be at the Bostic home together and though his curiosity begged him to ask, Greg did not.

He hopped out of the car and greeted them as he walked past, Eric following closely behind, while Jimmy squealed his tires during his departure. Greg avoided beginning any type of conversation. To him, Matt Collins was somewhat intimidating, though in a friendly sort of way. Maybe it was his position or the relationship he enjoyed with the Justice Department. Whatever the reason, Greg felt uncomfortable around the man, a feeling that Eric did not share or understand. But then, Eric dealt with the man more often, serving as the soccer coach for the Collins' son, Tyler, so he stopped to speak with him.

In truth, Collins was intimidating and he built a reputation among his peers as a master investigator and aggressive prosecutor. He earned the appointment to his position for his ability to break open investigations and obtain convictions on cases where most would fail. Because he was so successful, he was highly regarded by the Justice Department and would be asked to assist with many difficult cases in order to capitalize on his prosecutorial excellence, an excellence he attributed to the instruction he received in college at Duke and law school at the University of Virginia. And as the man concluded his conversation with Eric in laughter, entered the car with Greg's father and drove away, Greg questioned his own discomfort around the man who seemed so amiable.

The two boys walked into the house, dropping their duffel bags onto the floor in the entryway on their way to the kitchen where Greg opened the door to the refrigerator. He removed a drink container and a series of food items placing them on a table. "Are you hungry?" He asked, pulling two plates and glasses off a cupboard shelf.

"Do you really need to ask?" Eric replied, moving the food to the center island.

Greg looked backward toward his friend and chuckled. "No, not really." He said, tossing a loaf of bread on the island. "I hope you don't have plans for tonight because Jen wants us to go to the cages."

Appearing puzzled, Eric glanced at his friend. "She wants *us* to go to the cages." He repeated. "I thought *you* had a date tonight."

"Well, I do." Greg answered. "But, Jen wants to meet us at the cages tonight." He stated as he built a sandwich.

"And I'm supposed to go with you?" Eric asked, still puzzled.

"I see you understand the concept of us." Greg sarcastically stated. "She wants you to come as well."

Eric bit into his sandwich, chewed then swallowed. "On *your* date, she wants me there on *your* date." He said. "What's up with that?"

Greg grinned. "Nothin'!" He exclaimed. "I swear!"

"You swear." Eric repeated then began to laugh. "Every time you swear, you're lying. What do you have planned?"

Greg shook his head, and then conceded. "Okay look, it wasn't my idea, but we do have something planned."

Eric slowly nodded his head. "I know you do. So . . . who am I getting fixed up with?" He asked.

Greg took a drink from his glass. "So then you don't mind?"

"That depends on who I'm getting fixed up with." Eric replied. "I have standards."

"Yeah right, your only standard is if she's breathing." Greg replied.

Eric grinned. "That's not true."

"Now who's lying?" Greg interrupted. "But anyway, there's a hot girl who actually thinks you're boyfriend material."

"Really?" Eric asked. "Does she have a name?"

"It's Beth Wilshire." Greg answered.

"Beth Wilshire." Eric mimicked. "No, really who is it?"

"Beth Wilshire." Greg repeated.

Eric's eyebrows raised into a look of surprise. "Does she know she's getting fixed up with me?" He asked, an air of surprise in his voice.

Greg grinned. "It was her idea." He stated. "And I was just as surprised as you, but I take it you don't mind."

"You're fixing me up with one of the hottest girls in school and ask me if I mind. Hell no I don't mind!" He exclaimed.

Greg arrogantly nodded his head and smiled. "I didn't think you would." He stated, knowing Eric would be excited about a date with this girl more than any other.

For many years, Beth Wilshire unknowingly became the object of Eric's affection, the girl he could never conquer. From the first day that he met her in his first week of high school, his attraction to her strengthened. They gradually became friends, yet he avoided telling her of his true feelings for her. It wasn't his style. She would have to go to him, yet never did. Now, all that seemed to change.

He finished his sandwich and drink, placing his empty plate and glass in the sink, then thanked Greg as he picked up his bag and raced out the door. Elated with the thought of the date, he seemingly floated along the street past the four homes that separated his house from Greg's. He entered through the front door and raced up the stairs to his room, throwing his bag on his bed and pulling open his closet doors. If he was going out with the girl he desired for so long, the impression he made was all-important. He surveyed his wardrobe, carefully choosing a set of clothes then changing into a pair of shorts to return outside.

Standing in the driveway when Eric walked out of the house was Jimmy, leaning a bicycle against the garage. He looked at Eric and half raised his hand as he shuffled toward him. "What's up?" Jimmy asked.

Eric shook his head. "Nothing much." He answered, a puzzled look forming across his face. " Why this sudden switch to pedal power?"

"Ray said I burn up too much gas." Jimmy answered.

"He took the car away from you, didn't he?" Eric stated.

Jimmy slowly nodded his head. "Yeah. He's really pissed about finding that bottle under the seat."

"I'm sorry to hear that." Eric replied. "He didn't ground you too, did he?"

Jimmy shrugged his shoulders, simultaneously shaking his head. "I don't know. One thing I do know, if I could find a way not to be home when he gets back, I wouldn't be there." He said, pausing for a moment. "So, what are you doing tonight?"

Eric smiled. "I have a date tonight." He proudly stated.

Jimmy hesitated as if he didn't hear his friend correctly. "You have a date. An actual date or a carnal meeting between two bodies?" He asked.

Eric chuckled in an irritated sort of way, a snarled look pasted on his face as he squinted he eyes and shook his head. "An actual date."

Jimmy laughed. "I'm sorry buddy, it's just that I didn't think you could settle down to just one girl for a period of time." He stated. "But it's cool. I hope you have a good time."

Eric smiled, nodding his head. "Thanks. So what are you up to tonight?" He asked.

I was supposed to go out with Allison, but I don't know how I'm gonna do that now." Jimmy said.

"Get her to drive." Eric suggested.

Jimmy scowled at him. "And have her pick me up at the house with Ray all in my face? That's not a good idea, especially since my dad thinks she was the one with me." He answered.

"And you don't want it brought up in front of her." Eric added. "That's the big problem, isn't it?"

Jimmy nodded his head, dropping it lower until he broke off eye contact. He sighed deeply, a sullen mood overtaking him as he stared at the ground. "You know," He began, pausing for a moment to collect his thoughts. "Just to be an ass, he'll say something to her about it and that will end everything. Goodbye Allison."

"You think he would do that to you?" Eric asked in disbelief.

Jimmy raised his head and glared. "Of course he would." He coolly stated, his eyes swelling in a hurtful anger. "Listen...do you think I can stay at your house for the weekend? Ya know, until he cools off a little."

"Is it that bad?" Eric asked.

Jimmy pressed his lips together and nodded. "You know how he gets." He began. "Well this morning, I thought he was gonna kill me. He threw me against the wall dude."

"He threw you against the wall?" Eric repeated. "All right, go pack some stuff and come on back. We'll figure things out when you return, but you can stay here this weekend."

"Thanks." Jimmy said as he half-hugged his friend. He grabbed his bicycle, hopped on and turned. "See you in a little bit." He said as he rode away.

Eric watched him as he pedaled down the street, angered that his friend experienced another conflict with his father, though he was not completely sure of the severity of the incident. Jimmy tended to exaggerate at times. Lately, however, Ray and Jimmy Thomas constantly seemed to be at odds with each other, getting into verbal battles that, on at least one occasion, turned physical. It was that incident that Eric thought about and caused him to become concerned. The memory of seeing Jimmy beaten by his father with no attempt to defend himself flashed through his mind. It was an episode that exposed vulnerability in Jimmy that neither Greg nor Eric knew existed before and made them aware of a situation they could never believe would happen.

Ray was a good father. He cared deeply about his children and spent a great deal of time with them. But as Jimmy got older and began to assert his independence, tensions began to build. Maybe it was the way Jimmy did things. Admittedly, he could be an ass and probably deserved to get his butt kicked every once in a while, but not by his father. Eric hoped this was just Jimmy trying to avoid being disciplined and not something more.

He walked across the yard and sat under the tree, leaning against the trunk and scanning the neighborhood soaking in the warmth of the late May afternoon. In the distance, he saw his brother strolling along the sidewalk toward home. Kevin was a good kid, someone Eric loved deeply and felt proud to call his brother as well as his friend. And as brothers, they experienced some of the same problems that other brothers did. They argued, competed against each other with the fervor of ardent rivals and teased each other, sometimes unmercifully. But unlike so many of the brothers that Eric's friends had, Kevin never became annoying in the many ways that brothers can be; wanting to tag along or instigate conflicts or invade privacy or the other thousand ways a brother finds. Instead he respected every aspect of Eric's life, earning that same respect in return.

Kevin approached the house, seeing Eric sitting under the tree then joining him. "I saw Jimmy ride by, was he over here?"

"Yeah." Eric answered. "He's getting some clothes so he can stay the weekend."

"That's a good idea." Kevin stated. "He needs to get away from his dad for a while."

"Do you know what happened?" Eric asked, staring out into the neighborhood then glancing back at his brother.

"Yeah." Kevin replied, nodding his head. "Shawn told me in school. Did Jimmy tell you the story?"

Eric shrugged his shoulders. "He told me his side of it." He stated. "What did Shawn tell you?"

Kevin hesitated for a moment. "Shawn told me that his dad and Jimmy got into a fight this morning, a real fight." He answered. "Ray hit him a couple of times Eric and then threw him against the wall in the family room. Shawn had to break it up."

"Is Shawn okay?" Eric inquired.

Kevin nodded his head. "Yeah, but he made me promise not to tell anyone about it. So please don't say anything."

Eric scowled. "You know what's said between us stays between us." He stated as he stood and pulled his brother up with him.

"Yeah I know." Kevin replied. "So, was that what Jimmy told you?"

Eric slowly nodded his head. "Yeah, except for Ray hitting him." He replied as he placed his arm around his brother's neck and guided him toward the house. "But he'd never admit to that anyway."

"He's a tough kid." Kevin responded while directing his attention toward Jimmy who rode up the street, a backpack strapped to his body.

Eric watched him as he hopped off the bike and walked it onto the driveway, parking it beside the garage. He thought about talking to Jimmy about the situation but decided to respect his privacy, for now. Instead, he smiled at his friend and led him into the house.

CHAPTER 2

THE ALARM ON THE RADIO sitting on the stand next to the bed sounded as the numbers changed to five-thirty. Slowly, an arm escaped the cocoon of blankets and blindly searched, without success, for the button that would end the raucous that so rudely invaded his sleep. Eric pulled his head from the mass, squinting to find the switch to turn off the alarm finally putting an end to the annoying sound. For a moment, he laid in bed, eyes barely opened but staring at the ceiling with his arms cupped over the top of his head. He rubbed his eyes and attempted to sit up, his body feeling heavy as if fighting gravity, then swung his legs from beneath the blankets to hang over the side of the bed. As he sat motionless in the darkness of the room Eric thought how early it was for him to be doing anything, let alone going to work.

He reached to the nightstand and turned the knob of the lamp once to engage the light to it's lowest setting, casting a mellow glow throughout the room. Standing and shuffling away from the bed, he removed a pair of jeans and a shirt from his closet, separating them from their hangers and tossing them on his bed. He picked up a pair of shorts hanging on the back of a chair and put them on over his boxers, then walked to a chest of drawers, grabbed another pair of boxers and shuffled to the bathroom to quickly take a shower, careful not to wake anyone else.

After dressing, Eric walked downstairs toward the kitchen. Had his senses not been affected by the earliness of the hour, he might have smelled the aroma of fresh coffee brewing and not been surprised to see his parents sitting at the table. Instead as he shuffled into the room, the sight of his parents briefly startled him since he expected no one to be there. He smiled, realizing they woke early on their day off to prepare breakfast and have it waiting for him at his usual place at the table, something they didn't have to do. But then, they were always doing unexpected things like this, not only for him but also for his brother and sister.

He knew he had a special family, from caring and devoting parents who set the guidelines for each child to follow, to his brother Kevin, who he preferred hanging out with over many of his friends, and his sister Kristen, the baby of the family. And as he picked up a fork and began to devour the meal, he thanked them and conversed with them between bites knowing that he would have to eat quickly in order not to be late for work. When he finished, he apologized to his mother for having to leave so soon, then kissed her goodbye and hugged his father before he bolted out the door, jumping into the car.

As he drove the nearly empty roads of the Virginia suburbs on a Saturday morning just after six, Eric recalled his job last year as a line cook at one of the local restaurants, laughing that his greatest responsibility was making sure that some side dish found its way to the tray to complete an order. But then he was only fifteen and not expected to be very responsible. Now at sixteen, seventeen in two short weeks, his life changed to where responsibility was not only expected, but required.

As he approached the security gate of the employee's entrance to Saddlewood, he reached into his shirt pocket and removed his identification badge, a credit card looking piece of plastic with his picture and name on the front and a magnetic strip on the back. Eric inserted it into a slot on a control box and slid it downward, the gate blocking the passage through rising moments later. He continued on, parking his car in a space near a sculptured garden and walking toward the building.

There was a certain order to an employee's arrival to work, an order reflecting the importance of even the seemingly unimportant jobs. He entered the massive operations office complex through a set of security doors, again using his badge to gain entry and continued through the reception atrium to a set of stairs he descended. At the bottom, he followed a short corridor to the male employee clubhouse where he slid his badge through the slot of a panel on the wall, gaining access. Inside, where each staff member stops upon arrival and before leaving, a man at a service counter distributes the clothing needs for that day, pre-wrapped and packed according to the request of the work supervisor.

Eric examined his equipment and garment bags, seeing his pager, which he was required to carry while on duty, as well as his regular uniforms, a combination of navy blue and saddle tan shirts, trousers, shorts and socks, accompanied by black formal wear, clothing not often requested, indicating a special event. He walked to his assigned locker and changed into his uniform, storing his personal clothing inside. He was ready for work and exited the clubhouse, retrieving his electrically powered golf cart for his ride to the guesthouse.

The villa was magnificent, a French country style home wrapped by flower gardens surrounded by a variety of trees, all accessed from a deep crimson smooth stone lane that encircled a fountain in front of the house and was untouched by combustion engine vehicles. As impressive as the outside grounds, the interior of the villa boasted eight professionally decorated guest suites, private lounges and formal and informal dining areas, resembling a five-star quality private hotel within the borders of the resort. And though each guesthouse could function as such, the dozen villas that were spread over Virginia's rolling foothills contained within Saddlewood were designed to be privately leased by the world's elite.

Eric turned left onto the villa's service lane, concealed from the sight of the guesthouse by groves of trees and flowering bushes, and parked his cart in the underside open port tucked beneath a garden and outdoor terrace that flanked the formal dining room. He entered the villa through the port's service entrance and ascended a staircase to the main floor, walking into the employee center where he placed his gear into his assigned cubicle in the men's dressing room.

Inside the lounge the other service specialist, Aaron Butler, lay sleeping on the sofa. A junior political science student at Georgetown, Aaron was Eric's mentor and friend at Saddlewood, teaching him the nuances of concierge duties that formal training did not provide and intuition any other person couldn't. Aaron was brilliant, possessing a refined intelligence that impressed all who crossed the path of the extremely affable young man; and Eric greatly respected him.

Quietly, Eric walked to the opposite side of the room and seated himself in an overstuffed chair next to the window, careful not to wake his friend. On the table next to his chair sat the latest edition of the Washington Post, which he picked up and began to read trying not to crinkle the pages and make noise.

"You do know that I'm awake don't you?" Aaron asked, sliding his arm over his eyes.

Eric folded the newspaper downward and peered toward the sofa. "I do now." He answered, pausing as he briefly stared. "You look kind of rough over there."

Aaron pulled his arm away from his face, opening one eye to look. "Thanks." He sarcastically replied. "I only slept for a couple of hours but I thought I covered it well."

"You didn't." Eric said as he slowly shook his head.

"And again, I say thanks." Aaron quipped. "What time is this meeting supposed to start?"

"Eight." Eric answered.

Aaron lifted himself upright on the sofa, rubbing his face then standing. "What time is it now?" He asked.

Eric glanced at his watch while he replaced the folded paper on the end table then answered. "Five after eight."

Aaron shook his head and grinned. "Punctuality has never been one of Stephen's strengths. You want a cup of coffee?" He asked as he walked to an urn, flipped a cup onto a saucer and poured.

"No thanks." Eric replied. "What's this all about?"

Aaron grabbed his shirt that he had neatly placed on a hanger then took a sip from the cup, answering as he leaned against the table. "The people who leased this villa for the last couple of months requested some changes. I guess he's going to go over them with us?" He stated.

Eric stood and stretched. "Only us?" He asked. "I would have thought that he would call everyone in."

"He was supposed to." Aaron answered. "But I don't know where they are."

"They're waiting for you in the dining room." A man interrupted as he entered the room. It was Stephen Kearney, the manager and executive chef of the villa.

Kearney was somewhat of an enigma at Saddlewood. A graduate of the Culinary Institute of America where he earned a master chef degree, Kearney passed on many opportunities to manage and share ownership of some of the east's finest restaurants in order to secure this position within Saddlewood's borders, a position he held since the facility opened. It puzzled many as to why, but to Kearney, Saddlewood presented challenges unequaled by any independent establishment. Here, his talents were exposed to the world and because of that exposure, his skills as a chef became known throughout the diplomatic and corporate community. He built a reputation that emerged to be one of the most respected and one that he attributed more to where he worked than what he did.

Kearney led the two young men into the dining room, joining the remainder of the staff that assembled minutes before. Though this was by far not the first meeting he ever conducted, it was the most unusual. As it had so many times previous, the villa had been leased by an international group, though this time by a company headquartered in Liechtenstein named Terra Nova Recursa, Ltd. TNR, as it had listed itself, was an unknown in the corporate community and professed to be a world research consultant, in other words, a global think tank.

For the past two months while Eric had done the bulk of his training, contributors to the TNR collective shuffled in and out of the guest home. They were quiet and reflective in their stay, except for the scheduled meetings they held once per week, requesting nothing but the solitude the villa had to offer. Now, as a condition of extending the lease for the next six months, they requested additional services.

It wasn't the request for additional service that struck anyone as odd. Many previous guests amended their agreements. It was the type of service requested that surprised the staff, all geared to protect the identities of the guests and control their interaction with the staff. And as compensation for the execution of these unusual requirements, TNR offered to pay the staff a significantly higher rate, a covert bribe to be left alone.

As the small staff exited the dining room following the meeting, private discussions concerning their compensation dominated the activity. It was an exorbitant amount that Eric quickly calculated in his head, his eyes growing larger as he realized the figure. And within two steps, he smiled, planning the distribution of his newfound fortune.

Preparing for the group's arrival for the day, he walked through the house checking details in these last minutes, hoping that all was in line. Satisfied with its look, he returned to his desk patiently waiting for his pager to sound the warning of an arriving guest and within minutes, it signaled. He stood and checked himself in the mirror, then moved to his position standing outside of the front door waiting for the guest shuttle to arrive.

Emerging from between the tree line on the stone lane appeared a vehicle that circled around the fountain in front, stopping at the entrance to the villa. One man climbed out of the shuttle, straightened his personally tailored clothing and spoke to the driver who was removing the man's luggage to bring inside. As the man scanned the grounds, Eric watched him. It was not that the man just looked around; he appeared to be memorizing every detail of the area, obsessively searching for an unknown object in the style of the Secret Service. Once he rotated a full three hundred and sixty degrees seeming satisfied with the surroundings, he continued forward, meeting Eric at the door.

"Welcome to Saddlewood and Une Maison de Campagne sir." Eric greeted as he opened the door. "Right this way please."

"Thank you." The man replied as he entered the building. "But I hope you don't have to do that every time I come here, do you?"

"What sir?" Eric asked, puzzled by the question.

"Formally greet me to Saddlewood and this particular villa." The man answered. "I have been here before."

"Yes sir, I'm sorry. I'll make sure that it does not happen again." Eric replied.

The man smiled. "Thank you." He said. "What is your name son?"

"Eric sir." He answered as he closed the door behind them.

"No no, your last name. First names are far too informal." The man stated, scanning the interior as he stood in the entrance hall.

"It's Lynch sir." Eric replied. If there is anything you need, please feel free to call for me. May I show you to your room?"

"Thank you. That would be fine." The man said as he followed the boy. "Mr. Lynch, you seem to be a little young to be working here."

Eric stopped before he ascended the staircase. "I'm sorry?"

"You seem to be a little young to be working here. I'm sure you are of legal working age, it is just that I was expecting someone a little less... puerile?" the man stated.

Eric turned and began to lead the man upstairs. "I certainly understand that sir. Would you like me to find someone closer to your age to work with?" He offered.

"Are you able to do that?" The man asked.

Eric stopped at the top of the stairs, turned to the man and smiled. "Actually, no. You're pretty much stuck with me."

The man returned the smile before he replied. "I am. What makes you think that you are able to work with me?"

"Other than the fact that I taped a kick me sign to your back when you called me puerile, what makes you think I am not able to work with you?" Eric answered as he opened the door to a suite, placing the man's luggage that sat outside the door on the stand in next to the sofa. "I assure you that my maturity far exceeds my youthful appearance."

Again the man smiled. "I respect a man who does not back down to me as well as one who possesses a sense of humor. You will do just fine Mr. Lynch and I apologize for any indiscretion in my choice of words."

"Thank you sir. If there is not anything else at the moment, I need to prepare for the arrival of the remainder of your party." Eric announced.

"Again, thank you Mr. Lynch. Please inform the other gentleman that I expect to see them at the brunch I've arranged for noon. By the way, what time do you leave this evening?"

"Four o'clock sir." Eric answered. "May I ask why?"

"I wanted to inform you that I will be expecting a late arrival, sometime after five o'clock." The man stated. "However, he will not be staying with us this weekend."

"So then you only need seven rooms." Eric concluded.

The man shook his head in disagreement. "No, there are nine people in our party this evening. Only eight are staying."

Eric nodded his head. "Yes sir. I'll inform my replacement. Will there be anything else?"

The man paused for a moment, looking around the room, then directed his attention back toward the young man. "No, thank you."

"Thank you sir." Eric replied and he turned, leaving the room. As he descended the stairs, once again his pager signaled the imminent arrival of additional guests.

Two larger shuttles appeared through the trees on the lane as they approached the guesthouse, rounded the fountain and stopped in front. Seven men, their suits also personally tailored, sat in the passenger compartment of each vehicle waiting for the chauffeurs and attendants to open the doors to let them out. As they exited the vehicles, they stood on the deep crimson stone of the drive and quickly surveyed the grounds before walking toward the villa. They were an interesting collection of people, their ages the only common characteristic among them.

As the men gathered around the shuttles speaking with one another, Eric quickly studied the four most boisterous of the group and attempted to figure where these four men came from. After serving so many people from around the world, he became good at determining, from just a quick observation, from where a person hailed and how that person would act before ever meeting him. And he wondered this time how close he could come to actually guessing the personalities of these four people correctly.

As a group, the men walked toward the door, their luggage carried to their rooms by the four operators who unloaded the shuttle. Eric greeted the men at the door, introducing himself, and then guided them to their rooms, reminding them of their brunch meeting in the dining room, but gaining no response other than the occasional thank you. The coldness of the men irritated him, but he half-smiled and nodded his head, maintaining his professionalism as he returned downstairs and entered the kitchen.

Kearney stood at a stainless steel counter preparing food when the young man entered. "Did you get our guests all settled in?" He asked.

"Yeah. They're a real friendly bunch by the way." Eric answered, the sarcasm in his voice showing his displeasure with the men.

"Did you have any problems?" The man inquired, stopping his work momentarily.

"Other than the brief conversation I had with the first man becoming a little condescending, no." Eric replied.

"Though I'm sorry that happened, you understand that every once in a while, a guest may treat you that way without realizing it." Kearney said, resuming his work. "You just have to let it run past you and work harder to show them you are on the same playing field with them. And you are Eric, don't let anyone tell you differently."

Eric nodded. "Thank you sir. Do you need anything from me right now?" He asked.

Slowly Kearney shook his head as he concentrated on his work. "No, we're covered until after brunch."

"Then if you'll excuse me, I've got some work to do out back. If you need me, please page me."

"I'll see you later." Kearney replied.

Eric turned and walked out of the kitchen, returning to the employee lounge. He logged onto the computer at his desk to check for messages, and then entered the men's dressing room to change into his outdoor uniform, a more comfortable, less formal wear consisting of navy shorts, a tan polo-type shirt and sneakers.

After descending the stairs to the lower lever and removing a small kit and a skimming net from a storage room, he strolled outside to the pool, inspecting the patio and landscaped terraces that provided privacy on either side. Once he completely circled the area, he bent over, placed the kit on the patio floor and opened it, removing a small vial and dipping it into the water.

"The water looks crystal clear." A voice sounded from behind him.

Eric looked over his shoulder to see the first man who arrived at the villa peering over top of him. "I like to keep it that way." He said as he continued, dropping several drops of a clear liquid into the vial that colored the water. "Is there something you need sir?"

"You're not the same young man who worked here back in March." The man stated.

"I'm sorry?" Eric responded, implying to the man to repeat the statement.

"You aren't the same one." The man restated. "I visited this exact villa in March and do not remember a Mr. Lynch working at Une Maison de Campagne."

Eric stood, reassembled the kit and placed it on a nearby table. "No sir, you would not. I didn't start her until April." He answered as he picked up the skimming net and began plucking small petals and bugs out of the water.

"I see." The man said, pausing for a moment then continuing. "Did you replace someone or do the other gentlemen continue to work here?"

"I replaced someone." Eric replied as he continued his work. He retrieved a leaf out of the water and picked it off of the net, and then looking at the man he continued. "I get the impression that you were expecting a different person to work with and am disappointed that I am working here."

The man shook his head, keeping silent until Eric moved to the opposite end of the pool. "No, that's not it at all. I struck a good working relationship with one of the people and was looking forward to meeting with him again. Which one did you say remained?"

"Actually, I didn't." Eric replied, realizing that the man was fishing for information. "However, Aaron Butler is the other service specialist for this villa."

"Thank you. He unfortunately isn't the one I dealt with before." The man stated, pausing for a moment before continuing. "You know, I hope my speaking with you now is not hindering your work."

Eric smiled. The man wasn't keeping him from work. No, it was more that, in addition to the man clearly uncomfortable with Eric's employment at the villa, he had become irritating, following Eric closely around the pool and watching his every move as if he were being studied. And yet Eric knew that no matter how annoying the man became, he had to remain polite because his job required a special diplomacy. So he continued feigning a smile as he answered, masking his sarcasm. "No sir, not at all. In fact, I must apologize for working during this conversation."

The man interrupted, shaking his head and waving his arm. "No, no you do not. I know what your responsibilities entail and should I require some service from you, I am confident it would be handled promptly." "Thank you sir." Eric replied, momentarily halting his chore. "I assure you that would be the case."

"I am positive it would." The man agreed. "Do you have many chores left to do?"

Eric scanned the area and shook his head. "No sir, I don't. The only things I have left to do are to double check the pool house great room and the stock you requested for the bar inside."

"Excellent. When you are finished, would you consider showing me around the pool house?" The man asked.

"I would be happy to sir." Eric stated, though he thought about the oddity of the request. The pool house consisted of only the great room, a bathroom, an employee locker room and storage closets. So if the man had visited the villa in March, surely he would have entered the pool house at sometime during the stay and scouted the layout. The request didn't make sense.

Eric spotted a stray flower petal from a nearby azalea floating in the water and removed it from the pool, then placed the skimmer against the wall of the pool house. He grabbed the handle of the door, pulling it open in the same motion and entering the structure leading the man inside. "I take it that you intend to spend some time in here."

"In all likelihood, yes I do." The man responded as he followed. "This is why I would like to become familiar with it even though I had been inside on my previous visit. I must succeed in my endeavors and success is all about preparation, Mr. Lynch. Do you participate in organized athletics?"

"Yes sir." Eric answered as the two stood inside the great room.

"In what sport?" The man asked.

"Soccer mostly, though I swim as well." Eric reported.

"Very good." The man complimented. "So then you understand the necessity to prepare before you compete."

Eric grinned. "And what exactly are you competing in?"

The man walked around the room, examining every corner and piece of furniture, then turned to answer. "You greeted the other guests, did you not?"

"Yes sir, I did." Eric replied, curiously watching the man search behind potted plants and furniture.

"Then you observed the gentlemen with whom I will be conducting meetings. Probably made some judgments of your own about them and me. Am I correct?"

"I wouldn't say that." He answered.

The man moved closer, his voice strong and clear yet subdued in volume, the expression wiped upon his face far more serious and more thoughtful. "I know you did, just as I made judgments about you. You see, Mr. Lynch, not every competition is an athletic one. You and I are in competition. With these men, every word, every sentence and every subject is a competition. Government is a battle of ideals and diplomacy, a war with words. Even science becomes a struggle between two opposing energies. There is no part of life that avoids one force being thrown into opposition with another and if one fails to properly prepare and take even the smallest of advantages when available, then it will be the force that folds first. And I am never *that* force."

"So then you're saying that you always win?" Eric asked.

"Essentially, yes. I always eventually win." The man arrogantly replied, unconsciously puffing his chest out as he spoke.

A grin grew across Eric's face as he turned away and walked across the room, not sure if the pompousness of the statement of the man's actions amused him. "What you see is pretty much the entire building." He said, avoiding a response that would no doubt cause the conversation to escalate into a debate, or worse, a conflict. Instead, he directed the man's attention to the three doors inside and continued the tour. "That door leads up to the tennis court. The second..."

The man interrupted. "I saw you smile Mr. Lynch."

Eric stopped and turned toward the man. "I'm sorry?"

"I saw you smile when I told you that I always win." The man stated. "I expected a far more vocal response from you."

Eric approached a grouping of furniture, stopping near the sofa where the man stood. "I did not realize that I gave you any response at all. However, if I did, I apologize as it would be inappropriate for me to do so sir."

"But you would like to respond, wouldn't you?" The man concluded, staring at the boy and observing another grin grow upon his face. "Mr. Lynch, I expect to be conducting business here for quiet awhile. So I am requesting...." He paused, looking across the room away from the boy before he continued. "No. A service that I require from you is that you speak your mind around me, at all times. Is that understood?"

"Yes sir. It is." Eric responded. He turned and led the man outside, cognizant of the man's attempt to goad him into a discussion.

"Good. With that in mind, what was your comment?" The man asked as he followed Eric along the pool, watching him stop by one of the tables to pick up the skimmer.

Eric stared at the man and smiled. "If there is nothing else, I've got to go."

"But you haven't answered me." The man stated.

"Sure I have." He said as he turned and began to walk toward the villa.

"No, you haven't." The man argued.

"Then I guess you don't *always* win." He shouted as he disappeared into the main house, leaving the man standing speechless. As he walked through the storage area and replaced the skimmer on the wall, he chuckled to himself, reveling in the fact that he used the man's pompousness to win his point and the relative ease he experienced in doing so. The unexpected pleasure he felt from the surge of adrenaline that pumped through his system as he walked away from the man knowing he had gotten the best of him, rivaled that of any goal he scored while playing soccer. The natural high carried with him as he ascended the stairs to the employee lounge, wanting badly to share his victory with everyone around, but knowing he could not.

After he stepped into the dressing room, washed and changed into his formal attire, he walked into the service area of the dining room to prepare for the scheduled brunch. First glancing at the hand-written menu Kearney hung on the message board, Eric carefully set eight places at a large rectangular table next to the fireplace in the center of the expansive room, inspecting every piece of silver, crystal and china positioned on the navy blue tablecloth. He slowly circled the table, checking that no piece was awry. After reporting to Kearney on the readiness of the dining room, he walked to the lounge where the guests had gathered and announced that meal's service, leading them to the entryway of the dining room.

As the first man who arrived at the villa approached, he stopped, smiled and tilted his head toward Eric in acknowledgment before quickly continuing inside and seating himself at one end of the table. Eric turned toward the room and stared at the man until he caught his attention, then nodded his head in return and smiled, somewhat gloating as he did so. And while the men were being served, Eric quietly turned and disappeared from the room.

He entered the lounge where the men had been waiting and folded two newspapers that were left out on one of the tables. As he moved two arm chairs that the guests slid out of place, he quickly scanned the room searching for needed adjustments, finding the room in acceptable order. He slowly backed out and began to turn, coming face to face with the man who quietly sneaked behind him, a very stern expression pasted on his face.

"From our limited conversations, I can see that you are going to be a challenge for me intellectually." The man stated, his powerful and imposing voice purposely held placid by his desire to keep the discussion discrete.

Eric eased back from the man, answering quickly but retaining his composure despite the fact that his insides had transformed into liquid. "And how did you determine that? We've never participated in an intellectual discussion."

The man cocked his head to one side, squinting his eyes in confusion. "So then what you did to me at the pool was a mistake?" He asked, staring into the boy's face.

Eric grinned. "No, that was intentional." He replied, his arrogance momentarily overcoming the nervousness he felt seconds before.

"I see." The man responded. He pressed his lips together as he constructed his next thought. "You know, only a gifted intellect would have conceived such a response, Mr. Lynch. And since I am considered to possess a gifted intellect by a great many people, I must regard you with respect for having out-witted me. So, I look forward to additional discourse. And Mr. Lynch, you will not get over on me again. I'll see to that." He continued as he feigned a smile, turned and walked away.

Simultaneously, Eric shrugged his shoulders and shook his head as he watched the man return to the dining room, the drain of energy from the encounter causing him to become speechless and his body to freeze motionless. Whether a warning or a challenge, the conversation made him uncomfortable. Had he crossed the line with this guest? If the purpose of slipping in behind him was to intimidate him, the man succeeded. The exhilaration Eric experienced after speaking with the man at the pool disappeared, realizing now that he may have erred in his actions.

He stood stationary in the hallway staring toward the dining room wondering the atmosphere of his ensuing confrontation with the man, becoming more anxious, more confused about what the man was attempting to accomplish or what he would plan next. Eric turned away from facing the dining room, forcing air out of his mouth as he began to walk through the lounge toward the service hall, the questions concerning the man consuming his attention.

He entered the kitchen, ignoring the conversation around him, and retrieved the lunch he earlier ordered, shuffling into the empty employee lounge absorbed by the thoughts that raced through his mind. Why was the man making contact so often when the meeting that morning specifically stressed the opposite? What did he want? Or better yet, what did the man expect from him?

He sat in the overstuffed armchair next to the window overlooking the pool and turned on the television with the remote control that sat on the table in front. As he slowly munched on his sandwich alternately peering out the window and gazing at MTV, he realized that Aaron could help unlock some of the mystery surrounding the man. Since Aaron worked at the villa during the man's previous visit in March, it only made sense that he met the man, maybe knew his name.

He took another bite of his sandwich and stared out the window, seeing that two of the guests walked out of the main house and sat next to the pool at a table. Eric watched intently, the discussion between the two appearing heated.

"You look a little too comfortable." Aaron said as he walked into the room, startling Eric who twitched in his seat almost knocking over a glass. "Anything going on?" He asked.

Eric shoved the final bite of his lunch into his mouth and stood, grabbing his plate and empty glass before he swallowed. "What are you doing here already? It can't be three o'clock." He excitedly asked.

"No relax." Aaron replied. "I had to come in a little early for a meeting at the consulate. Any changes to the schedule?"

"You're going to have nine for dinner tonight instead of eight. I told Stephen already. Everything else is listed on the computer, but it's pretty much the same." Eric answered, walking to the desk.

"Good." Aaron replied. "You have plans for tonight?"

Eric leaned against the desk, placing the plate and glass on top. "I've got my practice at five and then the under-ten team I help out with has a practice at seven. After that, I'm supposed to go out with this girl that Greg set me up with last night."

"Do you like her?" Aaron asked as he sat at the desk and began reading the computer screen.

Eric smiled widely, his eyes sparkling as he nodded his head. "Yeah, she's pretty hot. We had a good time last night, a real good time."

"Excellent." He replied. "So, when is your next game?"

"At six tomorrow." Eric answered as he leaned over the desk. "Hey Aaron, I've got to ask you a question."

"Shoot."

"One of our guests has been a little....I don't know, intense I guess, and I wanted to know if you knew anything about him. He said he stayed here in March." Eric stated.

"What do you mean by intense?" Aaron asked.

Eric cocked his head to one side and gazed toward the ceiling, pausing before he answered. "He's been following me around, asking a lot of questions and kind of challenging me. I just wanted to know if I should be concerned about it."

Aaron stood from the desk and walked to the window, peering outside. "Is he out there right now?"

Eric joined him and looked toward the pool house. "Yeah. You see the one walking over to the men sitting at the table?" He asked.

Aaron smiled as he quickly returned to the chair and sat, identifying the man only as the general. He called him the general because of the way he directed others and organized himself, not because of a commission he earned in military service, though it was evident that the general possessed military experience from his disciplined actions and perfectionist lifestyle. Yet for all the instances that Aaron interacted with the man, he never learned his name and that remained a mystery for the entire staff.

The information eased Eric's mind. Though he would never admit the man's actions concerned him, they did. Now at least he felt he could be less suspicious and more comfortable around the man. Apparently, the general was looking for an intellectual challenge and he decided he found it in Eric. But what made him special?

He thought about the oddity of the situation. Until now, no one had ever recognized him strictly for the intelligence he knew he had. And other than his parents, no one ever pointed that intelligence out. In fact, he never gave himself credit for his own abilities even though his accomplishments far surpassed those of his friends. Instead, he tempered his intellect to fit his needs or surroundings. And maybe that was what the general thought was so special about him.

CHAPTER 3

ERIC STOOD ON THE PATIO next to the pool mesmerized by the device at the bottom wriggling its way slowly across the floor sucking any sediment into its several vacuum hoses. Today was his birthday, his seventeenth to be exact, and the anticipation of the celebration fostered the preoccupation that plagued him throughout the day. And the fact that for the first time in weeks, no guests stayed at the villa, allowed his mind to wander undisturbed as well as permitted him to complete his tasks in peace and in the comfort of not wearing a shirt on a day that sizzled with a heat and humidity that induced perspiration by even the slightest of movements. This was the last of his chores for this shift at the guesthouse and as the time wound closer toward four o'clock, his mind drifted further away from Saddlewood, imagining the dinner with his family and the date he had with his girl afterward.

He smiled at the thought of the phrase "his girl" because it was not something he expected or planned, yet, for the moment, it was so right and so perfect. Beth captured his eye long ago, the first girl he ever liked enough not to act upon with passing desires. Instead, he continued using his charming personality to date a harem-like number of girls while concealing his true feelings. Now, for whatever reason, she held feelings for him and acted upon them, the irony of the situation causing him to chuckle to himself as he peered into the water seeing that the device had completed its sweep.

He retrieved the vacuum from the pool, water dripping onto the stone patio instantly drying as it hit, then disassembled the device for storage in the pool house. "I hope you're about finished." Aaron said, coming onto the patio from the villa. "You've got to go over to the consulate before you leave." Eric stood, quickly swiping his hands across his shorts to dry them off. "Yeah, I forgot about that. Thanks." He replied. "Do I have to be dressed up?"

Aaron looked at the young man and nodded, a sarcastic smile spread across his face. "Well...think about this for a second." He began. "You are going to the Consul's residence. The man entertains heads of state and mixes with the world's elite. And even though the ceremony will take only about a half an hour and there will be other new employees there, look at yourself and tell me if you think you are properly attired to meet with this man?"

Eric nodded his head. "*That's* why there was a suit and tie in my garment bag today." He said. "I guess I didn't realize the importance of this occasion."

Aaron shook his head in disagreement. "It's not the occasion Eric, it's the man. Not to say that the meeting today is not important, because it is. You are being formally welcomed to the Saddlewood staff by the official representative of the United Nations. But the formality of the occasion is for respect to the man."

Eric grabbed his shirt and pulled it over his head. "I'm sorry. I didn't understand the significance of today or fully appreciate the importance of the man I'll be meeting."

"No need to apologize." Aaron replied. "It was difficult for me to grasp all of this as well when I began working here. Go grab a shower and get ready. I've got you covered and already told Steven I was relieving you for the day."

"Thanks." Eric answered.

"Oh, and by the way, happy birthday." Aaron stated as he grinned and nodded his head.

Eric smiled, acknowledging the wish by nodding his head in response. He turned and disappeared into the guesthouse, quietly returning to the lounge to pick up his equipment, leaving for the operations center clubhouse where he could shower before the reception.

Maybe he would have been more excited about meeting with the Consul had there not been so much else on his mind. For a moment, he thought about the many people who never get the opportunity to meet with an individual so connected to the world but would give anything to be in the position he is in now. He felt guilty, not about being in the position he was, but for not being excited or honored as other people expected him to be. The fact was, he failed to be impressed with a man because of a title, especially one that retained no real power and appeared purely ceremonial. And though Eric never met him, he figured the Consul was a man in the twilight of his diplomatic career and given his position as a reward for past service. It never occurred to him that the Consul was more than a figurehead, that the man possessed true skill for assuaging volatile situations or that he was widely respected in all corners of the world. Instead, Eric believed that the Consul was just an aging gentleman set to retire in the peace of the Virginia countryside.

He stepped out of the shower and removed the black suit packed in the garment bag, carefully inspecting his clothing as he dressed. He peered into a mirror for a final look before he walked to the reception area of the operations center where he reported with a receptionist who called for his escort to the consulate.

He stood alone for several minutes in the atrium-like space staring into a fountain that trickled down a formation of rocks into an awaiting pool filled with colorful orange fish and losing himself in thought as he waited.

"Mr. Lynch?" A female voice inquired from behind.

Her unrecognizable accent caused Eric to turn, his eyes meeting upon a classically beautiful young woman, her flowing dark hair and deep brown eyes so exquisitely accenting her delicate features that he stopped speechless, smiled and stared at her forgetting to answer.

"You *are* Mr. Lynch, are you not?" She again inquired.

Eric caught himself staring and sheepishly answered. "I'm sorry, yes. And you are?"

"My name is Maria and I am here to accompany you to the consulate." She replied. "Are you ready to go Mr. Lynch?"

Again he smiled, nodding his head. "Yes I am and please, call me Eric." He said.

She tilted her head in acknowledgment as she turned away. "Thank you Eric. Please follow me." She stated, leading him outside to the awaiting vehicle parked on the paved stone semi-circle drive.

As they rode toward the consulate, Eric gazed at the woman, quickly looking away from her when she glanced and smiled at him. Again, from the corner of his eye he attempted a glimpse of her, trying not to make her feel uncomfortable as well as not being detected, yet he thought about her smile. Was she attracted to him or just being friendly? Clearly her beauty captivated him and her accent, the unidentifiable intonation of her speech that augmented her mysterious elegance, caused his heart to palpitate faster with each word she spoke.

He silently sat in the passenger's seat of the vehicle planning in his mind some conversation that would avoid the appearance of a pick up line. As they approached the consulate, he realized that if he wanted to get to know this girl, he would have to say something and hope that it would not sound stupid.

"You have a pretty accent." Eric awkwardly stated, a tightness forming in his stomach as he considered whether she could take the comment as an insult, and quickly continued. "Where are you from?"

"I am from San Marino." She answered as she turned toward him and smiled, driving past a security officer who waved the vehicle through the gate. "Do you know where that is?"

"Honestly I do not and I am sorry about that." He stated.

"There is no need to be sorry Eric. Not many people are familiar with my country." She said, stopping the vehicle on the circular driveway in front of a building resembling an old English manor house.

Eric stepped out of the vehicle, quickly surveying the flowered gardens and sculpted shrubbery that surrounded the grounds before he joined the young woman walking toward the entrance and its large wooden doors. "So where exactly is San Marino?" He asked.

She grabbed the handle of one of the doors releasing a latch and swinging the door open. "If you are sincerely interested in my country or as I suspect, in me, then I suggest you take some time to research the answers to your questions." She replied, smiling at him as she guided him through the door and into a large reception hall. "Sir Charles will meet with you shortly. Please make yourself comfortable."

Eric watched her as she walked the marble floor down the expansive hall and turned, disappearing out of sight. He sat alone in the quiet space wondering where the other employees the Consul was greeting might be. He stared down the long hallway then fixed his eyes slightly to the right at a painting hanging on the wall across from him. For some reason, not knowing anything about art, he found the work exquisite. The boldness of the colors jumping off the canvas into shapes that resembled nothing he could comprehend captivated his imagination and he lost himself in it nearly becoming oblivious to his surroundings.

"It is a beautiful work, is it not Mr. Lynch?" The Consul stated, his refined British accent snapping Eric's concentration.

The young man quickly rose, directing his attention to the distinguished older gentleman who stood next to him, his arms cupped behind as he studied the piece of art. "Yes sir it is." Eric agreed.

The Consul gazed at the work for a moment longer before he turned toward the young man. "Please come with me, Mr. Lynch, and sit in the study for a moment." He said, directing the boy down the hall to a corner room of one of the sections, sitting at a grouping of antique wing chairs placed centrally in front of a gray stone fireplace. "Would you care for a beverage?" He asked.

"No sir, thank you." Eric answered. "I'll wait for the others."

The man looked at him somewhat puzzled. "I'm sorry, are you expecting someone else?" He asked.

"Well, yes sir. I was told you would be welcoming a group of us today." Eric explained.

The Consul nodded. "Normally, that would be correct. However, you are somewhat of an anomaly here in Saddlewood and because of that, I decided to take the time to speak with you one on one." He stated as a man carrying a tray with a glass entered the room, placing the glass on a table next to the Consul. "Mr. Lynch, are you sure I can't get you something? A soft drink perhaps?"

Eric held his hand up in front of him. "No, thank you. I appreciate the offer."

The Consul shook his head at the man who then turned and left the room. "As I was saying, I wanted to speak with you one on one. You see, Mr. Lynch, we have a policy that states in order to work here, one must be at least eighteen years of age and must have completed a secondary level education, as well as other requirements of course. Though you fit all of those other requirements, you do not meet or exceed our age and educational standards."

Eric interrupted. "Excuse me sir, I do not mean to be impolite, however, are you letting me go?"

The Consul smiled. "No, not at all Mr. Lynch. In fact I approved your provisional employment, provided you demonstrate the maturity and intellect we require in a position such as yours. You have done so and I wanted to meet you personally to see what makes you so special."

Eric grinned in embarrassment. "Thank you sir. I am honored to work here."

The Consul tilted his head in acknowledgement. "We are quite honored to have you. As I have been told, you are quite a footballer. I know you call the sport soccer over here in the colonies, but I do not know exactly what you call one who participates in the sport."

"A soccer player, sir." Eric replied.

"Thank you." The man replied. "Now as I was saying, I understand that you excel in the sport. Is that correct?"

Eric hesitated, avoiding an answer that would appear conceited and yet, be accurate at the same time. He was an excellent player and proud of his accomplishments in the sport. However, it wasn't until recently that he began to excel as a player and he partly attributed this success to his physical training at Saddlewood, a training that cultivated confidence. So he quickly constructed a humbled response that still exuded the confidence he possessed. "Though I appreciate the complement, I could not have gained any success that I am experiencing now without the training that I received here."

The man smiled. "Such a mature answer for one who celebrates only his seventeenth birthday today. I am quite impressed. With young people such as Maria and yourself, the world has hope for a brighter future." He stated.

"Maria?" Eric repeated.

"Yes Maria, the young lady who escorted you today."

"Yes sir, I know who you meant. How old is she?" Eric inquired.

The man grinned as he delayed in answering, staring at the young man for a moment. "I believe I sense an attraction toward my personal assistant." He stated. "You have good taste Mr. Lynch."

Eric shook his head in denial. "I didn't say…."

The Consul interrupted. "You didn't have to. I've spent a lifetime reading other people." He said matter-of-factly before continuing. "We do not discourage our employees from getting involved with each other as many are young and away from their families for as much as a year at a time. It is only natural that a certain amount of bonding occurs, so long as that bonding does not cross the lines of decency."

Relieved at the Consul's response, Eric leaned slightly forward in his chair. "Then with that in mind sir, may I ask you a question?"

"By all means."

"Where exactly is San Marino?" He asked.

"So you *are* attracted to her." The man stated as a grin grew across his face. He paused for a moment, contemplating whether to respond to the boy's question or to force him to research the answer, keeping Eric in suspense. "I should not make this so easy on you, however…it's a small country near the Adriatic Sea surrounded by the north central part of Italy."

"Thank you, sir." Eric said with a relieved grin.

The Consul nodded in response. "You know," He began. "I met her father when he served as one of the co-regents of the republic and found him to be a completely delightful, well-educated and fascinating man. In fact, he was the first official from any government to formally congratulate me on my appointment here."

"He sounds like a good man." Eric commented.

"He is." Sir Charles agreed. "And his daughter is a fine young lady. Incidentally, Maria does not normally escort my guests to the consulate, but on this occasion she requested to do so. My guess is that she is enamored with you as well." The man suggested.

A smile raced across Eric's face now realizing that the attraction he felt for her was mutual. "How does she know me?" He asked.

"Mr. Lynch, your employment initiated a great deal of discussion within this office. Out of curiosity, she observed one of your weight training sessions to see what all the fuss was about and I believe your actions and appearance surprised her. Since she is my personal assistant, she has access to some of the records and being the resourceful young lady that she is, I guess she took it from there." The Consul explained. "Of course, all of this is conjecture on my part."

"But I'm sure an accurate one." He replied. "One thing though, she didn't give me the impression that she was interested in me when she drove me over here." Eric stated.

"Well Mr. Lynch none of this is any of my business, but as you will find out sooner or later, women are like that. Whatever the case, please do me one favor." The man requested.

"Yes sir?" Eric asked.

"Should the two of you decide to spend some time together, do not cause an international incident that would require an explanation to her father." He requested.

Eric grinned, knowing what the man meant. "I promise I will not sir." He answered.

The Consul smiled as he nodded his head in appreciation. He stood, extending his hand toward the young man and continued. "Well Mr. Lynch, I have a meeting I must prepare for and I am sure you have plans for your birthday. It was a pleasure meeting you and I look forward to our next visit."

Eric shook the man's hand as he replied. "Thank you sir. It was a pleasure meeting you as well. I appreciate the opportunity to sit and converse with you."

The Consul guided Eric out of the room and down the hallway toward the door. "Thank you Mr. Lynch. Now if you will excuse me, I must return to my duties. I will call Maria and have her escort you back to the operations center."

"Thank you Sir Charles." Eric replied.

"You're welcome." The man stated. "And Mr. Lynch, have a happy birthday." He said then turned and disappeared down the hallway.

Eric stood, anxiously waiting for Maria. However, the nervousness was not so much that he grew impatient to leave Saddlewood for home. Instead, his apprehension centered around meeting this girl, the Sanmarinese goddess with the sensuous Italian accent. And as he fantasized about forging some kind of a relationship with her, his anxiety heightened, as from the back of his mind he thought of Beth, the girl he pined for during most of his pubescence, the girl he never figured he would date, only now to have her all to himself. He began to pace, the nervousness playing games with his body causing him to perspire and his stomach to quiver as he contemplated his options.

As he made the turn for his next lap, he spotted Maria walking down the hallway toward him and he knew that whatever decision he planned on making, he would have to do so quickly. Would it be right for him to attempt a relationship now that he knew Maria held feelings for him? And what about Beth? Though he did not know what love felt like, he knew he felt some way about her that was far stronger than friendship. But aside from his feelings for Beth, dating two girls at the same time made him feel uneasy for the first time in his life.

"Are you in that much of a hurry to leave that you must pace?" Maria asked.

Eric stopped moving and stared into her eyes for a moment, his decision becoming abundantly clear. "No. I have something else on my mind." He answered. "Sometimes that's how I work things out."

She smiled at him. "Is there something I can help you with?"

He paused and again looked at her. "In fact there is. When you take me back to the op center, do you have to come right back?"

"Well, Sir Charles does have a reception for this evening. Why do you ask?" She inquired.

"Because today is my birthday and I was wondering if you would be interested in having a quick soda with me?" He asked. "Maybe I can get to know about you and your country a little better."

Maria nodded her head and smiled. "I would like that." She answered. "Unfortunately I can stay for only ten minutes."

Eric opened the door and held it for her. "Ten minutes would be great." He said as he followed her outside, climbing into the cart after her.

She turned the key of the vehicle, guided it along the drive past the decorative gate and drove to the operations center, the awkward silence that consumed the trip to the consulate replaced by a comfortable conversation that hinted a promise of something greater. They entered the center and walked to the employee restaurant, the thoughts of Beth vanishing from Eric's mind as he sat across from Maria, being captivated by her every word. And as the two talked, Eric leaned toward her and stretched his arm across the table, his palm open and facing upward. She reached toward him, placing her hand in his and it closed around her as he coolly attempted to conceal his delight. But as the two relaxed into each other's companionship, Eric became conscience of the fact that they exceeded the ten minutes she promised to stay. And though he thought about ignoring the time, wanting to extend this moment with this girl as long as possible, in fairness to her he knew he could not.

Reluctantly, he rose from his chair, holding gently her hand as he led her from the table and out of the restaurant. Slowly, they walked to her vehicle, stopping in front as they gazed into each other's eyes before he softly kissed her then watched her drive away. He followed her with his eyes along the path until she disappeared into the woodlands, an emptiness filling his body that called for him to chase after her. But he would not.

Unaware of the actual length of time that had passed, he glanced at his watch, shaking his head as he abruptly turned and trotted into the building. When he entered the men's clubhouse, he quickly changed his clothes and returned his equipment, racing out the door to his car to begin his journey home, frustration building as each minute rapidly passed.

He felt guilty but was unsure why, or at least failed to admit to himself the cause. So as he drove toward home, he began to justify in his mind his actions, debating his case to himself. Beth was his girlfriend, but he wasn't married, or engaged, or even mutually exclusive for that matter. And sitting with a co-worker after work for a while certainly could not be considered unfaithful, even if that co-worker was a drop-dead gorgeous young woman from a small European country. No, he wasn't unfaithful and he slowly convinced himself of that position the closer he drove toward home.

After fighting the congestion of a Washington area rush hour that exacerbated the anxiety of accounting for his lateness, Eric guided the car onto his street, a feeling of relief engulfing him as he approached his home. He organized his thoughts into sequence, arranging in his mind what he had to do in hopes of recovering the time he lost while sitting with Maria. And though that time, a little over a half an hour, put him far further behind in his schedule than he could compensate, in his mind he knew it was time well spent.

He admitted to himself that he held feelings for Maria, strong feelings that rivaled or equaled those he shared for Beth. But now, it was Beth he needed to concern himself with. Within a few short minutes, he would have to repress his thoughts about Maria and prepare for dinner and his date with Beth afterward, allowing no one to suspect that anything had changed between them, if it had.

He parked his car in the driveway, rushing into the house and racing past his waiting family to his room, apologizing for his lateness along the way but avoiding any questions concerning it and the answers that could generate suspicion. He opened his closet and removed the clothes he set aside that morning before he left. They reminded him of Beth, the shirt he bought the last time the two of them went to the mall, and the pants he wore on their first date. And again, he felt guilty about meeting Maria.

Satisfied with his look, he calmly walked downstairs masking his thoughts about his tale of two women. His father might understand, his mother, never and his brother... well Kevin would applaud him just because he's fourteen and filled with raging hormones. Nevertheless in nearly ten minutes, he would have to face Beth.

As his father pulled in front of Beth's house, Eric's stomach tightened. The plan was to not let either girl know about the other and he fought with himself as he realized his hypocrisy concerning the situation. For years, he criticized Jimmy for cheating on girls he dated. Eric never cheated, just dated many girls, one after another, being very open about it. And though he hadn't officially begun dating Maria, there was no question that after today, a more intimate relationship was the very next step.

He walked to the door of her house as it opened and she appeared in the shadows of the entryway, her angelic face hosting a smile that could tame the wildest of men. He halted in his steps, his breath taken away as he stared at the beauty of the young woman before him wearing a black low-cut dress which hugged her body so perfectly that one would guess was made as she stood in it. And with that one long look at the woman before him, all thoughts of Maria left his mind.

He patiently sat through dinner. Though the thoughts of the time spent alone with Beth afterward rushed through his mind and the anticipation of the evening caused his heart to race, Eric remained confidently composed displaying an impressive refinement previously unseen by his family. And as the night continued, his charm dominated an evening that placed him squarely in the spotlight until he could be alone with Beth.

The lighting from the Jefferson Memorial reflected off the Tidal Basin as several people sat along the steps gazing across the mall. The dinner ended and as planned, the two separated from Eric's family to be alone. They strolled past the memorial on the walkway that hugged the shores of the basin, the illusion of quietness that a city provides resonating in the background like the discordant beats of alternative music. She led him to the marble steps and sat near the top, staring out into the water as she nuzzled into him.

Silently he wrapped his arm around her, holding her tight and making the most of a date that fell short of expectations. Though somewhat intimate in the idea that the two were alone, this spot was not his choice, the openness inhibiting the closeness he imagined this night would proffer. However, for a reason she did not disclose, she insisted on coming here.

She glanced at her watch and turned to him. "Do you want to take a walk?" She asked.

Eric cocked his head to one side and shrugged his shoulders. "Sure, that would be cool." He said as he stood, lifting her up with him. They descended the stairs and turned, following the walkway past the Roosevelt Memorial and along the tree-lined sidewalk.

"You're not having a good time, are you?" Beth asked.

"Why would you say that?" Eric replied as he grasped her hand, gently holding it in his.

She hesitated, the two of them walking several steps before she softly answered. "I just don't think this was exactly what you had planned for tonight."

Eric slightly turned his head, keeping notice of the path in front while glancing at Beth. "So that doesn't mean that I'm not having a good time. I'm with you, and that's cool enough for me." He stated.

She smiled. "That's very sweet but I'm sure you think coming here was kind of a strange request."

He nodded his head and grinned. "Well, I have to admit that this was probably one of the last places I would have thought about going to." He said. "But it's cool. We're kind of alone and I respect what ever reason you have for being here."

"That's very noble of you." She replied as she pulled him off the walk behind the line of trees and along the water's edge. "And I'm happy you want to be alone with me."

He shook his head and chuckled. "Why wouldn't I want to be?" He stated, deliberately drawing his face toward her, kissing her gently.

She moved her hand onto his waist slowly sliding her hand underneath his shirt. Breaking away from the embrace, she stopped and stared into his eyes. "That was very nice."

"We didn't have to stop." He said as he smiled at her.

She held him closely, her hands caressing his skin. "Yes we did." She replied. "May I ask you a personal question?"

He hesitated for a moment. "Sure" He replied. "Go ahead."

"Are you still a virgin?" She asked.

He pulled away from her, looking into her eyes. "If I answer yes, are you going to try to change that tonight?" He answered, a huge grin forming across his face.

She quickly looked at her watch, stared at him and smiled while she rubbed her hand inside his shirt. "Maybe not tonight."

"That's kind of disappointing." He replied, realizing that she checked her watch. "Is there somewhere you have to go?"

She shook her head, then quickly glanced across the water before looking back toward Eric. "No, why do you ask?"

"Because that was the second time you looked at your watch since we got here." He replied. "Either you have somewhere to go, or you can't wait until this date is over."

She grabbed his hand and led him onto the sidewalk, continuing in silence. As they turned around a series of bushes near the edge of the water they stood before a small group of people that included Greg, Jimmy and their dates.

"Happy birthday!" They shouted, walking up to Eric who stood motionless in his tracks, the girls hugging him.

Beth turned toward him and smiled, seeing the stare of surprise upon his face. "I guess I had somewhere to go." She stated. "Happy birthday."

Eric stood, his mouth agape. Then he turned toward Beth, smiled and hugged her tightly.

CHAPTER 4

THE HEAT OF THE SUMMER afternoon baked the gardens along
the approach to the gate like pottery curing in a kiln. Mist from
the spray nozzles hissed onto the shrubs and flowers, in an
attempt to keep them from burning in the midday sun, forming
small puddles of water that lined the road along the curb and
washed the tires of each passing vehicle. Slowly the driver's
side window of the car lowered and Eric reached his arm into
the sticky, humid air inserting his identification badge into the
slotted box next to the guard station. The gate hummed as it
retracted into the fence line and he removed his arm from the
oppressiveness of the afternoon into the coolness of the air-
conditioned vehicle, quickly closing the window and driving
into the complex. It was a typical sultry Virginia mid-summer
day, one that causes beads of perspiration to slide down the skin
during the slightest of movement and where floating in a pool
while eating ice cream was the only logical outdoor activity.

He pulled into a parking slot and opened the door, the rush of the heat hitting him as if he suddenly opened a furnace as he stepped out from the cool vehicle. It was too hot to hurry, so he sauntered to the operations center, careful that the excess of humidity not cause a river of perspiration.

He was hours early for his shift on this Friday, three hours early in fact because he planned on meeting Maria. The two of them became inseparable over the summer, forging a tight friendship, which masked the mutual attraction that existed for each other, an attraction that they chose to suppress out of respect for Eric's relationship with Beth. He told Maria about her, an unnerving task that reaped a reward in its own way by the growth of trust he built with the young woman. But because of his honesty, her feelings toward him intensified, respecting greatly the maturity he exhibited in telling her.

He walked into the complex, excited about his news of being offered an athletic scholarship to the University of Virginia for soccer, an accomplishment that just a short time ago would have seemed unlikely, and being able to share it with Maria. She joined in his excitement, showing his importance to her.

Every minute of their time together was meaningful as there were so few of those minutes remaining. At the end of summer, she was scheduled to return home until next spring, an occasion neither looked forward to. So they picked a secluded spot under a grove of trees near a trickling stream where they could sit and talk in the coolness of the shade.

As the time drew closer to his shift, they returned to the operations center, holding hands until they were forced by the hour of the day to part company, doing so with a long and passionate kiss. Again, as like the first day that he met her, he watched her until she disappeared from sight, knowing now they were more than just friends.

He hustled into the clubhouse, again a little late from the encounter with the Sanmarinese goddess, an encounter worth any admonishment for being tardy. As he picked up his equipment at the desk and continued to his assigned locker, he noticed a blockade at the entrance to the showers. A sign announcing their closure for routine maintenance was plastered across the barrier, a minor inconvenience that could be managed by using facilities at the villa. So he thought nothing of it as he rushed by to change into his uniform, dressing quickly to jog through the operations center and drive to the house to prepare for the guest's arrival.

The group from TNR remained guests of the villa and as their stay continued, the mystery of their purpose and identity grew daily. Their reason for the extended occupation of the house was never clear and it became apparent that the eight people who occasionally stayed overnight were not on some corporate retreat or company vacation. They were busy, seemingly using the villa as a base of operations for some special project, shuffling packets of information in and out of the house. There were secretive weekly meetings, sometimes with one or two of the guests and the general himself. Unlike the other guests who rarely spent more than two consecutive days at Saddlewood, the general rarely left. And it was his continued presence that cost him his identity.

Undoubtedly, the general was a man who sought and valued privacy. Though he appeared to forge a close friendship with Eric, his life was never a topic of discussion, yet he made it a point to discuss Eric's, showing interest in even the most mundane aspects of it. The general restricted his meetings, making their locations off limits to every Saddlewood employee no matter who they were. He orchestrated every detail of the group's movement at Saddlewood, painstakingly protecting the identity and business of all who visited. But on a day when he alone stayed at the villa, all of his work to secure his and his group's privacy became compromised by one seemingly harmless action. When he used his cell phone to order flowers for some unknown person or reason, he left his credit card out in the open on a table in the den. During Eric's rounds, he spotted the forgotten card and picked it up, glancing at it to read the name listed. Realizing it was not a staff member's, he walked toward the man and called him by name, alerting him of his loss. Maybe the card was left there on purpose for him to find, a thought that crossed his mind. Whatever the case, Mr. James Hamilton, though grateful the card was returned to him, strongly requested the young man respect his privacy and keep the knowledge of his identity to himself. It was a request that Eric understandably honored.

By far the biggest mystery concerning the group was the alleged ninth man. He was alleged in the fact that in all of the time that this man supposedly spent at Saddlewood, Eric never saw him. It was as if the man's appearance at the villa directly correlated with Eric's work schedule, or more to the point, his time off from work. Was this just a silly coincidence or an intentional act of the group? Whichever the case, it bothered him.

He entered the villa and stored his equipment, as well as the street clothes he brought with him because of the shower closure, in the wooden storage unit in the men's dressing room, and then quietly walked into the staff kitchen. Kearney stood at a preparation table, oblivious to the world around him as he concentrated on decorating the dessert that rested on the crystal pedestal in front of him.

"Hey Steve." Eric calmly greeted as he neared the table and observed the man work the pastry bag he held in his hand.

The man refrained from speaking until he completed the decoration. "Good afternoon Eric." Kearney replied. "Aaron is down by the pool house setting up for tonight. He'll give you the rundown on the plans because I'm really busy. Also, your favorite guest requested your presence as soon as you arrived."

Eric nodded his head as he slowly backed away from the table. "Thank you Steve." He said then he turned and walked away, descending the stairs to the patio outside, looking beyond the pool. On the other side near the pool house doors he could see Aaron sitting on the stone patio, wearing a baseball cap turned backward and sweat beading off of his shirtless body as he read a pamphlet and muttered to himself. Eric neared the building, realizing the pamphlet was a set of instructions to the industrial-sized grill Aaron was attempting to construct, the several remaining pieces of which lay across the patio. He walked up behind his friend, carefully stepping over two of the larger sections as he approached. "What's this for?" He asked.

Aaron peered over his shoulder and smiled. "It was your buddy's idea." He sarcastically replied. "The general ordered some sort of Middle Eastern barbecue, so we had to acquire a grill."

Eric laughed. "And you get to assemble it."

Aaron connected several of the pieces together and smiled. "You laugh too hard my friend." He replied. "Though I get to assemble it right now, you have the honor of breaking it down and cleaning it later this evening."

"How thrilling." Eric responded, pressing his lips together as he slowly nodded his head.

Aaron completed the project, stood and adjusted his cap. "I thought you'd like it." He facetiously said. "So, I guess Stephen sent you down here for instructions."

"Yeah, he looked a little aggravated." Eric replied.

"I'm sure he was." Aaron stated. "He isn't exactly accustomed to hosting barbecues."

"No, I'm sure he isn't. So, what's going on for tonight?"

Aaron grinned. "That's it. You have an outdoor barbecue." He answered. "Set up two large round tables and a total of seven settings, a prep station for Stephen and serving table."

Eric interrupted, "Seven settings?"

"Yeah, apparently one of the men had a little altercation with the general last night, so he won't be joining them tonight." Aaron answered, and then continued. "But anyway, after dinner, the gentlemen are going to a reception for the rest of the evening, so you have an early night tonight in case you want to make plans with someone later."

Eric smiled. "I wish I would have known that earlier." He replied. "You have a good time this weekend though."

"I plan to." Aaron said, wriggling his eyes and smiling widely. He grabbed his shirt that lay on a nearby chair, sliding it over his head and arms while walking toward the main house. "Have a good night tonight. I'll see you Sunday." And he disappeared into the house.

Eric moved the grill, connecting it to the propane receptacle in the wall of the pool house and creating the outdoor workstation Stephen requested. He quickly scanned the patio then entered the house looking for the general. For what little he knew about the man, Eric found him fascinating, telling detailed stories of the places he visited and the battles he witnessed in Eastern Europe and the Middle East to the ethical and philosophical discussions that usually followed. The man challenged Eric to think, and he did.

He entered the study finding Hamilton sitting in a wing chair reading a book and walked up to him. "Good afternoon sir." He greeted. "I was told you were waiting for me."

"Ah yes, young Mr. Lynch! I *was* waiting for you." The man stated. He inserted a marker between the pages and slowly closed the book, carefully placing it on the table next to him. "How are you today?"

"I'm doing well, thank you sir." He replied. "Is there something I can do for you?"

Hamilton leaned forward in his chair and smiled. "Yes, in fact, I have two requests of you." The man stated. "The first one should be quite simple really. Though I am sure that your Mr. Kearney has a variety of fine wines selected for this evening, I am equally confident that, considering my choices for dinner, a Leibfraumilch will not be one of them."

Eric interrupted. "And you would like me to have Mr. Kearney serve one with dinner tonight, is that correct?"

The man smiled. "No, actually I would like to enjoy a bottle now, if you could find one." He stated. "All I could find in the house is either French or domestic, fine wines in their own right, however not measuring up to the fruity delight one gets from a good bottle of this distinctly German masterpiece. Have you ever enjoyed a glass?"

Eric shook his head. "No sir, I can't say that I have."

"That would be a shame. Fine wine is a pleasure of life to be savored among nobility and treasured by the noble. Do you know who said that Mr. Lynch?" Hamilton inquired.

"No sir, who?" Eric asked.

The man paused for a moment, a befuddled expression covering his face. Quickly, he rose from his chair and stepped behind the desk, turning to face the young man. "For some reason, the author's name escapes me at the moment. However I can guarantee you one thing, he was not an American. Most Americans, I have discovered, take wine for granted and do not value it as the distinguished art that it truly is." He lectured. "May I ask why you have not enjoyed a glass Mr. Lynch? I would have surmised that a young man with your breeding would have toasted some social occasion."

"Yes sir, except that I'm only seventeen." Eric answered.

Hamilton shook his head in disapproval. "And of course drinking a fine glass of wine at your age is illegal here." He said. "How utterly barbaric. I imagine you've never experienced the simplicity of a beer either."

Eric hesitated, and then answered. "Yes sir, I have."

"But you're only seventeen." Hamilton mocked. "Mr. Lynch, if you are going to break a law of this country, may I suggest that you do so with some style instead of in some prosaic fashion."

Eric smiled but did not respond.

"I see I have you speechless for the moment." The man observed. "Maybe my second request of you will prove to be more conducive to discussion." He stated.

"And what is your second request?" Eric asked.

"It is a question for you actually." Hamilton replied. "What is your purpose for working here?"

"My purpose." Eric repeated.

"Yes, your purpose." The man said. "You cannot secure a position in the facility at your age without serving some purpose. The young man you replaced was a foreign relations graduate student and is now working at the U.N. in Geneva. Mr. Butler is preparing to secure an internship for next summer in New York. Their training here prepared them for those positions. You are still in High School. What are you preparing for?"

Eric stared at the man. "How do you know all that?"

A smug grin formed across Hamilton's face, his eyes piercing through the young man's zone of comfort with a menacing glare that chilled the air of conversation. "It's my job to know all that." He stated.

Movement momentarily escaped Eric's body as he stood staring at the general, the sudden uneasiness feeling far stronger than when the man first arrived. He tried to make sense of it, but it puzzled him. Why now did Hamilton's posturing disconcert him? What was it that signaled his senses to become wary of the man? He had no answer.

Looking at Hamilton for a moment longer, he hoped that the general's smugness would cause the man to forget the original question; a question Eric's instinct advised him to avoid. Therefore, he did not respond but instead forced a smile; turned and told the man he would retrieve the finest bottle of

Leibfraumilch he could find as he headed out of the room. The diversion succeeded. The relief he felt as he exited the study was unexplainable. Eric felt threatened and it was odd, because at no time was Hamilton threatening.

Calmly he walked into the staff room to a computer terminal at his desk, punching in keys searching Saddlewood's wine lists silently scanning the monitor and reserving several bottles. After informing Stephen of his plans to retrieve them, he got into his cart and drove off the villa's grounds. It gave him time to think.

He returned to the guesthouse placing all but one of the bottles of wine in the cellar then preparing the remaining bottle for the general, but stalling for time. Eventually he would have to face the man knowing that in all probability Hamilton would again focus on Eric's reason for working at Saddlewood. Obviously Hamilton realized that this was more than just a summer job. And it was.

For Eric, it was all laid out before him. He could experience the incredible opportunities and adventures of working in the diplomatic world without ever straying too far from home while gaining an impressive entry to his resume for college. And if this position at Saddlewood generated a chance at a position with the United Nations or preferably the United States in the future, then it was a benefit far more valuable than any ordinary job could provide. But he had to ask himself, why did Hamilton care? Why was it so important for him to know? And again, he could not answer.

The general quietly sat behind the desk in the study, focusing on the content of the small pile of papers that lined the top. Absorbed by his work, Hamilton was incognizant of Eric's entrance into the room, becoming startled by the young man standing next to the desk with the bottle of wine grasped gently in his hands. Coolly, the general slid the papers into one pile and concealed them under a folder, smiling at the young man and approving the bottle with a slight nod of his head.

Without inducing conversation, Eric placed a tray with a silver wine bucket and long-stemmed glass on the corner of the desk, smoothly uncorked the bottle and set it gently into the ice-filled container. Quickly he glanced at Hamilton, smiled as he tilted his head, and then backed out of the room.

He returned to the patio and began preparing for the dinner party to be held there, first setting the two tables then stocking the service area. It was the beginning of evening and the sun sunk behind the scattered clouds, the air cooling to a more comfortable temperature as the sky began to darken toward twilight. The men, as they had so many times before, returned to the villa one by one and gathered at the bar waiting for dinner to be served. But there was something different.

An excitement circulated throughout the room. Whether the result of a productive week that no one talked about or the gala the men would attend tonight, Eric did not know, nor did he care. The mood of the group had changed, the secretive and cautious giving way to the lively and more outgoing. Maybe they concluded their project, celebrating an end to a seemingly endless task. Maybe they were always outgoing and he never noticed. For some reason, now he did.

It was strange to see these men full of laughter, especially considering the argument that had taken place. Throughout dinner, conversation was light and jovial while the men were pleasant, none of them mentioning the previous night's event or the missing member of their group. It was as if he no longer existed.

The dinner wound down and the group left the villa for the reception at the consulate, leaving Eric in the solitude of the peaceful muggy night to restore the barbecue area to its garden-like state so he could leave. His family had gone away for his brother's weekend tournament and thoughts raced through his head. Maybe, if he got out in time, he could still enjoy some of the night. It would be a perfect time for he and Beth to spend time alone together, and he smiled when he thought of the comment she made to him the night of his birthday. Getting laid was not all that bad of an idea.

He quickly retrieved his gear from the storage unit in the main villa and placed it in the small room in the pool house, remembering he could not clean up at the operations center. Returning outside to begin his tasks and anticipating the dirtiness of the job, he removed his shirt hanging it over one of the chairs. The barbecue grill's smell of burned mesquite emanated from its soot-encrusted shell and Eric stared at it for a moment hoping it would go away.

Knowing it was the last chore he needed to complete before he could leave, he began to carefully disassemble the large metal appliance, first sliding the charred mesquite chips into an awaiting garbage bag before he started cleaning. Again he smiled while he imagined the remainder of his night, if he could contact Beth, as he cleaned piece after piece before repacking the unit in its crate that he hurriedly tossed into the mechanical room. He finished and he lifted his arm to glance at his watch, peering at his body below. He was filthy, but had plenty of time to enjoy a hot shower.

He entered the shower room of the pool house, a small chamber recessed deep behind the bar and accessible only by the staff. He undressed and climbed into the stall, relaxing as the hot water danced across his tired body, his thoughts focused on the night ahead. After soaking under the gently falling water for as long as he could, he quickly washed, rinsed, then shut off the water, the indistinguishable sound of heated voiced muffled by the hum of the pool filter running in the mechanical room drawing his attention toward the pool house great room. Still wet, he eased toward the room, grabbing a towel along the way to quickly dry his hair and wrap around his waist. Positioning his ear near the crack of the door, the voices he heard became clearer and more distinct. It was Hamilton and his men.

Eric turned and silently retreated to the small dressing area by the shower. He removed the towel from his waist, placing it on the floor and standing on it as he opened his equipment bag, careful not to make noise. Quickly dressing in his street clothes and packing the bag that he hoisted over his shoulder, he cautiously walked to the door, again placing his ear next to the crack and eavesdropping on the conversation in order to prepare for his surprise entrance into the room. The boisterous discussion the seven men held transformed into a wrathful deliberation, the anger that encompassed the room causing Eric to pull back from the door. Now was not the time to leave.

He turned off the light, set his bag on the floor and crouched next to it, leaning against the wall as the conversation continued, hoping the men would either leave or calm down as he listened.

Each voice that sounded he recognized as one of the TNR guests, each giving an opinion on some yet unidentified subject. He sat patiently listening with little interest until one muffled voice rang above the others, a voice he never before heard here but for some reason recognized. And he figured this was his mysterious ninth man.

Suddenly Eric became more intent on listening to the conversation, the enigma of this ninth man supplying a new interest in its content. Why was this one man so clandestine in his actions? What was his purpose in being here? He pressed his ear closer to the door hoping to find the answers to his questions.

One of the men sarcastically laughed. "If you think they will just let this happen, you are far crazier than I ever thought you were." He yelled, his unidentifiable accent hindering his quickness in speech.

"I do not think that at all." Hamilton answered. "But then I do not believe I plan for them to find out."

"Do you believe they will not investigate?" Another man asked.

"Of course they will investigate." Hamilton stated. "And once they do, they will realize exactly what happened and not be able to do anything about it."

"And we have the people we need in place to take over?" A third man inquired.

"It would be automatic." The ninth man answered.

For a moment, the room went silent. "Can we not try to resolve this through their hierarchy?" Another man inquired.

"Their conspiracy with this man is why we have reached this point." Hamilton stated. "And that is why we have one less with us tonight."

"And if they do not agree to our proposal?" The same man asked.

An eerie silence filled the room while Eric felt the beating of his heart become stronger as it pounded within his chest from the rapidly building tension. He inhaled deeply as he waited for the answer that could clarify the subject of the intense discussion, but carefully exhaled to not make noise and signal the men to his presence.

"If they do not agree to our terms, then an assassination is our only option." Hamilton coldly stated.

Eric sunk against the wall, tilting his head backward looking toward the ceiling, quietly saying the words 'holy shit' to himself as he placed his hands on either side of his head. Instantly he became frightened, his stomach tightening as the thought of his discovery wrapped around his brain. There was no doubt that they would kill him.

He froze, thoughts racing through his mind as he sat motionless in the lightless room, terrified to make any noise. What should he do? What *could* he do? He stared into the endless darkness searching for an answer as the discussion raged on from the other side of the door. Whatever the decision, it would have to wait until he was sure the men had gone.

Minutes turned into hours as Eric crouched in the room. He soaked from the nervous perspiration that poured from his body, wiping it off his face and arms with his towel. His usually steady and capable hands quivered and his chest pounded with every word a man would speak when he neared the door. The fear of being discovered unmercifully heightened each instance someone pounded his fist on the table or on one occasion, the door to the room. And as the conversation heated into an argument, he received a reprieve.

"Look!" Hamilton shouted. "This is getting us nowhere. We should stop for now and pick this up tomorrow night. Maybe we can all clear our heads."

The room became anxiously silent as the sounds of people standing and shuffling about overpowered the sudden quiet. One by one Eric heard the men depart the pool house, the last one turning off the light to the great room and closing the door behind him. Still, he dared not move, at least not until he positively heard nothing.

He sat for a moment longer, then crawled onto the floor and peered underneath the door, scanning the pool house. Determining he was now alone, he cautiously opened the door ever so slightly, just enough to survey the entire great room. He swung the door further open to enable him to look toward the patio and the villa beyond. He saw no one and carefully grabbed his equipment bag, sliding it toward him until he could lift it above his shoulder. With the bag secured tightly next to him, he crawled onto the floor of the great room, gently closing the shower room door, avoiding the chance of making a sound.

In the darkness of the pool house, he crept around the furnishings heading toward the staircase leading to the tennis court in back, constantly scouting the villa for any signs of movement. As he reached the stairs out of the sight of the patio and guesthouse, he stood and stretched his cramped body, his pulse racing wondering if he could leave without being detected.

He slowly ascended the stairway and opened the door to the tennis court, easing the door shut behind him. The cyclone fence encompassing the court stood between Eric and his escape from the villa. To say that he was nervous understated his feelings as he stood for a moment planning his movement away from the house. His stomach churned and perspiration poured from his body as he quietly unlatched the electronic gate allowing him to pass onto the surrounding grounds. As silently as possible, he closed the gate behind him, taking great caution to prevent it from making any noise. Quickly moving across the walkways that connected the garden adjacent to the dining room to the gazebo on the knoll overlooking the interior of the complex, he ducked into the cover of the woods carefully walking to his cart, hopping in and engaging the accelerator. Quietly, he drove away from the house with the lights off in the electrically powered vehicle, looking back toward the villa twice as he rode along the path checking to see if anyone had noticed his departure. He appeared to be in the clear.

With the accelerator pressed down to the floor, he sped toward the operations center, his mind an ocean of apprehension. He haphazardly parked his vehicle and jogged through the building to the clubhouse, throwing his equipment bag onto the counter for the attendant and racing out the door, the shock of the night wearing off, his nervousness turning to fear and paranoia. Every person became suspicious, every delay a crisis and he fumbled with his keys as he slid them into the ignition of the new sports car.

He cleared the security gate and sped down the winding county road toward the center of the small village ahead, his hands so soaked with sweat; he found it somewhat difficult to grasp the steering wheel of the vehicle. When he reached town, he ignored the traffic signal and raced onto the main highway toward Washington, driving until he pulled into a convenience store several miles away and sat in the parking lot.

He peeled off his sweat-soaked shirt and leaned back into his seat, trembling as he recalled the discussion he mistakenly overheard. He tried to convince himself that he made an error, that he did not hear the conversation correctly. But there was no error. He knew what he heard and had no idea what to do.

Taking a deep breath and wiping the perspiration from his face and neck with his shirt, Eric started the car and continued toward home. Though the stereo spewed out song after song, he remembered none of them. As he drove, his eyes focused on the road passed, peering into the rear view mirror, nervously scrutinizing every vehicle that pulled behind him, yet watching ahead staring into the dark Virginia night as his mind stared into the darkness of his thoughts. And his thoughts consumed him, thoughts of what he overheard and the inevitable outcomes of every scenario he played within his mind, none of which comforted him.

He pulled into his driveway and scurried into the empty and lonely house where every sound threw his heart into his throat. He was scared, turning on every light and almost unconsciously, inspecting every door and window, silently praying he'd find none disturbed. Then, after walking through the entire house and peering around every corner, he nearly as systematically turned off every light, sitting in the darkness of the living room, peering out a window every time a sound was heard from outside the house. He could not continue like this. Carefully he opened the front door and ran to Greg's.

Above the light fixture at the back door sat an extra key and Eric stretched, grasping it and unlocking the back door, carefully opening it as to not wake anyone within the house. Quietly he ascended the stairs and walked down the darkened hallway, watching his step to avoid tripping on any unexpected object. He opened the door and entered Greg's room, which was illuminated from the moonlight piercing through the window. Silently, he closed the door behind him, slid to the edge of his friend's bed and gently shook him.

"Greg." He strongly whispered. "Get up!"

The boy rolled over to the side facing away from Eric and covered his head with a blanket, mumbling some indiscernible phrase.

Eric harshly poked him. "Greg! Get up man, I'm in trouble!" He nervously stated.

Greg pulled himself out from underneath the covers, turned his head and stared, groggy from being awakened from a sound sleep. "Eric, what the hell?" He said, his voice cracking. He grabbed his clock, pulling it closer to him to read the time. "It's almost two thirty!"

"I know, but I think I might be in some trouble." Eric said, his voice quivering as he began to pace in front of the bed.

Greg sat up and slid his legs over the side. "What's wrong?" He asked, seeing his friend clearly distressed.

Eric deeply sighed as he stopped and turned toward the bed. "It's these men at work." He stated, but began shaking his head, staring at the floor.

"What about them?" Greg asked. "What did they do?"

He resumed his pacing as he began to slowly and deliberately speak as if every word and every syllable encumbered his mind. "I was in the pool house shower and the men who had been staying at the villa didn't know I was in there. They returned early from some reception and came into the pool house great room to have a meeting. I got out of the shower and was getting ready to go when I heard them and before I could get out the door and apologize for interrupting their discussion, I heard what they were talking about." He said, pausing and gulping, trying to maintain his composure. Again, he took a deep breath and exhaled strongly before Greg interrupted him.

"Look, I know you weren't supposed to be there, but I doubt that you are going to get into trouble for overhearing what they were talking about." Greg stated.

Eric stopped and stared at him, shaking his head. "You don't understand. They were planning an assassination and I think it was the President's."

Greg's eyes grew wide and he stood, stepping closer to his friend. "You're kidding, right?" He said. "I mean, you couldn't have heard that correctly."

Eric gazed into his eyes and squinted, pressing his lips together as he attempted to control his emotions. "Yeah, that's right. I decided to come to your room at two thirty in the morning to make some absurd joke."

Greg placed his hands in front of him and nodded. "Okay, okay, I know you're not kidding, but are you sure that's exactly what you heard?" He inquired, a hint of disbelief in his voice.

"I assure you I heard them correctly. Do you think I would make this up?" He asked, becoming irritated.

Greg shook his head. "No bro, I don't." He answered, pausing for a moment. "Did they see you?"

He shrugged his shoulders. "I don't know. They could have as I was leaving." He answered. "But I didn't stay around to find out."

"I can understand that." Greg stated. He stepped back, walking over to his desk and throwing his arms into the air. "So what are you going to do?"

Eric chuckled in a nervous sort of way and shook his head. "I don't know. That's why I came over here. I don't *know* what to do." He emphatically stated.

Greg returned to his bed and sat. "Are you scared?"

Eric leaned against the wall opposite from the bed and sunk down until he was sitting on the floor. He stared toward the window, his eyes in a fixed gaze as if he was searching for words from within himself. Cocking his head toward Greg, he answered, an unsettling calmness filling his voice. "I've never been this scared in all my life."

Greg sighed as he watched his friend sit in the emptiness of his mind and occasionally tremble from the fear that invaded the boy's body. For once, he could not think of anything to say that wouldn't sound trivial or would even be helpful. Then he realized what needed to be done. "Look, I don't have a solution to this, but the smartest thing I think we can do right now is to tell my dad."

"What's he going to do?" Eric inquired.

Greg shook his head and leaned forward. "I don't know, but it will be far better than the solution we have right now."

Eric looked up at his friend, the few tears that rolled down the sides of his face leaving trails that glistened in the occasional light that filtered into the room, and he nodded his head in approval.

Grabbing a shirt and throwing it over his shoulders, Greg got up from the bed and left the room, patting Eric on the shoulder as he walked past. When he arrived at the door to his parent's room, he stopped, sinking his head to think for a moment what he would say to his father. How could he explain what he just heard?

He looked toward the door and, ending his hesitation, gently knocked before going in. His father woke, looking up from a sound sleep wondering what his son wanted.

"I'm sorry for waking you like this…" He began and he loudly exhaled before he continued. "But dad, I need you to come to my room. Right now." He stated as he slowly nodded his head.

"What's wrong Greg?" Dan asked as he rose then sat on the side of the bed.

Greg glanced at his mother sleeping on the other side of the bed, and then whispered. "Just come to my room."

Dan stood from his bed and grabbed a robe that had been draped over a chair in the room, following his son down the hall to his room not knowing the cause for his son's concern, but preparing for the worst. He entered, immediately spotting Eric sitting on the floor and staring into space, his legs folded into his chest and his arms wrapped around his knees. He could see, even through the lack of light in the room, that something had gone awry with the boy's life from the blankness in his face and he carefully slid the desk chair to position it in front of the young man. "Eric," He began, his voice strong but calming. "May I turn on one of the small lamps?"

Eric stared up at the man and nodded, though remaining silent.

Bostic sat in the chair across from the boy and motioned to his son to turn on the desk lamp. "What's wrong kid?" Dan asked.

Eric looked into the man's eyes and pressed his lips together for a moment as he bobbed his head. "I heard something I wasn't supposed to hear Mr. Bostic." He began, the tranquil tone of his voice masking the distress that appeared in his eyes. He continued with the same deliberate calmness as he detailed every moment of his time trapped in the shower room and the conversation he felt unfortunate to overhear.

Greg and his father concentrated on every word of the boy's story, at no time interrupting him and becoming further intrigued until the report concluded. Then, they sat in total disbelief, not of what they heard, but of the circumstances in which they heard it realizing that if their relatively unremarkable lives had not just changed, Eric's surely had.

Dan stood and returned the chair to its place, the silence he practiced unnerving the two boys as they looked to him for an answer. He turned and stood in the middle of the room, his arms crossed appearing to search for a solution. Instead, he motioned to them to follow him, leading the two downstairs to the family room and ordering them not to move as he left the room. There was a certain protocol he needed to perform and Matt Collins was the first on his list.

CHAPTER 5

DAN BOSTIC WAITED AT THE front door talking on his cellular phone, briefcase in hand and ready for work. Normally he would drive himself into the office, however on a day like today where everything was anything but normal, he waited for a ride. It was seven o'clock in the morning on a Saturday and instead of waking up for a round of golf or some other weekend activity, he prepared himself for a long day, already being awake for over four hours deciphering information Eric Lynch dropped onto his lap so unexpectedly. And while Eric slept inside, Dan hurriedly assembled a meeting that was scheduled to begin in about an hour.

Matt Collins pulled his car onto the Bostic street for the second time in the early morning. He called some three hours earlier to hear the unimaginable story a seventeen year-old neighbor had to tell. The account astounded him and he thought for a moment that maybe the boy erred in what he reported.

It seemed so unlikely that a presidential assassination scheme would rear itself in this manner, with this young man and in Collins' jurisdiction.

After he left the house for the first time this morning, he spent a moment reflecting on what he heard, realizing its magnitude. The question for him was not whether to react, but how? Unfortunately, the young man's information was terribly incomplete, devoid of names of the meeting's participants other than that of James Hamilton. And James Hamilton didn't ring a bell. But aside form a vague recollection of the muffled conversation, the entire report lacked specifics. It wasn't much to go on and though he felt deficient about not having additional information, according to protocol, he had to communicate the incident to the appropriate agencies.

Though the FBI and Secret Service showed an understandable interest in the situation, their responses remained surprisingly unimpassioned, and it disappointed Collins. As he drove the car, he thought about what happened, expecting a more aggressive reaction instead of the professionally stoic response he received. Was his office alone in expressing their concern and outrage? No, that was unlikely. Clearly these agencies were more experienced than his youthful staff and therefore more accustomed to investigating and managing such a delicate situation, making them appear unmoving when they were not. And though each would likely launch an investigation, neither indicated its intention to do so, leaving Matt and his staff with a responsibility to investigate the incident. Would this be the defining moment of his career, or just the beginning of the end of it? And for the second time he stopped his car in the driveway, this time letting it idle while Bostic jumped in the passenger seat.

The house inside remained quiet. Eric woke from his deep but nervous sleep, realizing that a mere four hours passed since he closed his eyes. He carefully rose from the bed, his clothes from last night now wrinkled on his body. He put on his sneakers and carefully left the room, silently walking down the hallway to not wake Greg or Greg's mother.

He left the house into the golden sunlight of the early morning, squinting his eyes as he shuffled toward his home. He had stayed with the Bostic's for two reasons, primarily because he was scared but also because by the time he finished answering questions, he was too tired to return home.

As he approached, he removed the key to his house from his pocket and inserted it into the lock. The door opened to the stillness he left, everything in its place undisturbed. He picked up the newspaper from the walkway and entered the house. Clearly no one came after him last night and he sighed in comfort at that thought. Still, he wandered through the house for his own peace of mind, then walked up to his room and sat on his bed, grabbing a remote control and turning on the stereo.

He stared across the room deep in thought. Did Mr. Collins take his story seriously? Or did the lack of any specific information of a discussion that he allegedly overheard hurt his credibility? Allegedly, he thought. Now he was questioning himself and he shook his head upset with the notion that even though he was positive of what he heard, he still doubted his own accuracy.

How could anyone else confidently believe his story when his own confidence wavered? He needed to do something to restore his credibility, if only for himself.

He laid back onto his bed and stared up at the ceiling, recalling last night's interrogation and, in his mind, hearing Matt Collins repeating the same question time after time. Did they at any time reveal the specifics of their plan? And the same answer haunted him after each question; he could not remember. He was sure they mentioned some detail; he vaguely recalled that part of the discussion. But the idea that he could remember no facts or give no names, other than Hamilton's frustrated him greatly. And he had to rectify that situation.

He squirmed in his bed, the music pushed to a space of his mind that muted the words of each song to an indistinguishable background of rhythms and chords as he thought. His thoughts were clear and organized, systematically calculating a result of one plan after another as he attempted to decipher his own credibility crises. Then he smiled, not the smile of happiness but that of success, sat upright on his bed and shuffled to his dresser, opening the top drawer and realizing that his problem had been solved.

He walked to his closet, removed his equipment bag then began searching through his clothes, tossing several black pieces of clothing onto his bed. He returned to his dresser and rummaged through the drawers until he removed two pair of black soccer socks and placed them next to the clothes he already laid on his bed. He stopped, sat on his desk chair across the room, and stared at the collection of clothing. Was he doing the right thing? He sighed and recalled in his mind the conversation he and Matt Collins held after the questioning was over.

It was a quiet and reassuring talk, one that somewhat reminded Eric of the talks he had with his father after something worried him, or scared him. And in that same fatherly tone, Collins urged him to go on with life as if the event did not occur, that nothing bad was going to happen and to let he and his staff manage the situation. But what would Collins manage?

There was no question that the information Eric gave him was far from complete and though Collins communicated his appreciation for the information, he emitted a feeling of disappointment. Or was that disappointment Eric's own in himself? Maybe it stemmed from hearing the plan then freezing and cowering in a darkened hallway like a little baby, so scared that he failed to retain any of the most important conversation. If he was really the confident and cocky young man he proclaimed to be, then how could he perform such a cowardly action? And it was that feeling that bothered Eric the most.

He rose from the chair and began packing his clothes and the rest of the gear he assembled into the equipment bag before he carried it downstairs. He placed the bag next to the front door and walked back to the kitchen to eat, surprisingly composed despite the weekend's events. Opening the refrigerator and scanning the contents, he pulled out three pieces of leftover pizza and tossed them into the microwave, then poured himself a large glass of orange juice before sitting down at the island counter to begin eating. The music from his stereo filtered into the room as he relaxed, scanning the newspaper he left there earlier. He was at peace with himself, slowly munching his food as he read, and then cleaning after himself when he finished.

He glanced upward to a clock on the microwave and, realizing that it was time for him to get ready for work, stood and trotted up to his room. After taking a quick shower and dressing, he rumbled down the stairway as if today was any other day. He grabbed the bag he placed next to the door and slung it over his shoulder as he bolted out of the house, slamming the door behind him and locking it before he walked to the car.

He lazily drove toward Saddlewood through the northern Virginia countryside, the scattered horse farms that dotted the landscape and the roadside attractions that entertained the host of travelers when U.S 50 was the main east-west thoroughfare in and out of Washington drawing his attention more than the traffic or the day ahead. He turned onto the side road that led to the staff entrance of the complex and fixed his attention to every turn and intersection along the way. He had driven this way so many times that the placement of almost every tree and sign remained etched in his mind, yet now he concentrated closer to the details of the route more then he ever had in the past.

At a sign announcing that the main road was restricted to authorized vehicles and before it began to ascend a small hill, a secondary road branched to the left and he stopped, turned his car onto it and slowly drove along its heavily wooded path. After riding a short distance, he stopped at a spot in the road where the berm widened to accommodate a parked car or two next to a mountain creek. He pulled onto the side and stopped, backing the car behind a grove of trees that concealed it from the road. The spot was serene as well as secluded and he stepped out of the car, leaning against its hood as he watched the water of the creek bounce across rock after rock until it calmed into a small and placid pool. He walked to the water's edge, bending down to stick his hand into the cool stream, wondering if it was the same waterway that ran through Saddlewood.

He stood, wiped his wet hands on the side of his pants and began following the creek upstream toward its source along a primitive earthen path that paralleled the water. As he ascended a small hill, he noticed a bridge ahead, recognizing it as the one that carries the roadway to the staff entrance of Saddlewood and he stopped. Going off the path to find a better vantage point, he climbed a small hill and stared beyond the highway toward the fence that separated Saddlewood from the rest of the world. He spotted part of a small waterfall and smiled, then descended the hill and returned to the path where he glanced at his watch and walked back toward his car.

When he arrived at the secluded spot by the creek, he walked past the car to the road and glanced both ways, first to the right and then to his left, noting that not one vehicle had passed by. He returned to the car and started the engine, again briefly glancing at his watch before he pulled onto the road and continued to follow it further into the woodland. After driving several miles along the winding country lane, he came upon a crossroads, one of them leading to an exit on the interstate highway that flowed into Washington. Again he smugly smiled, turned the car around and drove back toward Saddlewood. His plan was coming together.

Reaching the intersection where he first turned to find his secluded piece of forest, he made a left and headed for the security gate. After parking his car, he quickly entered the clubhouse, retrieved his gear for the evening and walked to his locker carrying both his bag of gear and his duffel bag. He opened the duffel and cautiously scanned the surrounding area. Seeing no one around him, he removed a small portable cassette player, placing it and its power cord into the equipment bag he picked up at the desk. He closed his bag and stuffed it into the locker, then changed into his work uniform before he continued to the villa, the equipment bag draped over his shoulder. When he arrived at the guesthouse, he entered the employee lounge, hung the bag in the closet and confidently walked into the kitchen.

"Eric, nice to see you looking so sharp and refreshed this afternoon." Kearney said as he peered up from his desk. "Especially since you apparently left here far later than I would have expected you to last night. Did something happen?"

"Sir?" Eric replied, surprised by the inquiry.

"Did something happen?" Kearney repeated. "I pulled the exit report from the computer to do payroll and I noticed that you didn't leave the clubhouse until well after one this morning." The man said.

"Oh." Eric began, hesitating before he answered. "I met with someone after I left here and forgot to turn in my gear right away. Sorry about that." He explained, pleased with himself that he prepared to answer such a question in advance.

Kearney smiled at the young man. "Ah yes, Maria. I hope the two of you had a good time." He stated. "However the next time you decide to go on one of your romantic rendezvous, please check out first."

Eric grinned. "Yes sir I will."

Kearney gazed at the young man for a moment as he smiled and shook his head. "Okay, we have an easy night ahead. The listing is on the computer so go ahead and do your thing."

Eric nodded his head and returned to his desk in the employee lounge, flipping the switch on his computer monitor and reading the schedule for the evening. It was exactly what he wanted to see. He grabbed a cleaning bucket from nearby and opened the closet, unzipping his bag and stuffing the equipment he brought into the facility inside the bucket then covering it with a towel before he left he room.

He walked alongside the pool, scanning it as he passed appearing as if he were checking its cleanliness. However, he had other activity dominating his thoughts. He opened the door to the pool house, his attention focused completely on the building's interior. In his mind he knew what he was looking for, yet the task was to find it; that perfect spot.

He entered the mechanical room, placing the bucket on a shelf inside, and removed the tape recorder with the other supplies he needed for this project. The pool filter engaged and the whir of the motor caught his attention; so he stopped, turned and stared at the piece of equipment realizing that now he would have to compensate for its noise and electrical interference when he chose his location.

He exited the mechanical room and slowly walked around the great room of the pool house, examining every wall and every piece of furniture just as Hamilton did the first day they met. It was Hamilton's actions that replayed through Eric's memory as he searched the room for the optimum location to set the recorder, one that the general would not suspect while providing an unobstructed account of the meeting. As he searched, clarity in his thoughts and actions dominated his once nervous body that now filled with an exhilaration that rivaled any soccer game he played. And he relished in it.

Behind the bar on the wall near the ceiling sat an air vent, its decorative cover concealed in the interior design of the room so as not to intrude coldness into an otherwise warm space. He retrieved a ladder from the closet and climbed to eye level with the cover, peering into the duct and examining its construction. Could he hide the recorder inside and tape the night's meeting?

He descended the ladder and entered the shower room, his heart beginning to race as he recalled his experience the night before. As he peered up along the wall, he noticed an air duct near the ceiling and an electrical outlet below. He took a deep breath and slowly exhaled as he thought for a moment. Did the two vents connect?

Picking up a screwdriver from the storage closet and grabbing the ladder from the other room, he ascended the ladder and removed the cover from the air vent, peering into the darkened shaft toward the left. A light dimly shined from inside and Eric grinned as he pulled away from the vent, carefully stepping down the ladder. He knew he found the solution he was looking for.

He walked into the mechanical room, retrieved the recorder and the remainder of his equipment then returned to the shower room. After using a long extension cord to plug in the recorder, he checked the tape inside then tested the voice activation system, setting the device on a rung of the ladder and moving across the room, speaking as he walked away. He stopped and turned around, picking up the recorder, rewinding the tape and replaying it. The recorder worked perfectly. Again he rewound the tape and climbed the ladder, pushing the recorder into the duct until it sat just behind the vent for the great room. He backed away from the duct and descended the ladder, removing the plug from the outlet to save the tape for the meeting, and then replaced all of the equipment into the mechanical room.

He returned to the villa as if he completed a series of chores and entered the study as his pager beeped signaling the arrival of a guest to the house. He walked outside to the circle and watched a shuttle pull around the fountain, stopping in front.

"Good afternoon Mr. Lynch." Hamilton greeted as he stepped out of the vehicle.

Eric hesitated for a moment, and then forced a smile at the man as he attempted to ignore the nervousness that bubbled from within. "Good afternoon sir." He replied. "Is there anything I can get for you?"

The man smiled in return, guiding the young man with one arm while carrying a briefcase in the other as they walked toward the door. "Not right now, well...maybe if you can find a particular bottle of German wine for me, a Reisling in fact, like you did yesterday with the Leibfraumilch, I would greatly appreciate that." He replied.

"I would be happy to." Eric stated as he opened the front door for the man.

"Mr. Lynch," Hamilton began, stopping at the door before he entered the villa and turning toward Eric. "you start school again soon, do you not?"

"Yes sir." Eric answered.

"You will be a senior in high school this year, if I remember correctly. Is that right?" The man stated, knowing he was right from the tone of his voice.

"Yes sir, that is correct," He answered.

Hamilton slowly nodded as he entered the villa. "I see. Are you planning to continue your employment here?"

"Yes sir," Eric said, following the man inside to the edge of the stairway where they stopped.

"Good." Hamilton replied. "I'll find my own way to my room Mr. Lynch. Thank you." And the man turned and walked up the stairs, disappearing into his room.

Eric stood at the bottom shaking his head. He was accustomed to conversations with Hamilton that seemed meaningless, though he wondered if any actually were. Hamilton was not the type to engage in useless or inane discussions, which caused him to believe that for some reason, the man wanted that particular information. Eric could only guess why.

He walked back to his desk, sat and scanned the wines available from the central cellar on his computer, ordering a case of a highly recommended Reisling as requested. He leaned back in his chair and stared at the wall across from him, a wall he had seen maybe a thousand times before. There was nothing on it to hold his attention, yet he sat gazing into its simplicity as if studying a Renoir or Monet, losing himself in thought until he popped onto his feet and raced into the kitchen where Kearney sat working at his desk.

"I need to go to the winery to pick up a case." He stated, the inflection in his voice unmasking his attempted to create a reason to leave the villa.

"They're not delivering today?" Kearney asked as he looked up from his desk, knowing the young man's intentions were not purely inspired by his diligence for work.

"I'm sure they would, but you know how long they take sometimes." Eric began. "I thought while there was nothing going on, I'd pick it up because you know they'll deliver it at the worst possible time for us."

Kearney chuckled, shaking his head. "You have a point, but I know that's not the impetus for your decision to go." He picked up an envelope from his desk and handed it to the young man. "Here. Take this to the consulate. At least this gives you a reason to be there."

Eric grinned. "Thanks." He stated, a puzzled expression covering his face as he wondered how the man knew.

Kearney shrugged his shoulders. "Hey, I was seventeen once too. I'll call and let her know you're coming."

Eric nodded his head as he turned to leave the room, scampering to his cart and driving away, his mind fixed solely on Maria. As he approached the consulate, he saw her, gracefully poised upon one of the marble benches of the Italian garden in front, her long slender legs tucked in a feminine fashion to one side as a gentle breeze fluttered through her dark flowing hair. Her face grew a delicate smile as her brown eyes sparkled the sun's rays to a twinkle the closer he came to her.

"Hi." She softly greeted. "Mr. Kearney called and said that you were on your way."

Eric jumped out of the cart, the bottles of wine he picked up on the way rattling. He sat next to her on the bench with the envelope clutched in his hand. "Yeah, I wanted to see you." He replied.

She looked toward the envelope. "Is that for me?"

Eric nodded as a grin formed on his face. "It was Stephen's way of giving me a reason to come over here." He confessed.

"I am happy you did." She stated. "I missed you."

The grin he formed grew to a shy smile as he drew closer to her. "I missed you too." He said, pausing and then pulling away, a more serious expression invading his face. "Maria," He began. "I need a favor from you and it might not be the only one I ask you for in the next couple of days."

She stared into his eyes and could sense his concern. "Is there something wrong?"

He glanced at the ground before he answered, slowly shaking his head and pensively contorting his face. "It's not that there is anything wrong at the moment, and there might not be anything wrong at all, but something isn't totally right and that could cause a little trouble."

"A little trouble." She repeated. "Here?"

"Not exactly." He answered.

"Oh." She replied. "Forgive me if I am not up on all of the trick American phrases, but what is the difference between something being wrong and something not being totally right?"

"There is a difference and I would love to explain it to you right now, but I can't." Eric stated.

She nodded her head in acceptance. "What do you need me to do?"

He hesitated for a moment, and then looked into her eyes. "If anyone asks if I was with you last night, I would greatly appreciate if you said yes." He requested.

"Okay, I will. What time were you with me?" She inquired.

"From about ten thirty until quarter after one." He answered.

She slowly nodded her head, and then tilted it to look into his eyes. "What is this all about Eric?" She softly asked.

"I can't really tell you that right now without getting you involved in something I don't want you involved in." He answered.

"I see." She stated, clearly disillusioned about the lack of information she was given.

"Look," He began, sensing her concern of a situation she knew nothing about. "You have to trust me on this, but I promise that as soon as I can, I will tell you all about it."

The sincerity in his voice and expression did nothing to quell the uneasiness that pierced her and she slid her hand onto his, grasping tightly to comfort her further. "Do you promise that you are not in any danger?" She asked.

He hesitated, as he looked deep into her eyes and attempted to control his own emotions. "I promise." He replied.

She smiled at him and slowly accepted his request. "Okay." She said, knowing he just lied to her.

The two of them sat in silence, Eric easing his arm around her and holding her tightly against his body. There was no need for words, no need for any discussion or need for any action other than to melt into each other because both knew that he was putting himself into danger. She didn't know why and she did not ask. Instead, she stayed close to him because he needed her to. She could sense his fear.

After several moments of sitting together in the garden, he gently lifted her off him and moved closer to her lips until they locked in a passionate embrace, breaking away from each other after Eric's pager sounded. "I have to go." He said as he stood and checked the number.

"When will I see you again?" She asked.

"I don't work again until Tuesday." He replied. "I won't be able to see you until then."

"E-mail me." She said. "Everyday so I know that you are okay."

Eric cracked a smile. "That I can do." He answered. He leaned over giving her a quick kiss, then jumped in his cart and drove away.

He felt an emptiness surge through his body as he passed through the gates of the consulate, an emptiness in the way that a person gets when he can't wait until the next time he sees someone, but knows that it won't be for a long time, if ever. He slowed the cart and looked back, catching a final glimpse of her as she stood in the vestibule of the residence before she turned, walking inside. And with the door closing behind her, the emptiness that all but invaded him swelled into a knot of twisted emotions. He stopped the cart and sighed. Should he continue toward the villa or turn back? And he knew he had to continue.

The stillness of the villa unnerved him when he entered and he hurriedly stocked the wine into the cellar before ascending the stairs into the main body of the house. It was quiet, yet the absence of typical activity concerned him, being paranoid of someone discovering his plans. He quietly roamed from room to room hoping to find someone in the house and not in the pool house. As he entered the study, he spotted Hamilton sitting in one of the armchairs reading and he stopped to slowly retreat from the room.

"I see you Mr. Lynch." The man stated. "Please, come in."

"I don't want to interrupt your reading." Eric replied as he cautiously entered the room, keeping his distance from the man.

Hamilton placed a mark in his book and closed it, setting it on the table next to him and picking up a cup and saucer, taking a sip from the cup. "You aren't really." He stated, replacing the cup and saucer on the table. "I trust that you acquired a satisfactory bottle of wine for me."

Eric nodded. "Yes sir, several bottles in fact. May I get you one now?"

"No, thank you. I am quite satisfied with coffee." He answered, crossing his legs and posing an inquisitive look toward the young man. "Mr. Lynch, is there something bothering you? You seem a little apprehensive today."

Eric forced a smile as he cupped his hands behind him. "No sir, I'm fine thank you, but I appreciate you asking."

Hamilton tilted his head in acknowledgment. "Well, should you have a problem that I would be able to assist you with in any way, please do not hesitate to ask."

The irony of the general's offer humored him and he stepped back nodding in appreciation, slowly turning and leaving the room. The general was his problem and he hoped that when he returned to work, that problem would be gone or at least under control. But for now, he would have to manage the night with Hamilton and his men.

He walked around the villa a final time before the guests were to be seated for dinner, his mind more focused on what he planned after work than work itself. And as he intensely thought about his plans for the evening, his focus transformed into anxiety, a feeling that must have become apparent to the general when he spoke with him.

As it occurred the night before, Hamilton and his men left the guesthouse after dinner, this time for a private party at one of the clubs located inside the resort. It was the perfect opportunity for Eric to put his plan into action. He casually walked outside, the reflections of the subdued lighting surrounding the pool danced on the breeze-caused ripples of the water that gently swept across and he sat for a moment in the peacefulness, contemplating what he was about to do for one final time. He puffed his cheeks, strongly forcing air out of his mouth, rose from the patio chair and approached the glass door to the pool house. Hesitating briefly, he turned the knob and opened the door, entering the great room then gently closing the door behind him. Quickly, he stepped into the shower room and plugged in the cord hanging down from the air vent above. The trap was set and with the one swift motion, the anxiety within him increased to a level he never experienced before.

He returned to the guesthouse and walked to the employee lounge, gathering his gear while announcing to Kearney and the remaining staff that he was leaving. It was imperative to him that everyone knew of his departure and he made sure they did. He drove to the operations center, changed into his street clothes then returned his uniform and equipment to the desk before he trotted out to his car with his duffel bag hanging over his shoulder. The air was muggy and the humidity generated a moon-obscuring haze that dulled the night sky to a more darkened hue, yet augmented every cricket's sound to produce a clear chorus of quick chirps. He stopped under the orange glow of the parking lot lights and listened before inserting his key into the lock, opening the car and hopping in. This was the easy part of the night.

After clearing the security gate, he slowly drove along the winding road to the intersection, returning to the secluded parking spot by the creek that he discovered earlier in the day. He opened the duffel bag sitting on his passenger's seat and removed his cell phone, quickly punching in a number then telling the person on the other end that he was leaving and he would see them in an hour. After closing the phone and tossing it onto the seat, he took out the clothing he had packed at his house, laying them across the seat back. When he emptied the bag, he pushed his seat backward and began to change, stripping down to his dark-colored boxer shorts. He was deliberate in dressing, sliding two pair of black athletic socks on his feet followed by a pair of black loose-fitting jeans and a white pullover collared shirt. A black sweatshirt and black tee-shirt remained on the passenger seat when he reached into the back of the car, grabbing a pair of black sneakers, putting them on his feet and tying them tightly. Leaving the remaining pieces of clothing on the seat, he stuffed his other clothing into his bag and tossed it onto the back seat, then started the engine and drove down the road, following it back toward the main highway. He had some time to kill.

He glanced at the clock on the face of the car stereo and he realized that three hours needed to pass before it was safe to return to the pool house. Happy that he left himself with enough time to do what he planned, he smiled as he drove through the countryside. He approached the intersection with the entrance ramp to the interstate and turned onto the highway, following it to an exit where all night restaurants and numerous motels catered to the hoards of travelers who visited the nation's capital on any given weekend.

He pulled into the parking lot of one of the all night restaurants and turned off his engine, hopping out of the vehicle and locking it. Walking slowly toward the entrance, he scanned the parking lot thoroughly, as if he were searching for someone or something specific. As he pulled open the right side glass door of the restaurant and entered the vestibule, he smiled. "Hey." He greeted, seeing Beth standing inside waiting for him.

"Hey." She replied, her face breaking into a wide smile as he walked toward her.

Eric stopped, leaned toward her and gave her a quick kiss. "I'm glad you came."

She turned toward him, a quizzical look preceding the question that undoubtedly filled her mind. "Is there some reason why you think I wouldn't?"

He shook his head and shrugged his shoulders simultaneously. "No, it's just...you know, kind of late." He stated as the two walked to a booth near a window and sat.

She stared at him for a moment, and then leaned forward. "It's not even eleven o'clock on a Saturday night." She softly replied. "It's not that late."

A waitress stopped by the table, unintentionally interrupting the conversation, greeted the two and handed them menus. "Can I get you both something to drink before you order?" She asked.

"I'll have a Coke." Eric replied.

"The same please." Beth answered. The waitress smiled and walked away as Beth paused to continue the conversation. "So why did you decide to come all the way out here?" She inquired.

"I have to go back to work tonight and I couldn't see you if we didn't meet somewhere in between." He explained. "And I really wanted to see you."

She tilted her head and a demure grin halted her from answering immediately. "That's sweet." She replied, pausing before she continued. "You have to go back to work?"

He nodded his head. "Yeah." I've got a special project I have to tend to and I can only do it tonight."

"A special project." She repeated. "Not to sound as if I don't trust you, but you are dressed nicely for a special project at work."

He shook his head. "It's nothing like that Beth." He replied, becoming slightly defensive. "I can't leave work with my uniform and I wanted to look good for you tonight."

She smiled as she leaned forward, twitching her head to signal to draw him near, and she gently kissed him. "You would look good to me even if you weren't wearing anything."

He wriggled his eyes and began to laugh. "Oh really?"

She gently smacked him on the side of his head. "You know what I meant." She replied, slightly embarrassed by her choice of words. "Everything with you is so sexual."

He grinned as he leaned back in his side of the booth. "It's difficult not to be, especially with you sitting across from me. But anyway, it's not like you aren't sexual, subconsciously wanting to see me naked tonight." He arrogantly replied. "You can't fool me Miss Wilshire." He began as he leaned forward to whisper to her. "You are as sexually charged as I am."

She grinned but did not answer. "I think we should order." She stated, clearly attempting to avoid escalating the conversation any further.

He smiled at her and slowly opened his menu, peering over it to peek at her. He didn't want to tell her what happened to him the night before or what he was doing when he left here, causing her to worry and over-react to the situation. Yet, he thought she had some right to know what was going on. The question was when to tell her. And for a moment, he considered explaining it to her while they ate, but decided instead to enjoy her company without the burden of the unavoidable questions that were sure to rise if he told her. So they sat, ate and talked until it was time for Eric to leave.

They stepped out into the parking lot and Eric escorted her to her car, his arm draped tightly around her body. She unlocked the door and opened it slightly. "I had a nice time tonight."

He grinned at her. "So did I." He replied.

"Are we still on for tomorrow?" She asked.

He nodded his head. "Of course." He said and he leaned toward her, kissing her passionately. Gently they separated and he stepped back from the car so she could get inside. "I'll see you tomorrow."

She started the engine and smiled at him, waving as she drove away. He stood for a moment, watching her as she exited the parking lot then speeding up the road toward the exit of the interstate. Again the feeling he experienced when he left Maria repeated in his body only this time, the emptiness was more profound. He slowly turned and walked to his car, anxious to get the night over with.

After filling the gas tank at a nearby station, he glanced at the clock in the car and shook his head. Still too early to return to the villa to retrieve the tape, he quickly thought of somewhere to go or something to do to pass the time. And though there was plenty of nightspots open into the wee hours of weekends, none of them catered to a person who was only seventeen and looked it. Instead, he was left to drive around a while before he could return to his staging spot by the creek.

As he drove, he reviewed his plan in his head, every step, every action, every detail painstakingly simulated including a contingency if, for some reason or another, his plan failed or was discovered. He returned to the spot in the woods by the creek and parked his sports car; backing it in as far as he could well out of sight from the road. As he shut off the engine, the nervousness that previously invaded his body circulated through it once again and he leaned his head back in his seat, took a deep breath, and then exhaled strongly to relax. He glanced at his watch and knew that it was time to go.

He grabbed the black tee shirt and sweatshirt sitting on the passenger seat, opened his door and stepped outside of the car; removing the white shirt he wore to see Beth and replacing it with the tee shirt and sweatshirt. Tossing the shirt he removed onto the back seat, he leaned inside the car and reached into the duffle bag, pulling out a small roll of black athletic tape, a plastic cassette holder, a pair of black batting gloves and a black knit hat, all of which he placed on the roof of the car. He stuffed the roll of tape and the plastic holder into his pants pocket, and then eased the door of the car nearly closed leaving the keys in the ignition to save time for a quick getaway. Putting the gloves on his hand and the hat on his head, he turned and began his quiet trek up the path that paralleled the creek toward Saddlewood.

As he approached the bridge that carried the road over the creek to the employee gate, he stopped and scouted the area knowing that a perimeter security vehicle that circled the complex could come riding by at any moment. After checking in both directions, he scampered along the creek and under the bridge, stopping once again to survey the roadway before he sprinted the ten or so yards of exposed land along the stream to the hillside that the fence perched upon.

The creek flowed out of the complex in a small cascade of a waterfall that eroded the earth underneath the security fence and created enough of a space to slide under. Eric ducked under the fence through the small trickle of water, then scaled the rocks and earth with the precision of a mountain ram, pulling himself up onto the level ground concealed by the wood line.

He stood among the thickness of the trees and looked around. The campus of Saddlewood sat quiet and empty in the early hours of this Sunday morning and he enjoyed the peacefulness for a moment before he started his walk toward the villa. Carefully he followed the creek through the trees and underbrush toward the first open space of the complex between the fence and the guesthouse, stopping as he reached the tree line. From the edge of the clearing, he studied the area between where he was standing and the tree line across the main access lane that wound through Saddlewood. He stared in each direction for several moments, the silence of the early morning interrupted only by the constant thudding of his beating heart as he searched for a hint of a security team inspecting the area. After assuring himself that he was in the clear, he darted across the open space and concealed himself between the trees.

Again he stood, stopping within the second row of trees to calm himself from the nervousness that caused his heart to beat so quickly. As he turned toward the clearing he just crossed, a security vehicle passed by and he realized that he narrowly escaped being discovered, yet he remained focused on his mission. He watched the vehicle until it disappeared further down the lane before he turned back toward the interior of the woods and followed the creek closer to the villa.

Carefully he stepped along the stream until he could see the lights that outlined the guesthouse in the distance to his left. Instead of changing direction and walking directly toward the house, he followed the creek until where he stood paralleled the villa, estimating the distance between the two points to himself. He moved closer, remaining under the cover of the trees as he examined the grounds surrounding the villa and the lighting from inside. Seeing no movement as he crept through the trees and underbrush, he circled behind the house to the tennis court slowly scanning every inch of the grounds before leaving the protection of the woods.

After confirming to himself that all was quiet within the villa, he sprinted across the open landscape to the side of the pool house next to one of the gates of the tennis court. Using a trick that Aaron taught him for when he accidentally locked himself out, he reached through the fence and tripped the electric security latch, the grinding of the gears that opened the lock shattering the absolute silence of the early morning. He quietly opened the gate to the tennis court and slid through, leaving the gate slightly ajar for his quick exit. Carefully he turned the knob of the pool house door and silently pulled it toward him exposing the stairway to the great room. He peered into the darkness of the downstairs, relieved by the silence, and entered the building.

Cautiously, he descended the stairs to the great room, pausing before he passed the French doors that led out to the patio. He was scared and the stillness of the room heightened his nervousness, so he swallowed deeply to recapture his heart that seemed to want to escape from his body. He scanned the room, peering out the windows toward the pool and seeing the dim accent lighting flicker its reflection off the water, but nothing else. Watching his step as he moved, he walked to the door of the employee shower room and removed his identification card from his pocket, sliding the plastic card through the slot and opening the door.

Not wanting to ruin his night vision for any amount of time, he entered the blackness of the room, left the main lights off and eased the door closed behind him. He turned and walked to the end of the room near the shower and turned on the dim auxiliary light over the stall, then returned to the wall under the air vent and grabbed the extension cord that hung down from above. As he slowly pulled the cord, he heard the faint sound of the recorder scrape against the duct as it neared the vent above him and he stood to peer upward to see how close the recorder was to the edge. Gently he resumed pulling until one side of the recorder appeared over the lip of the vent and again he stopped, grabbed the cord with both hands and strongly yanked it sending the recorder tumbling toward him. He caught the recorder in flight, then picked up the cord and returned to the lighted part of the room where he opened the storage closet, careful not to make much noise. He plugged in the recorder at a nearby receptacle and briefly listened to his recording, hoping for the important content that brought him here in the first place. It sounded perfect; every word and every voice of the ten or so seconds he dare play.

Disconnecting the extension cord from the recorder, he rolled the cord into a tight circle and placed it into the closet. Then, he opened the recorder, removed the tape from inside and stored the recorder inside the closet next to the cord as he held the cassette in his hand. He removed the small roll of athletic tape and the cassette holder from his pocket, kneeled down on his left knee and lifted the leg of his pants to expose his socks. He inserted the cassette into the holder, then lowered both pair of socks and placed the plastic case against his leg, taking the roll of tape and wrapping it around his leg to secure the cassette holder snugly to him. Raising the inner sock over the case, he sealed it inside the sock by wrapping an additional strip of tape around his leg, and then pulled his outer sock over the inner. After lowering his pant leg, he stood, placed the remaining roll of tape into the closet and quietly closed the door. He was ready to leave.

Eric turned off the shower light and stood in the room for a moment, listening for any activity in the great room and waiting for his eyes to adjust to the darkness. It remained eerily quiet and he eased to the door, pushing it slightly open to peer outside. As before, the stillness unnerved him. But now, as he neared the end of his mission, he ignored the nervousness and focused completely on getting out of Saddlewood without being seen.

Eric scampered across the great room to the stairway and climbed them to the tennis courts. Slowly and cautiously, he pushed the door open, slid outside and eased the door closed. He walked to the gate he left ajar and pushed it open, slid through then turned around to ease it closed until the electronic gears grabbed and secured it.

"Hey! Stop!" A man screamed from the end of the fence line, then began to run toward him.

"Shit!" Eric exclaimed as he turned and ran toward the obscurity of the woods. It was one of the Hamilton's men.

The older, slightly portly man began chasing after him toward the woods, yelling for him to stop as a gunshot exploded from behind. At any moment, Eric expected to run into any of Hamilton's other men hiding behind one of the approaching trees. Another shot pierced the silence of the early morning as he entered the woods and found the small stream that he followed to the villa, continuing his sprint to the clearing and increasing his speed to the opposite side. He couldn't stop running, even if he wanted to.

He followed the creek through the perimeter tree line to the small waterfall that trickled under the fence and slid down, clearing himself of the fence, but placing him into the open area between it and the roadway. Again he darted across the field along the water and ducked under the bridge, continuing into the cover of the trees on the opposite side and toward his car. As he ran deeper into the woods, he heard the security vehicles patrol the road behind and could see the reflection of the searchlights in the early morning mist.

He reached his car and jumped inside, starting the engine immediately. Without engaging his lights, he sped onto the road toward the interstate, only turning on his lights when he distanced himself from the intersection to Saddlewood, then increasing his speed the further away from the complex he drove. His heart pounded and sweat poured from his body, generated from the fear of being shot at for the first time in his life after being discovered breaking and entering into an embassy of the United Nations. And he thought about what he just did as he glanced into the rear view mirror hoping he wasn't being chased.

He reached the exit to the interstate but stopped before entering, pulling off the side of the road and engaging the parking break. He bent over, removing the tape from his sock and the cassette holder form his leg, placing the plastic case on the passenger seat. He then took his wallet out of his bag, tossed it into the cup holder next to him, released the parking break and entered the interstate toward Washington.

As he drew nearer to his home, he comprehended the seriousness of his activities and realized that his life had just changed forever. Hamilton would respond swiftly and decisively as he could not afford his plan being exposed. A man so exhaustive about details would definitely have prepared for such a situation. The question was, how well was he prepared?

As he approached the exit he would normally take to go home, Eric thought about Hamilton and knew he was in serious trouble. A man who prided himself on knowing so much about the people he associated with, certainly knew where each lived or where each would go. And he then realized he was left with the fact that he could not go home.

He grabbed his wallet out of the holder and opened it; looking for the business card he received from Matt Collins the night before. As he passed the exit, he pulled the card from the wallet then picked up the phone sitting on the passenger seat wondering if he should call or just show up at the man's front door. He glanced at the clock in the car and tossed the phone back onto the seat. He would show up at the man's front door.

The car raced into the driveway and quickly came to a stop. Eric shut off the engine, grabbed the cassette from the seat and rushed onto the front doorstep, ringing the bell then stepping back and staring at the house to search for some indication of a response. He anxiously waited a few moments, but seeing no movement from inside, he walked to the door and pounded on it several times. Suddenly, a light illuminated the doorstep and the door swung open.

Matt Collins stood before him and stared at the young man for a moment then shook his head as he stepped aside. "Come on in." He ordered, closing the door as Eric passed. "I take it we had some sort of a problem tonight."

Eric turned to face him and nodded his head. "Yes sir." He responded. "I'm in trouble and I didn't know what else to do."

Collins directed him into his living room and motioned for him to sit. "What happened?" He asked.

"You're not going to like it." Eric stated.

Collins sarcastically chuckled. "Eric, I already know that."

CHAPTER 6

As DARK CLOUDS MOVED FROM the west over the Potomac River, Collins walked out of the hanger onto the tarmac and toward a private jet sitting close by, its engines silently still and waiting for the order to fire up. He peered into the overcast sky and took a deep breath. It smelled like rain, the humidity of the air giving off that special fragrance which precedes every thunderstorm, and he thought to himself, hoping that the weather held off long enough to get the plane in the air. He didn't need a delay. He was busy and there was no indication that would change anytime soon.

He entered the jet and sat in one of the leather-trimmed seats next to Bostic and across from two other men, all of whom were engaged in conversation on their cellular phones. They were all tired, spending countless hours listening to the tape that Eric Lynch provided for them as well as questioning the boy about all he knew from working at Saddlewood. They could not stop, each moment becoming more valuable than the last and the next maybe more valuable than the rest.

As patiently as his tired mind could, Collins waited for the man to end his call, somewhat listening but not really paying attention. And while Bostic paused in his conversation, Collins leaned toward him. "Did you locate his parents yet?" He whispered, his patience fading as he waited for an answer.

Bostic nodded but did not answer. Instead, he raised his index finger and ended the conversation with the person on the phone. Closing the device, he slipped it into his jacket pocket and looked up. "They were in Greensboro for their younger son's soccer tournament. I had a Marshal discretely meet with them at their hotel and he's escorting them back home. Is Eric still sleeping?"

"Yeah." Collins answered. "I'm going to wake him in about five minutes. We need to get going."

"Where are you going with him?" Bostic asked.

Collins stretched out I his seat and exhaled strongly. "I've got a safe house and new identity set up for him, but for security reasons, I'm sure you understand that I cannot tell you where with your son involved in all this. I will tell you that we're going to have to hide him until this is over."

Bostic nodded his head in agreement. "I understand perfectly. However, since you're going to hide him until it's over," He began. "don't you think that it would be right to tell him that this may not be over for a long while."?

"Well," Collins began as he stood from his seat. "at this point I think we should keep that fact to ourselves. He doesn't need to know how long this could actually take." He said, and then he turned and walked out of the plane.

Again he glanced upward looking at a sky that appeared darker than just five minutes ago. He shook his head in a reaction to the weather then slowly began walking toward the hangar; his head sunk downward noticing a scattering of drops of moisture collecting on the concrete. He felt guilty and dishonest, a surprising first in his career as an attorney, as he knew he might be forced to mislead Eric if the right questions were asked. It's not that he hadn't misled anyone before, but they weren't seventeen, they were criminals and he had no connection to them. It was acceptable in those cases, but this. This was far different.

He entered the structure and casually walked toward the door at its rear where two military police attentively stood guard. He stopped in front of the door as one reached to open it, then quietly eased past them, entering the darkened room and turning on a dim light. The boy lay peacefully sleeping on a cot against the wall and Collins considered for a moment allowing him to remain a while longer, a rumble of thunder in the distance convincing him otherwise. He leaned toward the young man and gently shook him, calling his name.

"Eric, time to get up." He quietly called.

The boy rolled over on the cot and wiped his eyes. "What time is it?" He asked.

"About one o'clock." Collins answered. "We have to get going."

Eric sat upright and squinted at the man standing next to him. "Where?" He inquired as he put on his sneakers.

"Away from here for right now." He replied. "You'll be fine."

Eric slowly nodded his head as he thought, staying silent for a moment. He stared across the small room then stood and looked through the bars of a nearby window. "What's going to prevent them from finding me anyway. I know they possess that capability." He stated.

Collins moved next to the door and leaned against the wall, his eyes fixed on the young man. "We've created a new identity for you, enrolled you in school and have taken care of everything for you until all this is over when you can return to a normal life." He explained. "Nobody is going to be able to find you unless you allow it to happen."

Eric turned toward the man, a nervous smile forming on his face. "It kind of sounds like witness protection." He said as he chuckled.

Collins pressed his lips together and nodded. "That's exactly what it is."

The sobering tone of the man's voice caused a jump in the rhythm of Eric's heart. He stared toward the floor, thought about what was just said and after quickly processing the words, figured the move was probably best to guarantee his safety, though it failed to make him feel any safer. Instead he became anxious as a million thoughts raced through his mind. He knew what witness protection meant, at least the definition he learned from the movies as well as legend, and it scared him. How could he live without his family and friends? Would he ever be able to see them again? And what about his future? Would he even have one? Then he realized that his life, which was so certain and so orderly when the weekend started, was now anything but certain. He would have given anything to be able to turn the clock back in time.

Matt watched the boy struggle with his thoughts and wanted to find some way to make the situation easier for the both of them, but knew he could not. Instead, he opened the door to the room and cocked his head, a signal for Eric to go. Silently the young man shuffled to the door and walked out into the space of the hanger. Seeing the plane as he exited, he glanced back at Collins and gestured to the man, asking without ever speaking if he were to enter the aircraft. Collins slowly nodded and Eric's head sunk. He was nervous and scared and felt every emotion that accompanied the hollowness his life suddenly transformed into, being ripped away from the comfort of everything he had ever loved or experienced and thrown into the abyss of the unknown.

He was guided to the awaiting jet and climbed the stairs to the inside. He stopped as he entered and looked around the cabin, spotting Dan Bostic sitting in a seat near a window speaking into his phone. Eric smiled, the sight of the man momentarily tempering his anxiety, and he moved toward him. Bostic, he thought, represented his last connection to his life and he wanted to hold onto it for as long as he could. The man peered up and smiled at him, tightly grabbing the boy's arm as he gave a reassuring smile then returned to his conversation on the phone. It helped for a moment.

Silently Collins nudged the boy and directed him to the rear of the plane, escorting him to a seat across from two men dressed in suits, their sight heightening Eric's already immeasurable distress. He nervously fidgeted in his seat, adjusting himself until

Collins sat next to him and placed his arm on his shoulder to help ease the young man's discomfort. "Everything is going to be all right." Collins said in a calm and reassuring tone. He motioned to the man sitting across from them to the left and continued. "This is Jason Taylor. He's going to take care of everything for you and help you adjust to your temporary home."

"Where am I going?" Eric asked.

"Mr. Taylor will inform you about all of that when we get off the plane." Collins answered.

"You're not going with me?" Eric inquired, the cracking in his voice exposing the fear inside.

"No kid I'm sorry, but I need to take care of things here." Collins explained. "Mr. Taylor is the only one going with you."

"Oh." The boy sullenly responded. "What about my family?"

"Mr. Bostic will take care of them." Collins answered.

"No. I mean can I see them?" Eric asked.

Collins shook his head. "I'm afraid that's not possible right now."

Eric stared at the man for a moment and withheld a response, then turned his head and looked out the window of the plane avoiding any eye contact with anyone inside. Collins sat and studied the boy's actions, concluding that as tough as Eric was, the young man was more scared than upset. The overwhelming amount of care and activity to protect him finally caused the boy to realize the significance of what he did and what he mistakenly uncovered. And it was exactly that activity and that realization that caused Eric's fear.

Collins stood from his seat and motioned for Taylor to follow. Though completely confident of Taylor's planning and choices concerning Eric's safety, he needed to reassure himself as he held a personal stake in the operation. He had a history with the young man and he wanted to be certain there would be a future.

They walked into the small galley and Collins turned toward his associate. "Are you sure they're ready to take on this much of a responsibility?" He softly asked. "This kid is close to coming apart and I'm going to need him again when we put some faces with the voices we heard on the tape."

"He's going to be fine Matt." Taylor quietly answered. "There isn't anybody better equipped to manage this particular situation, and you know that."

Collins nodded in agreement. "Yeah I know." He replied. "I'm not questioning your choices, I'm ...."

"Too close to the situation." Taylor completed. "You've known Eric since he was seven and I am aware of your personal interest in protecting him in addition to your professional one. Let me do my job so you can do yours to get him back to where he belongs."

Collins pressed a smile between his lips and nodded his head. "Thank you Jason. You need to get going." He directed. Then he turned and walked to where the boy was sitting. "Eric, I'll talk to you soon. Hang in there. Okay?"

Eric nodded his head in acknowledgement yet remained silent starting out the window. For a moment, Collins stood and looked at the young man, then he turned, leading Bostic and the other man out of the plane toward the hangar and their vehicles. As they walked into the hangar, the whining of the engines starting broke the relative peacefulness of the early Sunday afternoon. The small jet sat on the runway ready for its departure and from their vehicles, the men turned to watch.

The aircraft began to slowly taxi along the runway and turned, stopping at one end. Within moments, the sounds from the engines changed in intensity from a high-pitched whir to the combustive rush of thrusters pushed to their limit before the jet began to rumble down the runway, picking up speed until it lifted into the air in one smooth continuous motion, slowly disappearing into the clouds.

"So where did you find him?" Collins asked as he turned away from the runway.

Bostic glanced at the man. "He's at George Washington having emergency surgery." He grimly reported.

Collins strongly sighed and shook his head. "I really didn't want to hear that." He said, "So what happened?"

Bostic leaned against his car and looked past the man, instead focusing on the activity taking place across the rest of the base. "He and his girlfriend were gunned down in their room at a downtown hotel." He reported. "His girlfriend was pronounced dead at the scene and Butler was still barely alive, so I hope that Eric was able to provide you with some idea on the identity of the ninth man because it doesn't look as if you are going to get it from Aaron Butler."

Collins covered his face with his hands and shook his head as he rubbed his eyes. "Eric never met him. Butler was the only one who dealt with the man on a personal level and was one of the few who even saw him." He stated, rubbing his forehead as though a headache began to from in his temples.

"Hence the reason Butler was hit." Bostic concluded.

"And the reason we have to protect Eric." Collins stated as he gently fell back against his car's fender. "Well, you know what you need to do. Who did you send downtown?"

"I sent Pachison to the hotel and Archeletto to George Washington." Bostic answered. "You know, we got lucky finding him at all."

Collins stood from his vehicle and walked to the driver's side door. "Somehow I think that Aaron Butler wouldn't call us lucky enough." He opened the door, sat inside and started the engine, quickly driving away.

The area around the hotel was filled with police, their cars clogging the driveway to the entrance as guests who had been questioned slowly made their way out. Collins carefully approached the scene and parked his car along the street, getting out and walking toward the barrier of yellow tape encircling the complex. He reached inside his jacket pocket and removed his identification card, flashing it as he neared the officer standing guard. The officer lifted the tape upward and pointed toward the hotel lobby as Collins ducked under.

He stopped and scanned through the activity inside the tape, then continued into the lobby. As he walked toward the registration desk, a large burly man, a badge sticking out of the pocket of his suit, came up to him.

"What red tape are you going to put me through now?" The man abruptly asked. "I thought this was going to be routine until I got word from your office."

"Routine?" Do you get a lot of college students getting shot up in the high class hotels John?" Collins flippantly responded.

"Not really," The police captain answered. "But then it isn't often the shooting of a twenty-two year old, no matter where it happens in my city, gets the interest of the FBI or the U.S. Attorney from across the river. Care to tell me what's going on?" He asked as he accompanied Collins into an elevator.

"I'm not exactly sure myself." The attorney replied. The doors closed and the elevator began to move. "Can you fill me in on what happened here?"

The elevator stopped and the doors opened onto a floor filled with uniformed officers gathered in an empty hallway. "The front desk," The captain began as the two entered the hallway. "received the hysterical call from the male occupant of room 710 gasping for help stating that he and his girlfriend had been shot. The desk clerk sent his security person to the room where he found Aaron Butler unconscious and nude on the floor in a pool of blood between the bed and the wall with the phone still clutched in his hand. The young lady was discovered in the bed on the door side. The clerk in the mean time had called nine one one. We immediately dispatched several units, including paramedics to the scene. When the first unit arrived approximately one and a half minutes after the call was received, they were directed to the room where the officers met with the security guard who had stayed to secure the room and attempt first aid. They requested backup and informed the dispatch officer of the situation. Two homicide detectives were called and took over the investigation." He reported, stopping in front of the room. "That is, until the Federal Government got involved. Do you want to go in?"

Collins shook his head. "I don't see any need to." He replied.

Captain Franklin nodded his head and reserved a smile. "Never been to a murder scene?"

Collins shook his head. "No, not really."

"I threw up at my first one." The captain said. "Can't say I blame you for skipping this. So, why is the U.S. Attorney in Virginia interested in a shooting here and I have FBI assistance when I didn't ask for it?"

Collins hesitated for a moment then directed the captain to a secluded section of the hall. "The young man shot in that room this morning was a witness in a criminal investigation we recently began. He wasn't aware of that fact and unfortunately we received information that only he could confirm. We were attempting to located him when all this happened."

Franklin nodded as a grin formed across his face. "It must have been a very recent investigation." He replied. "As late as Friday afternoon you would have found him working at the Saddlewood Resort outside of Middleburg, Virginia."

"We became aware of a situation on Saturday morning and began our investigation then." Collins stated. "Care to assist me with something?"

Franklin chuckled. "From the sound of the limited amount of information you gave me, I think I better."

CHAPTER 7

FROM OUT THE WINDOW, ERIC watched the ground slowly draw closer, an indication that the plane was landing sometime soon. He could see the terrain below, mountainous in spots and flat in others. Yet since the mountains reminded him of those in Western Virginia, rounded at the top and full of trees, he figured they hadn't taken him far from home even though it seemed they did. So he wondered where he was.

Where did they take him? He had asked Jason Taylor as soon as the plane began to rumble down the runway, but from the beginning of the trip, Taylor avoided answering that question. It didn't make any sense, Eric thought. What could he do, now that he was on the plane and thirty thousand feet in the air? When the plane left the ground, he attempted to guess where he was going, but the flight plan had them take off to the southeast and over the Chesapeake Bay. After that, he lost track mostly because the small jet soared above the clouds, but also because of the work he and Taylor accomplished during the flight. It wasn't until now, when he returned to his window seat, that he could stare out of the aircraft and again attempt to guess his destination.

His mind geared into overdrive and he began to think about what was going on even though Taylor explained to him the plan and made the preparations for it. Could there be restrictions the man failed to tell him about? He knew he was staying with a family without any children and instead of high school would be enrolled in college, having the freedom of any normal college student, with a couple of minor exceptions. So why the secrecy of the location of all of this? What sense did that make if he would have almost unlimited freedom? He became understandably suspicious. They were hiding something from him.

He looked away from the window and turned to Taylor. "You never did tell me where I'm going." Eric said to the man. "Is there some reason for that?"

Startled from the break in silence, Taylor peered up from the papers he was reading. "I'm sorry?"

"You never told me where you were taking me." Eric impatiently repeated.

"I never told you?" Taylor asked.

Eric shook his head slowly, simultaneously pressing his lips together in a pouty way. "No you did not." He answered. "What's the reason for all the secrecy?"

Taylor chuckled as a smile broke across his face. "There's no secrecy Eric. I assure you that not telling you was just an act of absentmindedness." He laughed. "So to ease your mind, in about five minutes we are landing in Latrobe, Pennsylvania which is a small town outside of Pittsburgh."

"Pittsburgh." The boy repeated. "Of all the exciting places you could have taken me to in this country, such as Florida or California, you chose Pittsburgh. He sarcastically inquired.

"The mountains east of Pittsburgh to be exact." Taylor responded. "Mr. Collins wanted you someplace quiet, safe and close-by. This fulfilled all of his requirements, as well as all of mine."

"Great." Eric grumbled as he turned back toward the window and buckled his seatbelt.

The jet neared the ground and smoothly touched down on the concrete runway, quickly slowing to taxiing speed. In the foreground, he saw a small passenger terminal, its gates, and planes from the airlines that serviced the airport, but his jet passed it by. Instead, the plane continued on toward a group of private hangars at the far end of the airport coming to a stop in front of the last in the line, then powering down its engines.

Cautiously Eric unbuckled his seatbelt and stood, picking up the duffel bag full of the clothes he had when he left Saddlewood that had been placed on the plane while he slept. He slung the strap over his shoulder then followed Taylor to the front of the cabin and the door of the plane. It was sunny outside; a far nicer day than it was at home and he stepped out onto the concrete, stretched and scanned the new surroundings. There were cars traveling along a highway and trees and buildings and everything one would expect to see. Yet, with all the nearby activity, it was peaceful.

He turned toward the hangar and stared inside. Except for two cars and a man standing in between them talking to Taylor, it was empty and he focused his attention to their activity, wondering if what was being discussed directly affected him. He moved closer, hoping to hear some of the conversation, but as he took his second step, the second man opened the door to one of the cars, sat inside and drove away.

Taylor turned toward Eric and motioned for him to join him at the other car. "It's time for us to go." He said. "Hop in."

Eric looked at the car for a moment. "I take it this is yours." He said as he opened the door to the convertible and sat inside, throwing the bag into the back seat.

Taylor smiled as he opened the driver's side door, sitting behind the steering wheel. "Not exactly." He answered as he started the engine. "Do you like it?"

Eric smiled. "Yeah, it's pretty tight. But this can't be a government car." Eric stated.

Taylor nodded. "You're right, it's not a government car." He agreed, putting the car into gear and driving to the security gate, where he stopped to wait for the gate to open.

"So who's is it? Eric asked.

"It's yours." Taylor replied.

"It's mine." Eric slowly repeated, not believing the man. "You're kidding me."

Taylor shook his head. "No I'm not. This is a perk of your new identity." He explained as the gate opened and they exited the airport grounds. "I thought it would fit your personality. So, how did I do?"

Eric grinned. "Pretty damned good."

"I thought you'd say that." Taylor stated as he turned the car onto the four-lane highway. "And I think that you will find I did just as commendable a job with the rest of your situation, including my choice of location."

"I'm sure you tried," Eric began. "And I don't mean to question you..."

"But..." Taylor quickly interrupted.

Eric hesitated for a moment then strongly exhaled. "But I just think that since *I'm* the one who has to go through all of this, you could have made it a little bit of fun. I mean, this place doesn't look much different from home and I don't want to think about home right now. Then I guess you can't possibly understand that."

The car slowed at a traffic signal and Taylor turned onto the road where a sign along side announced the entrance to Saint Vincent College. "You would be surprised what I understand about your situation." He sternly replied. "However, I have to look at the whole picture and I am sure this place is exactly where you need to be right now."

"Where?" He asked as the car crested a small knoll and from between massive willow trees, the college appeared in front of them to the left. "At this school?"

Taylor turned onto the main entrance driveway and slowed as he approached the security gate. "Not just this school, but the entire setup, where you're living, the people, everything." He replied, stopping at the gate and pulling out some unknown card from his pocket that allowed him to continue onto the campus.

Eric peered out his side of the car, studying the six-story antique brick building to his right. "I would have preferred the beach." He countered.

Taylor pulled the car into a parking stall near the athletic center, turned off the engine and got out, walking toward a picnic table that sat under trees and overlooked a series of athletic fields below. He sat on the top of the table, his feet touching the bench and motioned for Eric to join him. They sat for a moment staring across the fields before Taylor spoke. "Take a look around and tell me what you see." He asked.

"Just around the school?" Eric inquired, his eyes fixed on a group of men on the soccer field below.

Taylor shook his head and answered. "No. Everywhere around, including the school. Tell me what you see."

Eric stood from the car and began a slow and deliberate circle scanning the surroundings. From across the highway beyond the airport, he saw the mountains in the near distance, the greens and blues of their trees cooling the brightness of the day. He continued turning, taking in the sights of the campus and its old stone and brick buildings he imagined being built by monks hundreds of years ago mixed with newer structures and tree-lined walks, fitting together to beautifully create a simple touch of the classic college campus. For a moment, he lost himself in the beauty and serenity of the spaces until he completed the circle. He returned to the top of the table and peered across the baseball field in front of him, waiting for a moment before he spoke. "How descriptive and precise do you want me to be?" He asked.

"Don't go overboard." Taylor answered.

"Well," He began, sighing before he continued. "There are a bunch of rustic buildings behind us, what looks like dorms across from us past the baseball field, more dorms to the right, and a soccer field over there to the left. Then, aside from the highway and the stores, there are the mountains in the distance." He replied as he pointed to each area.

Taylor stood and stared across the fields as he spoke. "You chose to accept a soccer scholarship to the University of Virginia because of its proximity to the mountains, its academic and athletic reputation, its social settings and the beauty of its campus. That is correct, is it not?" He asked.

Eric shrugged his shoulders then nodded. "Yes, and your point is what exactly?"

"My point is that here, you'll find exactly the same things you wanted, just on a smaller scale." Taylor stated. "Look Eric, a beach is not going to help you forget your home, your past, or anything else you want to forget right now. Nothing will be able to accomplish that. But these people, and this place will help you adjust to the life you're going to have for a while because they are what you have already picked for yourself."

Eric silently sat watching the people in the distance then turned to Taylor as he sunk forward folding his arms into his body. "Do these people I'm going to live with know what I'm going through?"

Taylor leaned forward to draw even with the boy and rested his elbows on his knees, folding his hands between them. "Well, they know what you've been through." He softly began. "But, they're prepared to help you with what you're going through."

"And they want to help, they're not just paid to?" Eric asked.

"I won't lie to you, it is their job." Taylor answered. "But, they volunteered for this kind of government service and it takes a special kind of person to do so. And the people you are staying with are very special."

Eric briefly nodded his head as he sat in silence, staring out onto the now vacant field struggling to keep himself together. He felt as empty as the field before him and could think of nothing to rid himself of the insecurities that took over his body. He was lost, and scared, and nervous about anything and everything that could happen once he left the picnic table. Yet he knew that in a few minutes, he would leave behind not only the temporary security of the spot under the tree, but everything he knew of his past seventeen years of life.

Taylor watched the young man look out onto the field, the blank expression on his face signaling a need for something more to happen. "I think it's time we go meet the family. What do you think?" He asked, sensing the struggle within the boy and the obvious pain that the young man held within himself.

Eric stood from the table, stretched and deeply exhaled, still looking over the fields. He slowly turned toward Taylor and peered into the man's eyes. "Okay." He muttered, then shuffled to the car, sitting on the passenger's side.

Taylor rose from his spot on the table and joined the young man, starting the engine and carefully backing out of the parking stall. He slowly drove through the campus, returning to the main highway while occasionally glancing at the boy who quietly sat in the seat next to him. He was concerned about him, knowing well from his own experience that the boy's future would be anything but smooth.

Eric quietly sat in the car watching the scenery as it went by, the landscape quickly changing from small rolling hills to steep rocky mountains on either side of the four-lane highway, its east and west bound lanes divided by a wide rapid-filled creek. As they drove deeper into the narrow valley that the roadway wound through, the mountain's sides increased in height, blocking the rays of the late afternoon sun from reaching its floor. He sighed as he leaned back in his seat, the wooded setting reminiscent of family picnics along the northern edge of Skyline Drive in the mountains of Virginia and he fought the tears that swelled inside his eyes from escaping down his cheeks. He hadn't shed a tear in years, yet in the past couple of hours the urge to cry pierced his heart at least a dozen times.

The valley they had been driving through began to widen as the creek, which had split the road in half, passed under the highway and meandered to the right while the mountains spread apart. Within minutes, a small village appeared before them and Jason slowed the vehicle, merging into the left lane. It was a beautiful little town, its whitewashed wood-sided homes and gazebo dominated tree-lined public square seemed stolen from a Norman Rockwell painting and Eric, who had all but relinquished himself to sleeping in his seat, popped up to attention. He wanted to see more.

Taylor turned left toward the town square, resisting the desire to narrate a tour around the quaint yet obviously affluent village. Instead, he slowly negotiated around the square in silence hoping the sights would initiate conversation.

"How do you pronounce the name of this town?" Eric asked.

"Rhyme it with steer." Taylor replied. "Ligonier is French, but don't pronounce it as the French would."

"Is this where I'm going to live?" He inquired.

Taylor nodded. "Yes, but in a renovated farmhouse not far from here. I think you'll like it very much."

Though his interest heightened, Eric did not answer. Instead, he sat up in his seat, paying closer attention to the route taken. They passed a small ice cream store and further along the route, a mountain plaza on the right, with a bank and some other business until the two-lane road passed into more country-like surroundings. Mountains gracefully rose into the sky from behind scattered farms, their mixture of evergreen and broadleaf trees creating a lush but serene valley. Had he not known better, he would have thought he was near Middleburg, not in some small town in Pennsylvania.

The car began to slow and they turned left onto an old country road, not a smooth Virginia country road, but one appearing purposely unimproved with its scattering of potholes and ruts along the sides. It wound deeper toward the base of the mountain into a narrow valley of its own between the fencing and trees. In the distance to the left, Eric noticed an old farmhouse positioned to one side nestled between a grove of trees. There were horse stables and a riding corral with two horses situated behind the barn. As they neared the property, he could see a large garage to the rear, clearly recently renovated and perfectly matched to the exterior of the main house. They drew closer and the car slowed, nearly stopping completely across from a handcrafted rural mailbox on the right, the name Mason 2027 Foxridge Road scripted on the side, then turned onto the adjoining stone driveway.

As the car slowly drove past a glass-enclosed conservatory built into the side of the structure, a man and woman exited the house to greet them, following the car until it stopped next to the garage. Eric opened the door and stood grabbing his duffel bag from the back seat, the nervousness and awkwardness of meeting someone for the first time augmented by the fact he would be living with these people. He forced a smile as they approached and he closed the door behind him, stepping toward them.

"You must be Eric." The smiling man said, extending his hand toward the boy. "I'm Don Mason and this is my wife Carol."

Eric nodded as he shook the man's hand. "Nice to meet you Mr. Mason." He replied, then glanced to the women and smiled again. "Nice to meet you too, Mrs. Mason."

"It's good to meet you as well Eric." Carol answered. "Why don't you come inside and we can get you settled?"

Eric stepped toward the house. "There really isn't much to me right now." He dejectedly stated. "Everything I have is in this bag."

Carol opened the door to the house and held it as he entered. "We figured you wouldn't have much. In fact Eric, we didn't think you would have anything but the clothes on your back." She stated, closing the door and guiding him into the large country kitchen. "So, we have some things we think you'll like up in your room and we'll also go do a little shopping. Right now, let me show you to your room where you can take a shower and, as I hope you are hungry, get ready for some dinner."

Eric smiled and nodded his head. "Thank you Mrs. Mason. I am a little hungry." He said.

The woman smiled, and then led the young man up a staircase to a second floor bedroom. "I hope you find everything you need. If there is something else, honey, let me know." She warmly stated. "The bathroom is through that door and there are some clean clothes in your closet. So please relax and make yourself at home." She stood in the doorway for a moment watching him silently scan the room. Then she turned and closed the door behind her, leaving him to himself.

Eric stood stationary as he slowly looked over the room, silent, and still battling the vacant feeling within him. As he walked around to survey his new surroundings he thought about the Masons. They were nice and caring and genuinely interested in making him feel comfortable, though he was not. And it was evident from the time the Mason's must have spent to have the room ready with everything a teenager could want in it, a component stereo system with ten-disk CD changer, a flat-screen television with a DVD player and a fully-equipped computer station, that they were committed to making this transition as easy as possible. He shook his head in disbelief.

He moved to the computer and turned it on, noticing it connected to a cable jack. The Internet. Would he dare take the chance and contact Greg or Beth or Jimmy? How about Maria? Could he count on her answering her own E-mail? What if the wrong people intercepted his message? Of course, other than Hamilton and his men, who were the wrong people? It was a bad idea, at least maybe for now. He looked out the window next to the computer and stared toward the garage. He felt lonely and he knew the isolation from his friends and family would not end soon, so he sighed and turned off the power.

Deciding instead to take a shower, Eric retreated from the window and shuffled to the closet, opening the door. The large but nearly empty space held a few selections of clothing and he walked inside, removing a pair of pants and a shirt from their hangers. Both were his size, his style and in colors he would wear if he were home. The Masons did well, he thought, and threw the clothes on the bed.

Again, he peered out the window toward the back yard, spotting the man from the hangar speaking with Jason Taylor and Mr. Mason. He stepped away from the partially opened window and watched, sensing the discussion concerned him and was not just a friendly get together. Quietly he crouched to the level of the windowsill, peeking around its corner attempting to hear the conversation. It was short and businesslike, ending with Taylor and the man getting into the car then driving away without Eric hearing a word.

He sat on the floor for a moment and stared toward the wall across from him, his mind devoid of constructive thought but full of the frustration of not knowing the status of his family or having control over his own situation. He took a deep breath, forcing out the air as he pounded the floor. To say that he was upset would be a gross understatement. He was angry and scared and lonely and frustrated all at the same time as question after question invaded his mind until he could take no more.

He reached to the stereo and turned it on, finding a station of his liking after impatiently playing with the digital tuner. Then, he jumped on his bed and stared into the ceiling. What was really happening to him? What was the full picture? He tried to wrap his brain around the situation, but could not. He was overwhelmed and a tear of frustration slid down his cheek that he quickly and angrily wiped away. He would not allow himself to cry. That would be unacceptable and he spoke to himself in an attempt to control his emotions. Then he stood, stretched, and exhaled strongly, entering the adjoining bathroom to take a shower.

As his mind began to clear, he thought about the conversation outside. There was no doubt in his mind that whatever the topic of discussion between the three men, it was in his best interest. So he conceded to himself the fact there were people who cared and were concerned for his safety as well as his family's. The thought greatly calmed him and he began to relax as he stepped into the shower letting the hot water spray down upon him.

He stayed standing inside the shower, attempting to wash everything from the past two days out of his mind. He leaned his head forward against the wall letting the water run down his neck and back, closing his eyes for a moment wishing he could sleep until his stomach reminded him of his hunger.

After stepping out of the shower, drying then getting dressed, he slowly descended the stairs into the kitchen, the aroma of a hot meal caressing more of his senses with each step he took closer. He hadn't eaten in nearly a full day and the lack of food caused a pang in the pit of his stomach triggering a loud growl he hoped no one else could hear. Timidly, he entered the kitchen, finding the table set for a meal but no one nearby. He looked around, then shuffled to the kitchen door and peeked out, failing to see anyone outside.

"I thought I heard you come downstairs." Carol stated as she entered from the conservatory. "Dinner will be ready shortly, but for now, we need you to join us in the sunroom."

Eric nodded his head. "Yes ma'am." He respectfully replied as he followed her into the glass-enclosed addition. A grouping of chairs gathered around a fireplace built into the center of the glass wall that jutted out from the original structure where her husband sat reading a newspaper and she invited the young man to sit. He smiled at Don Mason and nervously took a seat across from the man. It was uncomfortable for Eric, to say the least, as he sat anticipating one of the two to begin some sort of discussion, the bit of comfort he experienced only minutes ago fighting to stay within his body.

He didn't know what to expect, but several questions crossed his mind. Was his family safe? Did they know where he was, or at least what had happened to him? And finally, what was going to happen to him? He sat on the edge of the wing chair waiting for their first words.

Carol sat next to her husband on the small sofa while the man neatly folded the newspaper and placed it on a nearby end table. He looked toward Eric and moved himself in the seat to better contact the young man's eyes. "Eric," He began, pausing for a moment. "There are some things we need to speak to you about and, as I am quite sure, you have many to speak to us about. Let me first tell you that we know that Jason explained to you the ground rules of the program. Is that correct?"

Eric nodded. "Yes sir it is."

"Then you know that contacting your family or any of your friends is strictly out of bounds as it would greatly jeopardize your safety as well as theirs. Is that correct?" He asked.

"Yes sir." Eric answered.

"Good." The man stated. "Then we can move on. To ease your mind, your family is fine. They returned from North Carolina with the safety of a U.S. Marshal and are under surveillance.

However, only your parents were informed of your situation and they do not know where you are or any of the circumstances surrounding the reason you entered witness protection."

Eric interrupted. "My brother and sister don't know?" He asked.

Don shook his head. "No they don't and they can't."

"Why not?" He inquired.

"Security reasons." Don answered.

"Security reasons." Eric repeated. He forced a smile as he slowly shook his head. "That's going to be a standard answer for a lot of my questions, isn't it?" He asked.

Don tilted his head in acknowledgement. "We were told you were a very perceptive young man. I see they were accurate in that description." He replied. "Yes, that is going to be a standard answer for a lot of your questions, but it will be the truth."

"Are you always going to tell me the truth?" Eric asked.

"As much as a normal parent would." Carol responded.

Eric grinned. "That could leave things pretty wide open." He answered. "So, I guess that my parents can't know where I am for the same security reasons."

"That would be correct." Don confirmed. "In fact, only the three of us, Jason and Mr. Collins know that you are here for the reasons you are. Do you have any other questions before we move on?"

"I have a million questions." Eric began. "But I'm sure you will cover most of them when you tell me how this works. The only question I want to ask you now is, did they find Aaron?" He asked. "When I went to Mr. Collins' house after I was shot at, the first thing he wanted to know was where Aaron was because he knew some information I couldn't provide. But I didn't have any idea, so they began to look for him. Did they find him?" He rambled.

Don paused for a moment. "I cannot provide you with any information about that at this time." He replied.

"You can't, or you won't." Eric stated.

Carol leaned forward and attempted to assuage the tension that began to build. "Honey, we aren't given information unless it directly involves you. Is Aaron one of your friends?"

Eric sat back in his seat. "Yeah. I worked with him at Saddlewood. I just wanted to make sure he was okay. Do you think you could find out for me?" He asked.

The Masons glanced at each other for a moment, and then redirected their attention toward Eric. They knew what happened to Aaron Butler and chose to answer the questions the young man had about his friend with intentionally misleading statements. It would be easier this way. Eric did not need to know the circumstances concerning Aaron, at least not yet. The shock could be too much for him to manage.

"We'll see what we can do." Carol answered.

"I appreciate that." He replied. "I guess now the only thing to do is to tell me how this works."

Don moved forward on the sofa and leaned forward. "Eric, the government developed the witness protection program a long time ago and continuously monitors its successes and accounts for its failures. I will tell you that the failures incurred were the result of participants failing to abide by the rules or conditions in each project. And though each project follows the same rules, each has its own set of conditions. You know the primary rule of the program, no contact of any kind with anyone from your former life, and Jason reviewed the remainder of the rules on the way here. Your conditions are what we are going to spell out for you now." He explained.

"And these are also set in stone." Eric stated, not actually asking a question.

Mason nodded. "Yes they are, for the success of this particular project, but they are by no means difficult." He answered.

Carol continued. "But because of your age, life and situation, certain adjustments had to be made. Instead of setting you out on your own, the program had to make you part of a family and that's where we come into play. From this point on until you leave the program, you are now Eric Mason, our son." She stated.

Eric sat back in his seat and shook his head. "And exactly how are we going to pull that off?" He asked. "My family and I have a history. We have pictures and memories and a whole lifetime of other things you just can't make up."

Don slowly nodded his head. "Well...actually we can."

CHAPTER 8

COLLINS SAT ALONE IN THE darkened office, his feet propped on a table across from the sofa he sunk himself into. It was quiet, except for the tape of the meeting that he repeatedly played for an uncertain number of times trying to decipher voices, words and anything else he thought might be helpful as he jotted notes on a legal pad. But instead of solving any of the questions he had in his mind before he listened to it, he developed more. So he shut it off.

There was no doubt something secretive had been planned in that house. The question remained, what? Could it have been a plot to assassinate the President of the United States or was it something far different? Eric had been so sure of what he heard the night before; he could not have made such a huge error. Could he? And what if the tape existed by itself and there was no eavesdropped account of the previous night's meeting?

Would Collins have acted at all, let alone inform the National Security Agency, the CIA and the FBI? Based just on the tape, the answers to his own questions concerned him.

He reached over to a lamp and turned it on, the sudden light piercing his eyes into a quick squint. He had been here all day and most of the night, fatigue becoming a sensation he passed hours ago. Still he continued, hoping to discover some quick answers to some of his new questions.

Lifting a tablet full of notes from the night he first interviewed Eric, Collins carefully reviewed page after page. Who were these people who met in the guesthouse? He requested names and addresses of all the guests of the villa from the Consulate at Saddlewood, but that request was denied citing diplomatic security. Though an irritating excuse, it was policy. Yet, it led him to wonder, what did the Consulate have to hide?

Then there was James Hamilton. What exactly was Hamilton's part in all this? Was he the organizer of the group or just a hired host? Collins paused for a moment then glanced at the folder on the table. Maybe he missed something, he thought, and he picked up the folder with the Seal of the FBI on the outside and opened it.

For whatever reason, the FBI had recently begun tracking Hamilton, a German-born Englishman who retained his dual citizenship. He was a veteran of British Army Intelligence in the Gulf War, but retired soon after, becoming a security consultant for a German company in Frankfurt. Yet most importantly, Hamilton became politically active. And it was that activity that prompted the FBI's interest.

As Collins read through the pages of the FBI file, he searched for the specifics of their interest in Hamilton's politics, but could not find any. So, what part of Hamilton's political activity concerned the FBI that prompted the active file? Why were they watching him and better yet, why didn't they share that information? Matt needed to know, not only to learn everything he could about Hamilton, but also to satisfy his own curiosity.

He returned the file to the table and stood, stretching as he walked to the window and peering outside into the darkness of the summer night. It was late and from his office, he could see the glow of the lights from the Capitol as he thought about all of the possibilities that opened with the existence of the recording. He turned away from the window and walked to his desk. It was time to go home.

He picked up his briefcase and started for the door when the telephone rang. Quickly glancing at his watch and setting the case back down on the desk, he lifted the receiver. "Matt Collins." He answered, listening for a moment then exhaling deeply, his face sinking as he shook his head. "Yes, I understand. Give me the directions?" He continued, pausing as he waited for the answer. He grabbed a pen and wrote directions on a piece of paper on his desk. "Okay, I'm leaving right now but it'll take me about an hour." He dropped the receiver back onto the base and picked up the briefcase, walking out of the office and slamming the door behind him.

An unsettled urgency built with each step as he hurried from the building to his car, his heart racing not from excitement, but more from the anxiety his thoughts produced. The man on the phone was vague, stating only that Collins needed to meet with a barracks captain of the Virginia Highway Patrol. Leaving so much to his imagination, the lone statement sent a chill through his body.

He sped down the interstate toward Front Royal, a small Virginia resort city at the northern edge of the Blue Ridge Mountains whose recent rise in population developed from people escaping the Washington suburbs for the peace of the country. He exited the highway and followed a winding road, reading the directions scratched on the paper as he drove. Within minutes, he came upon a flare-lit intersection where a Virginia Highway Patrol car blocked access to the highway ahead. Slowly he approached the roadblock, the humming sound of the electric motor winding the window downward breaching an otherwise still night as he stopped his car.

The patrolman held up his hand and bent over into the opened window. "Good evening sir. The road is closed ahead. If you make a right here, go about two miles and turn left on county road 643, it'll get you to the other side." He directed.

Matt smiled at the man. "Thank you officer, but I'm Matt Collins. I'm supposed to meet a Captain Porter at this location." He stated.

"Yes sir, he is waiting for you at the scene." The officer replied. "Follow the road about a half a mile. "I'll call you up."

"Thank you officer." Collins stated. He carefully passed the roadblock and slowly drove to where several emergency vehicles had surrounded what was left of a small sports car. He stopped his vehicle and walked toward an officer who had turned to meet him. "Captain Porter?" Collins asked.

"Yes sir," The man responded, extending his hand. "You must be Mr. Collins."

Matt shook the officer's hand as he nodded. "Yes Captain, nice to meet you." He stated. "I see you have the remnants of a pretty nasty accident, how exactly does this concern me?"

"I take it that my desk sergeant did not give you many specifics over the phone." The captain stated.

Collins shook his head. "All I was told was that I needed to meet you here for some type of emergency." He answered.

The captain opened a small notebook. "I'm sorry about the lack of communication, but my sergeant was only following orders. Did your office put out a bulletin about reporting suspicious activity related to the Saddlewood complex?" He inquired.

"Yes, we did. How does this accident fit with our bulletin?" Matt asked, his curiosity drawing him closer to the vehicle.

"The man driving this vehicle was Stephen Kearney, an employee of Saddlewood according to his identification badge." The Captain stated. "Now normally I wouldn't have given this accident a second thought, except you put out that bulletin and I wanted to be sure we didn't overlook something."

Collins nodded his head. "I appreciate your diligence Captain. Was there anything suspicious about this accident that caught your attention?" He asked.

Porter walked toward the wreckage and pointed to the skid marks on the highway. "You would think not with the marks on a curve like this." He stated. "But anytime someone slams a Porsche into a tree at about sixty miles an hour, you have to wonder why?"

Matt shrugged his shoulders. "I don't follow you. Couldn't he have just lost control of the car?" He asked.

"Have you ever driven a Porsche?" Porter inquired.

Collins shook his head. "No, I can't say that I have had the pleasure." He answered with a smile.

The captain turned toward the man. "I have. It's an incredible machine, handles perfectly. In fact, at sixty miles an hour, it handles with the stability that others do at thirty. That's why I have a gut feeling that you should look into this further." Porter explained. "According to his license and registration, Kearney has lived about three miles away from here for the past five years. The recommended speed for this curve is only forty, but I've done it at sixty before and I didn't have a Porsche. What are the chances that he lost control of the car he had driven for the past three years on a road he had driven over a thousand times, on a clear moonlit night under perfect road conditions?"

Collins hesitated for a moment, and then walked to the wreckage. "I would guess you don't think very good." He replied as he bent over peering at the mangled piece of metal.

"You're right, I don't." The captain agreed. "Now I don't know what you've got going over at Saddlewood and I do not want to tell you your job, but if this in any way fits into your situation might I suggest you order an investigation?"

Collins nodded his head. "Under the circumstances, that would be the prudent move. Can you secure the vehicle at a private facility?"

The captain nodded his head. " That would be no problem. Now I have done the preliminary C.S.I. work, but can I assume you will be sending your own investigation team?"

Collins nodded his head slowly. "Yes that would be correct. I'll have them contact you at your office." He replied as the two men retreated from the vehicle and slowly walked toward the parked cars. "By the way, where is the body?"

Captain Porter signaled to a wrecking crew. "Standard procedure with what I marked as a suspicious accident is to have it taken to Winchester for testing. Is there some other arrangement you need to have made."? He inquired.

"No, that will be fine." Collins replied as he opened the door to his car. "But relay to your team to treat this as if it were a murder and let them know that I will contact them personally tomorrow afternoon."

The captain nodded. "I will do that sir."

Matt sat in his care and smiled. "Thank you captain. You have a good evening."

"Thank you sir." Porter replied. "You do the same."

Collins shut the door and turned the car around, easing past the roadblock and following the road back to the intersection then continuing toward the interstate. Though he was returning to Washington with even more questions than what he had when he drove out, none of them were about Kearney. In his gut, he knew that Kearney was murdered because it made perfect sense. Aside from Eric and Aaron Butler, Kearney was the only staff member who could identify any of the guests of the villa. Therefore, he had to be eliminated.

Collins pounded the steering wheel in a moment of anger, his clenched first bouncing off the side hitting the door, and he gritted his teeth as he drove. And within that anger, he felt a moment of grief knowing that if Kearney had made it the three extra miles, he would have gotten the protection he needed. A Federal Marshal, who had been assigned to protect Kearney, was waiting at his home. And that made Collins feel even worse.

In a way, he hoped that Kearney actually died in an accident, not an act of murder. A morbid thought, he said to himself, but one that could relieve the tension of the circumstances that seemed to be in motion. Yet the longer he thought about it, the more he convinced himself that this was a murder. And he brought himself back to the same question. Who else, other than Eric and Aaron Butler, would know or could know the identities of the men in the villa? For a moment, he thought about the other employees of the guesthouse? They needed protection as well and he needed to make some calls.

As he pulled into the driveway of his home, he glanced at the clock in the car. It was almost midnight and it occurred to him, that with the exception of forty- five minutes he used to shower and change into other clothes earlier in the day, he had not been home or seen his family in over three days. He eased the car door shut and silently entered the partially lighted house.

It was quiet inside and he hoped that his wife had been waiting for him, but as he walked through the house it was apparent that she could wait no longer. He entered the family room, set his briefcase on the floor and fell back onto the sofa, kicking his shoes off as he sunk into the cushioning. Exhaustion consumed his body but his mind remained filled with everything that happened over the past several days. It haunted him during the few hours he slept and now, as his body collapsed, he reluctantly closed his eyes for a moment fearing his mind would prohibit him from resting. The tension augmented the ache in his temples, but as he stayed longer on the sofa, he became more relaxed and comfort began to set in.

"I thought I heard you." His wife softly spoke as she sat on the arm of the sofa and began to caress his shoulders. "I'm glad you finally came home."

He smiled as he opened his eyes and slid himself upright, pulling her next to him. "Thanks." He whispered, kissing her gently on the side of her neck. "I hope I didn't wake you."

She wiggled her body, snuggling in closer to him as she laid her head against his chest. "You didn't." She quietly answered. "I was waiting for you."

He looked downward toward her, stroking her hair away from her face as he held her in his arms. "I know I was supposed to be home hours ago, but …"

She interrupted. "You don't need to explain." She said, placing her arm around her husband's waist and massaging his stomach. "I know it's part of the job."

Matt breathed in deeply, forcing the air out of his mouth in one strong blow before he spoke. "I know, but I still could have called." He replied.

She grinned, and then quietly chuckled. "Okay." She sarcastically answered. "You know, you're not in trouble with me if that's what you think. I'm used to you not calling me when your plans change."

A smile grew across his face. "It was the thought." He flippantly stated. "So…how are the kids?"

She hesitated for a moment. "They're fine, but they miss you." She answered. "You were supposed to take Tyler to practice tonight."

Matt nodded his head in agreement. "I know, I'm sorry. There's just something intense going on right now."

"You want to talk about it?" She asked.

Matt slowly shook his head. "Jean, I wouldn't even know where to start." He replied.

She sat up on the sofa and turned toward him, having a question already prepared. "How about with why Eric came over here after two in the morning?" She suggested.

He rose from the sofa and walked to the edge of the room, lifting a glass from a wet bar along the wall and filling it half way with water. "I never did explain that to you, did I?" He inquired.

"No, you didn't." She quickly answered. "And since you hustled out of here with him minutes after he arrived, I figured that has something to do with your absence now and his absence at Tyler's soccer practice this evening. Am I right?"

Matt glanced at his wife. "You know you are." He sarcastically replied.

She slowly nodded her head, stood from the sofa and walked to the large picture window in the middle of the room as he followed her every movement with his eyes. She turned toward him, hesitating a response as if she searched her mind for the right words or to plan a series of questions, then stared directly into his eyes when she continued. "Is he in trouble?" She asked.

Matt slowly shook his head. "If you mean did he do something wrong, no he's not in trouble." He answered.

She cocked her head to one side and grimaced. "But if I mean is he in danger you would give me a far different response, wouldn't you?" She inquired, sounding confident that she already possessed the answer and was only attempting to confirm her suspicion.

He stared at her but did not answer, the stoic expression on his face signaling to her that the answer was apparent. And she knew from his lack of a response that he could not enlighten her any further. But now, the situation, of which she knew nothing about, scared her. For years she had accepted her husband's career as exciting and public, but distant from their actual lives. That changed as his job has now come closer to home.

She moved to a nearby chair and sat. She was worried and thought about what her husband did not tell her. "Is he safe?" Jean asked, assuming that at one time he was not.

Matt nodded his head. "He is now." He replied, taking a gulp of the water.

"Are we?" She inquired.

He set the glass down on the bar and exhaled deeply. "Of course."

CHAPTER 9

FOR OVER TWO WEEKS, A constant stream of information flowed in and out of Eric's mind, building a past life that previously existed only in the thoughts and plans of a creative government agent sitting in some office. It was like staging a series of tall tales, not so far different from that of fishermen or hunters relating their experiences in the wilderness, fabricating stories of the ones that got away. But this was life and it was real, though sometimes he wasn't sure where the truth ended and the lie his life was now based upon began.

It started the moment he landed at the airport, the abrupt transformation into Eric Mason that cut all ties to his former life. Aside from his first name, which he kept because it was easier not to change, there was very little that did not. Though he retained parts of him that could not be altered; his personality, his talents and his memories, everything else was wiped out with several easy steps onto the tarmac. No longer was he from

Virginia, or a senior in high school or even seventeen years old. No longer did he have a brother or a sister, or a girlfriend or even friends for that matter. Now, he was from Connecticut and moved to Pennsylvania after he left his New England prep school, was going to be a freshman in College and was eighteen soon to be nineteen years old. Now, he is an only child, has a phantom girlfriend and no other friends except those his new life created but has leaving at the school in Groton. The differences were funny, but not in a humorous type of way. And at times, he wondered when he got up on any given morning and looked into the mirror, would he recognize himself? Because now, his life was anything but recognizable.

Becoming Eric Mason was not just a switch of driver's licenses and birth certificates, then winging the story from there. On the contrary, an entire eighteen years of life had to be constructed within the two weeks he had before he again stepped foot on the campus of Saint Vincent College. It was difficult enough that he needed to get used to calling Don and Carol Mason his mother and father, but the work involved in creating this life mentally exhausted him.

There was the week-long trip to Connecticut where one day they spent hour after hour on the campus of the prep school taking pictures and memorizing the surroundings as well as the faculty and staff. They stayed, not in a hotel, but in an enormous older home hidden in the landscaping of an exclusive neighborhood bordering Long Island Sound. It was to pass for his old house, every moment spent there dedicated to family building, as Don Mason called it, including the walks along the beach and the campfire they built along the water one relaxed night. It was an intense crash course and one he had to pass.

Then there were the assorted activities and their locations, all appearing methodically planned as though scheduled for a production. Pictures were taken at only carefully selected spots at specific times of the day, the filled rolls of film then whisked off to some unknown address by way of special courier. Events were carefully chosen to fit what his social and economic background would have exposed him to; the theaters of Broadway, the Boston Pops and the New England countryside. It was an amazing coordination of events and time conducted into a space of a week, constructing a past that didn't exist.

Eric opened the door to his car and sat inside, the lessons and instructions from the previous weeks still fresh in his mind as he nervously pulled out of the driveway to begin his journey toward school. The early morning sun reflected off the dew of the leaves on the trees and he squinted in the light as the car rounded the top of the hill to the main highway, nervous in hoping he would remember everything. He stopped and paused for a moment, leaning back in his seat then exhaling as he looked to his left before making the turn onto the road, the thought of turning back and hiding in the house an option pushed to the deep recesses of his mind.

After passing through the quaintness of the town square, he drove through the narrow valley toward the college, apprehension slowly entering his body with each mile he drew closer to campus. It was more than his first day at school causing his discomfort. No, if that were the only event happening in his life at the time, he could easily manage the changes that were about to occur. However, he had more on his mind, though being seventeen and entering college when he had never finished high school certainly would have been enough to cause his anxiety. His concerns focused more on his identity and what brought him here in the first place. Would anybody recognize him? Would he run into somebody who knew somebody else who knew him as Eric Lynch and not Eric Mason? He slowly shook his head thinking that the people who placed him here must have considered exactly the same scenario. At least he hoped they did.

He turned onto the two lane road that led to the campus, slowing as the willow trees towered on his left so he could park in the lot at the right. Walking up the hill along the driveway, he glanced at the large, old but renovated brick building to his right called Aurelius Hall and he asked himself if this was the building his first class was in. He stopped, removed a paper from his pocket then read and checked a small map. Though this was not the building he needed to report to, the correct one was adjacent to it and he reached a walkway that led to the commons area of the two buildings. He stopped before he entered, turning to lean against the sidewall of the walkway, a nervousness bubbling inside he stomach and he inhaled deeply hoping to quell the feeling when he pushed the air out of his lungs. To his right, he stared at the soccer fields below the driveway, his first collegiate practice later in the afternoon another reason for his anxiousness this morning.

Grabbing the handle, he pulled open the door and shuffled to the lone elevator that would take him four stories upward to his classroom, a rustic but remodeled space with carpeted floors that still creaked from the wooden floor underneath and rows of wooden one-armed desks. He was the first one inside, sitting by the window, gazing outside watching drivers negotiate their cars through the inner drive that circled the campus. Slowly, several young men and women joined him in the room and within a few minutes, nearly every seat became filled.

The professor walked into the room, left arm full of books and the right carrying a briefcase that he flipped down onto the desk in front. He was an imposing man for a history professor, his better than six foot frame dominating the front of the room as he turned toward the chalkboard, silently scripting his name and title across it. Doctor Ronald Miles, Professor of History captivated his students for the next fifty minutes, his brilliantly worded lecture filled by stories told with a passion and emotion usually reserved for those around a campfire in the middle of a darkened forest. No one moved, or interrupted, or even noticed that the class had extended over its allotted amount of time until the man assigned his reading for the next class.

Eric stood from his chair and began to follow the other students out the door when he was stopped by the professor.

"Mr. Mason." The man called as he peered into his opened briefcase on the desk.

"Yes sir." Eric answered, surprised Doctor Miles knew who he was. The professor closed his briefcase and looked up at the young man. "Do you have a class now?" He asked.

Eric paused for a moment. "No sir, not until ten thirty."

He slowly nodded his head, picked up his briefcase and books, and then walked toward the door. "Good! Why don't you follow me to my office? I'd like to speak with you for a moment." Doctor Miles stated.

"You would like to speak to me." Eric repeated, following the man down the hallway to a corridor that connected to an adjacent building, stopping in front of another door. "Did I do something wrong?"

Miles grinned as he opened the door to a quiet hallway. "I should think not." The man replied, shaking his head and walking along the hall, stopping in front of a door a quarter of its length. "Step into my office. There are a couple of questions I would like to ask you."

Eric eased into the tiny, book-filled room and sat in an armchair that looked to be as old as the professor. He wasn't nervous, just curious as to why the man picked him out of the class. He did not think he looked out of place and actually felt as though he belonged there. So what was it that singled him out from the other students?

Professor Miles closed the door and took a place behind the cluttered desk, dropping his briefcase on the floor. "How are you today Mr. Mason?" The man asked.

Eric briefly hesitated. "Ah, just fine sir thank you."

A slight smile formed on the man's face and he pulled the briefcase up to the desk, opening it to face him. "That's good to hear Mr. Mason. However, the pleasantries aside, I am sure you are wondering why I wanted to speak with you." Miles stated.

"The thought did cross my mind." Eric replied.

The professor removed a file from the briefcase and carefully placed it in front of him on the desk. "I'm sure it did." He said. "You know, you were a last minute addition to my class and that had me a little curious as to why. You see, every section of all of my classes has been filled for quite a while. Until, that is, the registrar made a space specifically for you."

"Is there something wrong with that?" Eric inquired, the paranoia from earlier triggering a nervousness building in his stomach.

Doctor Miles leaned closer, staring directly into the young man's eyes, resting one arm on the desk as he softly but strongly spoke. "I suppose not, except for the fact that in my twenty some years as a professor at this fine institution of higher learning, it had never been done before." He responded. "So naturally, I wanted to know why it was done this particular time."

Eric inhaled deeply, trying to calm himself without the professor noticing. "And what did you find?" He asked, squirming in his seat trying to become comfortable.

The professor leaned back into his chair, pressing his lips together as he folded his arms across his body. "Oddly enough, I didn't find anything that would give you a special exemption to enter a filled class while there were other people on the waiting list who registered far ahead of you. Well, by now my curiosity has the best of me, so I pulled your file to hopefully discover why you received such preferential treatment. And do you know what I found?" Miles asked.

Eric shrugged his shoulders, simultaneously shaking his head. "No. What did you find?"

The man grinned widely as he again leaned forward and rested his arm on the desk. "Would you believe nothing!" He exclaimed, slapping his other hand on the desk so hard that the explosion of sound in an otherwise quiet room caused Eric to jump in his seat. Miles reclined in his chair and stared at the young man, intentionally attempting to disconcert him, yet seeing the young man remain in his chair emotionless.

Eric broke a smile across his face. "So there's nothing special about me and I got into your class. Are you going to have me removed from it?" He asked. "Because if you do, I'm sure I can take it with someone else if this is such an issue with you."

"A bit contemptuous Mr. Mason?" Miles inquired.

He slowly shook his head. "No sir, I certainly do not intend any disrespect." The young man answered, adjusting himself in the chair to draw closer to the man. "But instead of going round for round on what apparently has become a focal point, let's end the inquisition and get to the actual matter. Do you have problem with me being in your class?" Eric asked.

The professor smiled. "Very good Mr. Mason." He responded. "By no means do I hold an objection to you in my class."

Eric opened his hands widely, gesturing his displeasure with the discussion. "Then what's the real reason I am here?"

The professor drew closer as he sat straight in the chair. "I think you bought your way into this school and I do not appreciate the politics suggested by that situation." Miles stated. "What happened? Did you get into trouble and couldn't get into your Ivy League university?"

The young man shook his head. "I don't know what you're talking about." He stated.

"Sure you do." The professor replied, the insolent grin plastered on his face becoming more irritating and unnerving. "Your SAT scores are well above fourteen hundred, you graduated near the top of your class from a prestigious Connecticut prep school and you were a four year letterman in two sports as well as a division one soccer recruit. You have Harvard or Yale written all over you, yet two weeks ago you applied, were accepted and registered here. I grant you that we have an excellent school and you will receive an extraordinary education at this outstanding institution, but do not insult *my* intelligence by claiming this was your first choice. We are talking Harvard, Yale, Princeton, Duke, Stanford or anywhere else you could think of where the nations' elite scholar-athletes would matriculate. Yet, you came here." He stated.

Eric coldly stared at the man as he thought, planning a quick response and fabricating a supporting rage inside him that he drew from the anger he felt about his current life. He pressed his lips together in a furious pout. "Who the hell do you think you are that you can judge my life from a file and a few minutes of one-sided discussion?" He replied. "Now I *am* becoming contemptuous because you know nothing about me or my situation and frankly, it's none of your damned business. But if you must know, it was a personal family decision and this school, in its truly Catholic compassionate way, tended to our needs."

Miles grinned as he sat back in his chair. "That was a truly excellent response, Mr. Mason. I hope there's more of that in you when you actually need it." He stated, removing a cellular phone from the briefcase. "Do you have one of these on you right now?"

A confused look spread over Eric's face as he watched the professor place the device on the desk, the abrupt change of subject even more bizarre than the encounter itself. "No. Why do you ask?" He inquired.

The professor ignored the question and continued along his odd conversational path. "I didn't think you were issued one already and Matt insisted that you have one. Here, this is yours." He said and he slid the phone across the desk toward the perplexed young man. "I have it pre-programmed so when you press number one, it automatically calls me and when you press two, you can reach Don. We both carry our phones twenty-four hours a day so we can keep in touch with you. Just remember, it's for emergencies only."

Speechless and stunned, Eric sat in the chair and gazed at the professor. He reached for the phone then grabbed it, lifted it off the table and looked at it for a few moments, staying silent as he shook his head. He peered up toward Miles and cocked his head to one side. "Who the hell are you?" He calmly asked.

A grin cracked across the professor's face as he leaned back into his chair. "In addition to your academic advisor, I've been a professor here for over twenty years." Miles answered. "But I am also an Army Intelligence consultant and a friend of Matt Collins. You don't need to know any more than that."

"And you were hired to watch over me." Eric stated.

Miles nodded his head. "In a way. I serve many duties, one of which is to be Matt's contact with you." He said. "Open the folder." He directed.

Eric hesitated as he glanced at the man, then at the folder. He slid it around to him and opened it. Inside were several dozen of papers, small pictures of men in the upper left side of the page and a listing of names on the right.

"Take your time." Miles said. "Let me know if you recognize anybody."

Slowly, Eric picked up the first paper and studied it, assuming that anyone who appeared on one of the following pages could be someone who was a guest at the villa. After a few moments, he flipped it upside down on the desk, and then repeated the process with each page until he completed the stack, separating seven of them into a different pile. He lifted the pages he set aside and studied each of them once again, setting each picture face up on the desk as he finished.

Miles watched the young man handle the pages, waiting until he placed the final one on the desk. "I take it that you recognized these people?" Miles inquired.

Eric nodded his head as he stared at the papers. "Yes sir. I remember every one of them." He stated.

"From Saddlewood?" Miles asked.

Eric peered up, his expression revealing a relieved seriousness, and he looked at the professor. "Yes sir. The only one missing out of the group is Mr. Hamilton." He stated.

Miles collected the pages and glanced at each. "I thought Matt had told me he was looking for the eight people aside from Hamilton." He stated. "You're now telling me there was eight total? Did I misunderstand something?"

"No sir." Eric replied as he slowly shook his head. "There were a total of nine men who visited the villa. I just never saw the ninth man. The only people who saw him were Aaron and Mr. Kearney. Mr. Collins will need to speak to one of them."

The professor leaned back in his chair and glanced at each page once more before he placed them into an envelope. He collected the stack of unidentified pages and replaced them into the folder, closing both into his briefcase. "You have soccer practice today at four. I informed your coach about your abilities. You can make your own excuse as to why you are here, however the one you gave me earlier was very creative as well as believable."

Eric nodded his head. "Yes sir." He replied in a reserved tone, his voice signaling a continuation of the conversation. "So, why did you put me through the interrogation?"

"To prepare you." Miles began. "You never know when you may need to create a believable story on the spot and I wanted to be confident you had that ability. Just one word of caution, make sure you remember the stories you create." The professor stated.

Eric stared at the man for a moment then nodded slightly before he rose from his seat and walked out the door, heading for his next class the professor's advice replaying through his mind. He had heard it all before, Don Mason stressing consistency day after day for two solid weeks while Jason Taylor did the same in the short time they were on the plane. But this time it upset him, not for the advice itself but for the way Doctor Miles presented it, and anger built inside him as he walked down the hallway.

He entered the classroom, thoughts rumbling through his head wondering if the people connected to him now even credited him for possessing common sense in addition to the intelligence he exhibited. What was the necessity of reviewing the same point time after time? He knew what he had to do in order to succeed in the program and he understood the importance of their warnings better than they thought he did. He would show them that. However, their constant reminders weren't just to keep the stories straight and avoid problems for the program. No, it was far more than that and he wondered if they would ever admit to it.

By the time the class ended, he developed an entire series of questions and prepared answers for his first encounters with the people he met here, knowing that the opportunity to test those questions out would present itself at practice because his future teammates would undoubtedly ask them. Hell if he were in their position, he would have many of his own. Why should they be any different? He stood from his seat and exited the room to the now filled hallway, hungry from all the thought he put into his situation. Maybe instead at practice, the cafeteria would provide a first encounter.

He shuffled along the hall to an adjoining building, finding the corridor that led to the dining hall and entering, giving his identification card to the attendant as he passed through the door. This was far different from his high school cafeteria. The glass ceiling angled into the sky as antique bricked walls laden with artwork cloaked any semblance of an institutional food service facility and he stumbled onto the service line as he gazed through the architecture.

Following the line until it broke off into two separate directions, he wondered which he should choose, then deciding on the shorter one. He smiled to himself because of the irony of his decision, it being the road less traveled, which not only served as a recruiting slogan for the college at one time, but was one of the Robert Frost poems his last class was assigned to read. Was it a coincidence or a subliminal message that the school used for more students to eat what was offered in the line not serving cheeseburgers and French fries? And again he amused himself, shaking his head and smiling with the thought.

After choosing his lunch and retrieving his drinks, he entered the expansive dining area and stopped to search for a place to sit. He was uncomfortable to invite himself to a table with more than one other person, yet he was anxious to begin a conversation with one of his fellow students. Apprehension rushed over him and he decided to wait. Don't rush into things, he thought, it is far better to check the place out before attempting to meet anyone and he spotted an empty space in the back corner. He carried his tray and walked to the empty table, sitting with his back to the wall studying who associated with whom.

After lunch and his final class of the day, Eric returned to his car, placed his books on the back seat, then sat inside and drove to the area adjacent to the athletic center, parking it in nearly the exact place the first time he visited the campus. He got out and reached into the back seat, removing his equipment bag and setting it on the ground beside the car while he locked the doors. Crossing the driveway, he entered the building through the lower level and walked to the soccer locker room, changing into practice clothes. Though confident of his ability to play, the excitement of this first day triggered a nervousness he hadn't experienced in a long time that consumed every parcel of his thoughts until what brought him here was pushed far back into reaches of his mind.

The practice field sat below the campus several hundred yards from the locker rooms and Eric ran to it, his heart beating quickly more from his excitement than the sprint. He stretched then began to warm up by shooting the ball off the square of the post and juggling off his feet and legs, becoming so focused that he failed to notice three players watching him from the center of the field.

"You must be the new guy coach told us would be at practice today." One of them called.

Eric stopped and turned around, realizing he had an audience. "Hey." He replied. "I just thought I'd kick around a little before practice. I'm Eric Mason."

"Eric Mason." The young man repeated. "So you *are* the new guy coach told us about."

"I guess so." Eric replied, nodding his head in confirmation. "And you are?"

"Dan Brunelli. Nice to meet you." He said as he extended his hand, and then turned toward the two standing next to him. "This is Jeremy Rafter, we call him Jay, and the guy with the ball is Mike Woods. We heard you were pretty good."

Eric smiled in an embarrassed sort of way. "I don't know who told you that." He replied. "I would just like to make the team."

"The word is you already did." Jeremy stated. "So did you transfer from Connecticut?"

"I'm sorry?" Eric asked, thinking that he failed to hear the question correctly.

"Connecticut. Isn't that where you transferred from?" Jeremy repeated.

Eric shook his head and laughed. "I think you must have me confused with someone else." He stated. "I'm a freshmen and this is my first day in college, so I didn't transfer from anywhere."

The three of them quickly glanced at each other. "We don't have you confused with anyone." Mike replied. "If you *are* Eric Mason, then coach told us you were coming in from a division one program and he seemed pretty excited about the prospect of actually getting you here from Connecticut."

Eric nodded his head slowly then shrugged his shoulders. "Well, then I hope I can live up to his expectations. But as far as coming in from a division one program, I think someone erred.

I went to high school in Connecticut and then came to college here." He answered while other players arrived at the field and practice appeared only a few minutes before beginning.

The team formed a circle and began stretching exercises as two coaches walked around the outside. When they reached Eric, they stopped to confirm his identity, and then smiled widely with his response. There was no doubt the two men purposely had been passed information.

The practice was scheduled as an inter-squad scrimmage on the varsity field, a situation that Eric clearly did not expect. He had not played for over two weeks while the team had practiced together during that same period and he felt at a disadvantage. However, the few drills they ran before the game, he excelled in, possessing a skill level above the seniors on the same team. And as practice progressed, he became more confident, asserting his strength in the inter-squad scrimmage where his superiority stood out from the other players. His successes made him feel good and for the entire game, in front of a small crowd of people who gathered on the hillside, everything that had brought him here had slipped far out of his mind.

He walked from the varsity field up the hill toward the locker room, but stopping by his car. He opened the door and slipped off his soccer cleats, sliding them into a bag and pulling out a black pair of athletic sandals. As he shut the door, a voice called from behind.

"Eric!" Dan shouted as he, Jeremy and Mike ran up the steps, stopping as they reached the car. "What are you doing after practice?"

He turned around, leaned against the door and slipped the sandals on his feet. "Not much." He answered. "I figured that after I showered, I would go get something to eat, and then study in the library to get this college thing down before I go home. Why do you ask?"

"It's only your first day. You can get this college thing down tomorrow." Jeremy stated. "You don't need to jump into the studying habit so quickly."

"I take it you have a better idea." Eric replied, raising his eyebrows. "If so, you've got my attention."

Before Jeremy could answer, Mike interrupted. "Is this yours?" He inquired as he motioned toward the convertible.

"The car?" Eric replied. "Yeah, it's mine."

"It's damned sweet." Dan stated, stepping closer to get a better look. "Anyway, there's a first night party tonight. Y'know, beer, girls, everything a freshmen needs to kick off his path toward academic excellence but isn't really allowed to do."

"A first night party." Eric repeated, as he walked toward the door of the athletic center, not sounding at all interested.

"Yeah. You in?" Jeremy asked. "It's a great way for the new guy to get to know his fellow students, especially the girls."

Eric opened the door and stepped inside. "I don't know." He replied, still unconvinced. "I was kind of thinking I should get used to this whole college thing before I start an active social calendar."

Jeremy shook his head in disagreement. "You can get used to college on your second night. Look," He continued as he pointed to his wrist. "In about two hours, you're going to be the talk of the campus just because of the way you dominated the practice today. Think of this party as your opportunity to meet what will soon be your adoring public."

Eric grabbed the handle to the locker room door and pulled, smiling at his teammates in disbelief. "You know you're full of shit, right?" He said as he entered and shuffled to his locker, beginning to undress to take a shower. "First of all, I don't think I dominated practice out there. Secondly, I doubt that I'll be the talk of anything, let alone the campus. And finally, I'm no better than any of you."

"Now who's full of shit?" Dan interrupted. "I know that I'm a pretty decent player, but I have nowhere near the skill you do. You may not have come from a division one program, but you could easily play at one. And as far as being the talk of the campus, well maybe not the whole campus." He stated, becoming aggravated with Eric's unconvincing humbleness. "But definitely the sports-following public. Even you have to admit, in all what seems to be a self-serving modesty, that you were impressive out there. So humor us not-so-talented individuals and show up for the damn party. I'll even buy you dinner at the cafeteria after we shower."

Eric grinned and stopped undressing; glancing at the three and understanding that it was important to them, for some reason that he show up. "Where is it and what time?" He asked, giving an indication that he may be interested.

"Eight o'clock down by the lake." Mike replied. "Cost is five bucks."

Eric smiled. "Five bucks." He repeated in a disapproving tone. "I take it's not a school-sponsored function, but I'll go. And you may be right, it could be a good way for me to meet people, but I have two conditions."

"Only two?" Dan sarcastically asked. "I would have figured there would have been more than two. What would these two conditions be?" He inquired.

Eric glared at him for a moment, then continued. "First, after dinner until eight o'clock all four of us study in the library because I want to get this college thing right. And second, understand that I can stay for only a little while because I still have to drive home." He stated.

Dan briefly peered down at the ground, upset with himself that he misjudged Eric to be self-centered and condescending when in fact his first requirement revealed the opposite. "That's cool." He replied, quickly changing the tone of his voice to a more friendly timbre. "I think we can live with that."

Eric smiled, figuring he had won over the three as friends. "Good, then let's haul a little ass so we get all this in." He directed as he grabbed a towel and walked into the shower.

After eating then spending about two hours in the secluded lower stacks of the library to study, the four of them walked along a tree-lined back road to the lake. A small fire burned in a makeshift pit near the water sending a faint glow into the twilight as dozens of students sat on logs and rocks or stood near the shoreline. It was not the picture of a college party that Eric had etched in his mind, the raucous Animal House-like free-for-all featuring beer-guzzling men and half-naked women. Instead, this was a sedate gathering of people actually talking to each other, some drinking beer and others not.

As he walked through the crowd with his three new friends, people he didn't know or had never seen before stopped him to speak for a moment. They knew who he was, at least they thought they did, and they wanted to know more. But what more could he tell them? All night he listened to countless stories of someone's not-so-distant youth, wanting to participate because he had so much to contribute, even if it was just to be a part of the conversation. But the fear of making a mistake and exposing his friends to the fraud he was portraying prevented that. And it all came back to him being Eric Mason and not Eric Lynch.

He glanced at his watch, the discomfort he felt causing him to become more conscious of the time and he realized that he needed to go, not that it was all that late. He pulled the three to the side and discreetly told them he was leaving, inventing an excuse of having to go do some work at his house in the morning. Then he turned and began the journey back toward the main part of the campus.

After walking a short distance along the road, he heard footsteps coming up quickly behind him and he instinctively turned. "I'm walkin' back with you." Dan stated as he caught him.

"You didn't want to stay at the party?" Eric asked, resuming his walk toward the campus.

Dan laughed. "Let's face it. That was a pretty lame party." He replied. "I kinda expected a little more action."

Eric grinned as he nodded his head. "So did I. Mike and Jay decided to give it more time?"

"Yeah, Jay found a girl and Mike's still looking." He answered. "Anyway, I wanted to apologize to you for being an ass earlier."

"You were being an ass." Eric repeated.

Dan nodded his head. "Yeah, after practice...."

Eric interrupted. "No, I was agreeing with you. You *were* being an ass and the apology is accepted, but unnecessary." He said as they climbed the steps toward the Basilica and headed toward the center of the campus. "I would have probably been worse."

Dan smiled. "So, why did you really leave the party?" He inquired. "Because I doubt that it was on the account you had to work in the morning and the party wasn't that bad."

"Yeah, the party was that bad. But truthfully, I didn't feel in the partying mood." Eric replied. "I've got some things on my mind."

"Who is she?" He asked.

Eric chuckled. "Who said anything about a girl?"

"It's always about a girl." Dan confidently stated. "We do everything because of girls. So who is she, your girlfriend you left in Connecticut?"

Eric stared at him for a moment and faked a laugh. "You met me about six hours ago and you already think you know me?"

Dan shook his head. "I didn't say that. I said you have a girl on your mind."

"I don't have a girl on my mind." Eric replied.

"You don't have a girl on your mind." Dan repeated, unconvinced of the answer and remaining silent until his friend responded.

Eric stared at him again as he stopped under a walkway that connects the administration building with the dining hall and leaned against one of the arches, grinning. "Okay, so I have a girl on my mind, among other things. What's the big deal?"

"There isn't one." Dan replied. "Is she your girlfriend?"

"You could say that." Eric replied as they resumed walking.

Silent for a few moments, they passed through a flower garden and Dan looked forward, pointing to the building across the driveway. "Why don't you go sit in the shack and give her a call? You have a cell phone?" He asked.

"I can't call her." Eric answered.

"You can't call her." Dan repeated as he led the two to the building, opened the door and walked inside. "Why can't you call her? Don't you have a cell?"

"Yeah I have a cell, it's not that. I just can't call her so leave it alone." Eric sternly replied. "Look, if this is some attempt to make up for being an ass earlier forget it, I accepted your apology a couple of minutes ago. So, you can end this attempt at redeeming yourself."

They stood inside the lounge, stopping in front of a small group of chairs. "I'm not trying to redeem myself." Dan calmly answered as he pulled a cell phone out of his pocket, motioning with a flick of his head for Eric to use the phone. "I'm just helping a friend."

Eric glanced at him and then at the phone. More than anything he wanted to make a call, and not just to Beth or Maria, but to his family, Greg and Jimmy. Yet, he knew he couldn't. He glanced back at Dan then the phone and reluctantly took the phone from his friend's hand. He walked away for a moment, though out of the corner of his eye he could see Dan watching him, then punched in a series of numbers and waited until his call was answered, speaking for only a few moments before he erased the number from the memory, closed the phone and returned it to his friend.

"That's not exactly what I had in mind when I said to call her." Dan stated.

"She wasn't home yet." Eric answered. "I'm supposed to call her back in an hour."

"Are you?" Dan asked.

Eric nodded his head slowly. "As soon as I get home, which I'm going to do now."

"Good, then I'll see you tomorrow." Dan said as he turned and walked toward the fitness center.

"See you tomorrow." He replied and he went outside, walked to the parking lot and got into his car.

The night was clear and moonlit and it reminded him of so many of the nights that he spent sitting under the darkened sky, searching for stars with Beth by his side. He started the engine and carefully backed out of his stall, easing down the driveway until he exited the campus, his thoughts focused on his life in Virginia and if he'd ever return. What if he called Beth when he got home? He didn't want her to think that he just left her. No, if he just talked to her for a couple of minutes and explained what happened, what harm could that possibly create?

As he drove toward home along the part of the highway that was separated by the mountain creek, he thought about his situation. How long would he stay here? Would he be going home at all? And though he knew from the beginning that this becoming his permanent life was a possibility, the realization reserved itself until now.

He pulled off the road at an area on the left near the creek, shutting off the engine and getting out. For a moment, he leaned against his left fender thinking about a life as Eric Mason. It was not a question if he could manage the situation, should it occur he would have to. The question was, what exactly would happen to him? Would he be required to alter his idea of the future any further than it has been? He wanted an answer.

He walked down to the water's edge, sat on a large rock sticking out into the current and stared across the creek to the opposite bank. The water danced in between the stones creating a harmony of soothing sounds that helped him quiet his mind. He picked up a flat rock and skipped it across the water, grinning as he remembered that his father was the one who taught him the skill during a camping trip that his family took when he was ten. Now he'd give anything to go back to that time, and to his family. He picked up a handful of pebbles as he stood then tossed them slowly into the tranquil pool formed by the curve of the land. It was peaceful here and for a short moment he could be himself, forgetting about Eric Mason, Saddlewood and everything connected to the two.

The nighttime chill of the late summer air deepened closer to the running water and he skipped one last stone before returning to this car. It was time for him to go home and the people he now called his parents. He liked them. They were warm and caring and made him feel welcomed, truly treating him as their own son. He could not have asked for a better set of people to fill in as his parents and on some level, he felt love for them. But it wasn't the same.

He closed the door and sat behind the steering wheel staring out into the darkness. Again he thought, what if he actually did call Beth or Greg or Jimmy? Could he get away with it? Talking to them for even five minutes would relieve the pressures building inside from not knowing what was happening at home. Then he remembered every instruction he was given when he was rushed into the program and he knew calling anyone from home could not happen. He started the engine and pulled onto the highway, continuing toward his new home. There were questions he needed answered and he needed them answered soon.

He pulled into the driveway, absent of a memory of the remainder of the trip home as his thoughts were occupied by all the questions he had. He parked the car and pulled his gear out of the back, hauling it inside the house and setting it on the floor next to the kitchen door. It was quiet inside, but a light glowed from within the living room and he walked toward it.

"Hey," He greeted as he entered, seeing Don and Carol sitting in two armchairs reading while classical music played softly in the background.

Carol closed her book and set it on the stand next to her as her husband peered up from his and smiled. "Hey!" She replied, happy to see the young man. "How was your first day?"

Eric tilted his head to the side, gesturing with his hands. "Not bad. I made a couple of friends from the team." He responded, the tone of his voice suggesting the answer was far from complete. "We have our first home game on Saturday at two if you'd like to come."

Don smiled and nodded his head. "We'd love to be there. Thank you for including us." He answered as he looked at the boy standing in front of him, sensing that there was something bothering him but choosing to ignore it for the moment. He motioned for Eric to sit before he continued. "Did you happen to meet Doctor Miles today?"

Eric's eyes widened and he pressed his lips tightly together before he strongly exhaled. "Yes I did." He answered as he sat on the sofa across from the man. "In fact, he called me into his office and gave me an aggravating lesson in mental preparedness, which I did not appreciate."

Don remained silent for a moment. "Well, I'm certain that was just his way of being sure that you were ready. I assure you he meant no harm."

"I'm sure he didn't." Eric sarcastically replied. "However, I definitely believe that he enjoyed scaring the hell out of me. And with all that's going on right now, it wasn't something I needed or expected at this time."

Carol shook her head in disagreement. "I doubt that he enjoyed scaring you, but I believe that the point of your encounter was to see how you handled the unexpected." She stated. "You know, you aren't going to have the luxury to plan for every difficult situation you run into. I'm sure he wanted to confirm that you possess the equanimity one needs to have for a person in your position."

"So did I pass?' Eric asked, becoming agitated. "I mean, did I hold my composure well enough for this guy?"

"I'm sure you did better than you're doing right now." Carol sternly stated, hinting for Eric to calm himself. "And had you not done well, he would have informed us."

Eric slowly nodded his head, not as to agree with anything but as if he was carefully choosing his next words. "He would have informed you." He repeated, the tone of his voice barely masking his displeasure. "Well that's nice. Have you planned any other surprises to head my way?"

Don chuckled as he closed his book and set is aside. "Eric, we didn't plan this one. However if there were some surprises along the way, they wouldn't be a challenge if we told you about them, now would they?" He asked. "You have to understand that there is no way for us to know what you will face when you are out there by yourself. That is one of the risks this program takes, giving you the freedom it does. We have no one following you, no one to protect you, just a cellular phone with a GPS device that is programmed to call Doctor Miles or myself in case of an emergency. It's not comforting to Carol or myself because it's like preparing our son the best we can for his life and hope he learns from the lessons thrown at him?"

Eric paused, then stared into the man's eyes. "So you're preparing me for my life." He said. "Are you telling me that this is the way my life is going to be from now on?"

Carol leaned forward in her seat. "We aren't saying that at all." She sympathetically replied. "But we have to prepare you for every possibility because we have no idea how long this situation is going to take to resolve itself, if it ever does."

"If it ever does." He slowly repeated. "I know that is also a possibility." He stared as he stood from his seat and began pacing. He paused, gathering his thoughts before he continued. "That's why I need to ask you a few questions and I need you to be honest with me."

With her eyes, Carol followed him as he shuffled from one side of the room to the other sensing his anxiety. "Whatever it is, we'll be honest." She stated. "What do you need to know?"

He stopped pacing, standing in front of the fireplace and leaning on its mantle. "When I left, it was pretty sudden and I didn't have the chance to at least say something to a couple of people, especially my family and girlfriend. So I was hoping there was some way I could do that." He stated.

"To contact your family or your girlfriend?" Don repeated, the strength of his voice not signaling a positive response. "If we could arrange some way for you to have a little closure, we would do it. Unfortunately at this time, contacting either could jeopardize your safety and we can't afford to do that. Not with everything that is going on."

Eric walked slowly to the couch and sat. "What exactly is going on?" He asked, becoming a little unnerved. "I don't know how my family is, or how my girlfriend is, or anything for that matter. What if this situation doesn't resolve itself? Will I ever be able to see my family again?"

Don stood from his chair, grabbed a remote control and turned off the music, placing the remote back down on the end table. "You will get to see your family again, no matter what happens. I guarantee that." He answered, intentionally avoiding the first part of the boy's question. "If the worst possible scenario occurs, there are plans for you to have contact with your family through common vacations and other outlets. However, none of that can transpire at this time and as far as your friends, well that's just not going to happen."

Eric nodded his head in acceptance. "Out of curiosity, how did they explain me leaving?" He asked.

Carol shook her head. "We would not have been told, but I'm sure they created a believable story."

"I have no doubt they did." Eric replied, a sarcastic grin appearing across his face. "Can I at least ask you one favor?"

Carol smiled. She felt sorry for the young man knowing that whatever his inner strength, this adjustment could exceed what he could manage, and that greatly concerned her. It was her responsibility to help him, not only as the government employee who held the position to take care of him, but also now as his mother. And that was the job she most valued. "Of course you can." She replied. "What is it?"

Eric sighed as he leaned deep into the sofa. "Could you at least find out how my friends and family are doing?" He asked. "I would feel a lot better knowing something."

Carol nodded her head as she stood from her seat. "We'll do you one better." She replied. "Not only will we find out for you, but why don't you invited the friends you mentioned earlier over here after the game to spend the weekend?"

A wide smile broke on Eric's face as he nodded his head. "Thank you. I think I will."

CHAPTER 10

THEY WERE SUPPOSED TO MEET in Berkeley Springs, West Virginia. It was a cool rainy day and Doctor Miles was late. He wasn't usually, but on this day when nothing worked smoothly and an hour had passed since the normally prompt professor agreed to meet, Matt Collins became concerned about his absence. He paced the floor of the lobby, then ordered a drink, drank it and paced some more.

The day before, Collins received the pictures Eric identified, courtesy of Federal Express next day delivery guaranteed before ten in the morning, and they arrived at his home without incident, but with one very curious note. Doctor Miles insisted on speaking with the United States Attorney personally and privately. There was no explanation, no additional information other than a time and a place and Matt knew he had to be there. But now, he waited.

Miles chose the Berkeley Springs Hotel, a resort at the foot of a mountain in a small town of eastern West Virginia. It was out of the way, yet close enough to where both men could meet and return to their jobs all in the same day. But the professor was over an hour late and Collins waited for him, ordering something to eat.

He walked to the door and peered outside, seeing a familiar figure walking through the parking lot in the subsiding rain. The drizzle, intermittent with rays of bright sunlight that caused a twinkle on the moisture of the leaves of the trees in front, hindered his sight, but he knew from the distinctive gait that the man was the professor and the tenseness that built from his concern suddenly subsided.

He opened the door and guided Doctor Miles inside, ordering a set of drinks along the way. "I was beginning to worry." He stated. "Did you run into bad weather or bad traffic?" The professor turned toward him and stopped. "Neither." He answered, the stoic expression on his face hinting of additional discussion on the matter. "And you were right to worry."

The concern returned to Matt's face and he led the professor to their awaiting table in the dining room. Doctor Miles' comment generated an abundance of curiosity and now, in addition to the reason for this clandestine meeting in the first place, Matt needed to know what his remark was all about. They sat in the corner, secluded from the few patrons who remained after the lunch service and Matt leaned forward. "So, are you all right?" He asked.

A scowl formed across the professor's face. "Please Matthew, there isn't much that can fluster this old dog. But, I was forced to recall some of my old evasion techniques."

"What are you talking about?" Collins asked.

The professor reached for the glass that the waitress had delivered when she took his lunch order and he took a swig, blowing air out of his mouth in a deep sigh. "I was followed Matthew." He began. "At least someone tried to follow me. I lost them somewhere between Johnstown and Altoona."

Matt leaned closer so Miles could hear. "Who did you lose between Johnstown and Altoona?" He strongly but quietly asked.

"I can't say for sure." Miles casually replied. "But somebody definitely was interested in where I was going. That's why I took such a roundabout route."

Matt paused and sipped his drink. "Look, not that I doubt you, but are you absolutely sure you were being followed?" He asked. "Because other than the Masons, there is no one who even knows that I consulted you."

The professor bent forward, the expression on his face showing his displeasure with the question. "First of all, I know when I'm being followed." He indignantly replied. "But as far as who knows you've consulted me, well...the people at Federal Express do. And who knows who is tracking their packages."

Matt reclined into his chair deep in thought as he stared past the man for a few moments. Slowly, he slid forward pulling closer to the professor. "How many people do you think knew I would have sought your assistance?" He asked.

Miles raised his eyebrows as he sipped his drink. He set the glass on the table and looked up at the United States Attorney. "I don't think you're getting the point here." He answered. "What

I suspect is that *you* are being watched Matthew and whoever these people are, decided to check out what my connection was to you."

"Then I'm going to have to move Eric." Collins concluded.

The professor shook his head. "No you aren't. I already took steps to secure his safety and I do not believe that whoever is tracking you would even consider him being at Saint Vincent, if they even care." He stated. "If they did their homework, and I know they did, they've undoubtedly found out that I was an Army Intelligence Officer and that we have a history. Therefore, my connection to you should raise no questions in regard to Eric."

"You may be correct." Collins agreed as he nodded. "So then, why don't we get down to the original reason you called this meeting?"

The professor paused as his lunch was delivered, then continued, scanning the room almost instinctively. "It's about the pictures." He stated, pausing again to take a bite of his lunch. "Where did you get them because they were not surveillance, they were United Nations photos."

"Yes, I know they were." Matt replied. "I've acquired an anonymous source who sometimes feeds me information."

"An anonymous source?" Miles repeated.

"As strange as it may sound, someone who we're trying to identify occasionally sends me information." Collins reported.

The professor paused for a moment, staring at the man. "And you have no idea where your information comes from?" He asked somewhat in disbelief.

Matt slowly shook his head. "Not a clue."

"That's interesting." Miles responded. "Very interesting. You know, I recognized two of the men who Eric identified from my time in the intelligence world. Matthew, it seems very strange that these two would involve themselves in a plot against the United States."

"Why?" Collins asked.

Miles hesitated. "Well, it's just a hunch, but if you were planning an event against the United States, or any country for that matter, would you not include people who actually have some sort of knowledge about the country?" The professor asked. "These two worked exclusively in Western Europe."

Matt paused as he thought about the professor's comment, and then breathed deeply before he responded. "I haven't had the chance to dig deeply into their backgrounds, but maybe they were picked for some reason other than their knowledge of the United States. I mean all seven probably possess some special skill they were supposed contribute to this operation." He stated.

"I agree with you.' The professor replied. "But Mueller's days in German intelligence were strictly confined to Europe and Motilgin worked mainly in the Middle East." He stated.

"And now they're working for someone else." Matt said. "Mercenaries will work for whomever pays them the best."

Miles shook his head. "They aren't mercenaries Matt, they're professionals and there is a difference."

Collins took a sip of his drink and glanced at the man. "Yeah I know, but what you're suggesting makes this far more complicated." He said. "And I was hoping it wouldn't get any worse than it already is. I can see that's too much to hope for."

"It seems that way." The professor replied, pausing for a moment before he continued. "Now as for the second thing on my mind about your little situation. Eric identified seven of the men. You told me that there were eight, in addition to James Hamilton, for a total of nine. Is that correct?"

"Yes it is." Collins confirmed. "However, Eric never saw the ninth man, so he could only identify Hamilton and the other seven."

Miles silently nodded his head, a smug grin forming across his face as he stared at Matt. "I see. Why do you suppose that is?" He inquired, the grin growing into a cocky smile.

Matt hesitated as he realized the professor possessed his own theory, and then he quietly spoke. "Well, I have two theories." He announced. "The first is that avoiding Eric was purely coincidental. However, I am inclined to believe that nothing in this case is pure coincidence."

"I agree with you." The professor stated. "Nothing about this case is going to be a coincidence. What is your other theory?" He asked.

"Well, the other deals with what Eric told me about the beginning of his employment." Collins began as he readjusted his seat to become more comfortable, then leaned forward on the table. "Before Eric began his employment as Saddlewood, there were two service specialists, Aaron Butler and a young man names Patrick McCarren, who Eric replaced. James Hamilton had apparently stayed at the villa earlier in the year on what I now assume was a scouting mission. He got to know all of the staff and investigated them thoroughly. Then, after everyone checked out, he leased that same guesthouse for later in the year. However, between his visit and the beginning of the lease, Patrick

McCarren ended his employment at Saddlewood and accepted a position with the United Nations in Geneva, Switzerland. Eric was hired to replace him, which must have taken Hamilton completely by surprise, so much that he was uncomfortable with Eric's presence until they were able to investigate Eric's background to their satisfaction. My guess is that this ninth man is some high profile figure that requires specific security. So, they shielded the man from Eric by avoiding his shifts." Collins explained.

The professor took a bite of his food and shook his head as he swallowed. "I don't agree with you on this Matthew." He replied. "I do agree that this elusive ninth man did not feel comfortable about Eric's presence, but it was not because of an absence of a history with the young man. I think it's because of a lack of an absence of a history with him."

Collins ruffled his eyebrows as he straightened in his chair. He looked at the man then leaned forward and whispered to him. "You think Eric knows him?" He asked.

Miles widened his eyes as he tilted his head in acknowledgment. "Either he knows him or would be the only one to recognize who he is." He replied. "I know it might at first seem a little far-fetched, but it's quite logical if you think about it."

Matt silently sat at the table and ate the remainder of his meal as he reviewed the professor's suppositions in his head. The man made good points. Why were foreign agents who exclusively worked in Europe and not in the United States are now working in the United States? Then, of course, there was the mysterious ninth man. Could the reason Eric never saw him be because Eric already knew who he was and Hamilton protected the man's identity? And if Eric did know the man, was it personally or only as casually as by sight and name? They were interesting questions he'd like to have the answer to.

He took one last bite of his meal and swallowed, wiping his mouth with the cloth napkin sitting on his lap as his pager sounded. Reaching into his pocket, he pulled out a cell phone and pressed the button, looking at the paging number. His expression needed no explanation and Miles stood knowing that the meeting had concluded.

Matt walked to a public telephone in a secluded booth off of the lobby and made a quick call. After hanging up the phone, he rushed out the door and wished the professor well, the urgency in his step leaving the man following far behind. He hopped into his car and zipped out of the parking lot, speeding toward the Virginia border. Again he was to meet Captain Porter of the Virginia Highway Patrol, though this time it was not about an automobile accident.

He pulled into a parking lot of a locally owned motel outside of Winchester, Virginia, and stopped his car directly behind one of the many police cruisers and FBI vehicles that filled the small poorly paved lot. Stepping out into the drizzle of rain that had become steadier, he weaved his way through the mob of officers to an isolated room away from the view of the office and the highway in front. For the first time, his heart pounded so strongly that he could feel its pressure pumping through his body as he entered.

"Mr. Collins." Captain Porter greeted as the attorney walked inside. "I have to tell you that I'm not at all thrilled about the circumstances that appear to be unfolding around here if this ends up being one of yours." He stated as he opened the door to the bathroom, exposing a body, partially covered by a shower curtain, lying in an empty bathtub. "And if he is, I believe that you and I need to engage in a serious conversation."

Matt stepped inside the bathroom. There was no blood, no sign of any struggle and he wondered how the Captain decided that a murder had taken place until he discovered the burns at the bottom of the dead man's feet. He scanned the area once more before he closed the door behind him, signaling to an agent standing by the doorway to remove the body. Moving to the side of the room out of the way of the activity taking place, he turned to the captain. "I truthfully wouldn't know what to tell you at this point." He admitted. "But I will tell you that this is probably just the first."

The Captain paused as the black body bag passed by the two. "The first of how many?" He inquired.

Matt hesitated, and then stared at the man. "That would depend on how many of them made it out of the country." He replied. "Apparently, this one didn't."

"Apparently." The Captain sarcastically stated as the two exited the room and stood in the parking lot away from the others. "So, Mr. Collins, why don't you explain to me exactly what is happening at Saddlewood?"

Matt hesitated, feigning a smile before he answered. "Like I said before, Captain, I wouldn't know where to start."

Porter faked a smile in return as he guided the attorney out of the rain to a covered walkway. "I have an idea. How about starting with why I am now investigating two murders of people who either worked at or visited the United Nations Embassy at Saddlewood?" He suggested before he became far more animated.

"Or, if that isn't a good starting point for you, how about why two more people, connected with the resort, were mysteriously gunned down in their motel room in Washington?"

Collins stared at the police captain for a moment, stunned that he possessed information that had not as yet been released. "How do you know about those?" He inquired.

Porter sarcastically grinned. "A very nice and very interested reporter from the Washington Post paid me a visit about twenty minutes before I got called out on this." He answered. "She asked me about the connection between the Kearney accident and the shooting in Washington. Of course I didn't know there *was* a connection to a shooting in Washington, which is how I answered. That naturally made me look very foolish when she proceeded to inform me about the incidents and how they were connected. So I decided to refer her to your office."

Collins shook his head as he pressed his lips together, showing disapproval for the action. "I wish you would have consulted with me first." He stated.

"And I wish you would have informed me about all the facts." Porter countered, the irritation in his voice growing with each exchange. "You know, Mr. Collins, I do not enjoy being made to look like we don't know what we're doing out here."

Matt understood the Captain's anger. Like Porter, he also did not appreciate appearing unprofessional or uninformed, and his intent was not to have the Captain appear as such. But with the delicate nature of this situation, he did not possess the luxury of jumping to conclusions such as the one the reporter from the Washington Post apparently did. After all, it was only this morning that the FBI lab confirmed that someone attached a device to Kearney's Porsche that altered its ability to perform, or that it collided with the tree closer to eighty miles an hour and not sixty as it was recorded on the speedometer. And though his gut feeling told him that Kearney had been murdered, he had to know for sure before he connected Butler's shooting to the accident. With the lab report and now this death, he could connect all three.

He informed the Captain on most of the events of the past couple of weeks, excluding information concerning Eric or the subject matter of the meetings that took place in the villa at Saddlewood. And for the moment, Captain Porter appeared satisfied with his explanation, not that it mattered if he was. Now, the looming headache of the Washington Post and the avalanche of media to follow dominated his thoughts as he walked to his car.

Driving back toward Washington to his office, he organized his thoughts in preparation for the reporter who should be waiting for him when he arrived. He knew what to do; the task was to convince her to cooperate with him without revealing his goal. But what if he couldn't persuade her? What if she asked the right questions at the wrong time? He could avoid revealing the assassination plan. The question that lingered was; would she uncover it on her own? That was a risk he'd have to take.

He pulled into the nearly empty parking lot of his office building and parked his car, walking to the elevator and pressing the call button. Except for the security guards and few workers remaining, the lobby was quietly devoid of people and he welcomed the lack of activity knowing that it wouldn't be like this much longer. As soon as the story broke, the building would host a flurry of activity and he entered the elevator somewhat relieved for not having to face the press, at least not right now. Instead, he could go to his office and think about what he needed to do next.

For several hours, he worked at his desk under the light of the green desk lamp in a steady and sometimes eerie silence. Broken only by the illumination of his computer screen and the soft surrounding incandescent accent lighting, the darkness of his space intensified a small yet aggravating headache that recessed in his temples. It was tension and, though he realized that the coffee he was drinking to stimulate his brain was doing nothing for the small throbbing in his head, he stood and walked to the wet bar in the corner of the room and poured himself another cup. Staring at the start of a tiny mound of paper that he carelessly stacked on his desk, he was interrupted of his thoughts by a strong knock on the door. He called out for the person to enter, seeing the door swing open and Dan Bostic came into the room.

"You did a good job." Matt stated, stirring powdered creamer into his cup.

Bostic walked to the bar and poured a cup for himself. "You know already?" He asked.

Collins smiled, reaching to a switch on the wall and turning on the overhead lighting in the office. "We had one asking some questions earlier this afternoon." He replied. "I fully expected a reporter to be stationed here waiting for my return, so I'm kind of disappointed."

Bostic laughed. "Don't be." He said. "Kincaid was here earlier and asked for you, so I did just as you planned and gave him the extra information you wanted disclosed."

"Good." Collins responded, taking a sip from the cup and walking toward his desk. "So long as they don't know that this office is responsible for leaking the story."

Bostic shook his head. "They don't." He answered, taking a seat by the desk across from the man. "I used the correct people and took the right steps."

Matt smiled. "One thing for sure, they've taken this story seriously sending Kincaid here and at the same time, sending Evans out to speak with Porter." He stated. "Maybe we'll get the action we need out of it."

"Maybe." Bostic agreed, pausing before he continued. "So, what's this about you being monitored?" He asked.

"It's a notion that Ron Miles related to me today." Matt answered. "He was tailed while he drove to our meeting. He lost them, but he thinks that the only reason someone would follow him was because I contact him."

"What's so crazy about that?" Bostic inquired.

"I didn't say it was crazy." Collins replied. "It's possible."

Bostic nodded. "So much that it might be time you start carrying a weapon." He suggested.

Matt grinned. "I'm not carrying a weapon Dan. If I bring a gun home from work, Jean is going to assume that we're in danger and we don't know if that's the case. No need to stir her up if I don't have to." He stated, lifting one of the papers off his desk and handing it to Bostic. "By the way, you can scratch the German off the list. He's not going to give us any more problems."

Bostic took the paper and glanced at it. "The dead body out in Winchester?" He inquired.

Matt slowly nodded his head. "Yeah. He was electrocuted in the shower." He reported, somewhat unmoved by the death of the man. "Kind of a neat operation. The only thing left at the scene was a blank computer disk."

"How convenient." Bostic stated. "I take it that it wasn't accidental."

"No, there was no accident." Collins answered as he slowly shook his head. "We just don't know exactly how it happened because there were no electrical devices around, but then that doesn't really matter. The killer took it with him. The one thing that does matter is that they've started covering their tracks."

Bostic folded the paper in his hand and placed it in his jacket pocket. "Then I hope we can draw them toward us soon, because we'll never catch up to them." He said.

Collins sat behind the desk and began spreading the papers across its top. "That would all depend on whether we know our young friend as well as we think we do." He replied, peering up from the stack and widening his eyes.

Bostic nodded, staying silent for a moment as he thought, then he moved toward the door. "Yes, I guess it does." He agreed and he walked out of the office, closing the door behind him, leaving Collins standing by himself in the silence.

Matt shuffled to the window and peered outside. How contradictory his feelings have been, he thought, worried about keeping Eric safe while using the boy as bait to lure Hamilton or his men. Was it even an intelligent move, depending on the actions of the young man in order for the plan to succeed? In a short time, he hoped to find out.

He returned to the desk and sorted through the papers. Placing them into neater piles to gain a semblance of organization, he noticed an unopened legal-sized envelope underneath the stack that was addressed to him, yet had no return address of its own. Lifting it off his desk, he studied the foreign postmark and collection of stamps in the upper right corner, and then carefully turned the envelope over, seeing that it had been professionally sealed. Why was an anonymous individual from Italy writing him personally? Curious, he carefully slid a letter opener under the seal and opened the small package, removing the contents. Inside were sets of papers, all documents from Saddlewood containing privileged information of which there would be no way to gain access through normal channels, as well as an unsigned hand-written note in English from the person sending the package. It was all very mysterious.

Collins glanced at the note and placed it to the side, slowly lifting each page of information and studying its contents. How did the person who sent him the package know what to send to him? He replaced the papers into the envelope then picked up the note and began to read.

The note was very clear and worrisome. The author knew about Eric's trouble, the men of the guesthouse and insisted on helping. The unknown person sent information classified by the United Nations as confidential, including the entity responsible for leasing the villa, a fact that he did not know nor thought important until now.

He read the final paragraph of the note, an invitation to meet with the author the second weekend of October and he thought about the conditions of that invitation. Was it necessary to meet with the author and worth the risk the conditions set forth in the note? Could the entire offer be nothing more than a trap? He would have to consider all the possibilities before he made a decision. For now, he slid the note into the envelope, rose from his seat and left the office for the night.

Chapter 11

ERIC SAT IN HIS LAST class of the week, the lecture taking place in the front of the room distant in his mind. His focus lie far from the white plaster and antique brick walls of school. No, instead he thought of home and all the people who were in his life before he came here as well as the urge he battled each day to contact them. He thought of the game tomorrow afternoon and the first weekend in a month that he could spend freely with people his own age, doing anything he wanted to do, within reason.

He glanced at his watch, relieved that this tortuous class was scheduled to end in under five minutes, and he restlessly wriggled in his chair, fumbling with his pencil and notebook doodling a haphazard design on the paper as a mini cassette player recorded every word that the professor spoke. He briefly stared at the device, realizing its significance in his life and the irony of its use at this moment. A fleeting anger swelled in him, not toward the device itself but the fact that his prior use of a similar recorder caused him nothing but anguish.

Reaching onto the desk from the relaxed position in his seat, he clicked off the button and slipped the small machine into his backpack sitting on the floor next to his chair. As soon as the professor dismissed the group, he would hustle out of the classroom and scurry through the crowded hallway until he reached the stairway and the exit outside.

Maybe this was what Fridays in college were all about, the excitement and expectations of the weekend as each student prepared for an unstructured, unchaperoned and uninhibited two and a half days before the obligations of higher education resurfaced on Monday. And if it was, then he quickly became the typical college freshmen, getting caught up in the newness of it all. In the back of his mind, as he ran toward his car in the lot, he regretted inviting Dan, Jeremy and Mike to his house over the weekend. It was not because he did not like them or that he didn't want them to spend the weekend, but because he wanted to spend the weekend on campus. There was excitement here or at least a change in environment that invited him to forget everything difficult about his life. And to him, forgetting about what was happening to him was more than just appealing.

He jumped in his car and drove it to the upper parking lot next to the entrance of the locker rooms, removing his duffle bag from the back seat and carrying it into one of the dormitories. He planned on staying overnight in Dan's room and remaining on campus until after the game was over. Until then, after the team's scheduled light practice this afternoon, he would enjoy the activities a normal college freshmen would on any given weekend night.

Following a shower after practice and dinner, Eric and Dan walked from the dining hall past the athletic center and between the athletic fields to the main freshmen dormitory in relative silence. They climbed the stairway one level and crossed a corridor, opening a metal fire door leading to a brightly painted and well-lighted dormitory hallway. They shuffled across the carpet of the hall floor, passing several doors until Dan stopped and knocked on one, not waiting for someone to answer, but opening it and walking inside announcing himself as he entered.

It fulfilled Eric's expectations of what a college suite should look like, a tattered couch along a poster-filled wall and a misfit of bar lamps placed in corners on off-colored milk crates serving as combination bookshelves and end tables. Yet in spite of its seedy appearance, it was strangely well kept, looking as though it were recently cleaned. Eric followed inside and closed the door behind him, sitting on the small sofa in the central room as Dan crossed the confined space to the window, peering outside.

"Yo Danny!" Mike answered, slipping a shirt over his head as he entered from a connecting room. "What's up?"

Dan turned away from the window and answered. "What's goin' on tonight?" He asked as he leaned on the exposed radiator underneath the opened window.

"Jay said there's a party up in Rooney." Mike replied as he sat on the arm of the sofa. "Five dollar cover. Otherwise, there's not much else happening."

"Where *is* Jay?" Dan inquired.

"The shower." Mike said, the door opening the moment he finished his answer and Jeremy walking inside, a towel wrapped around his waist with shower shoes on his feet completing his dress.

"Hey fellas." He greeted, moving past them and entering an adjoining room. "I'll be right out."

"Ya want to go to the party in Rooney?" Dan called into the other room.

"What else is there to do?" Jeremy inquired.

"Nothin' really." Dan began. "And the party doesn't start 'til nine so we've got to burn some time until then."

Eric stood and stretched. "Why don't you pack your stuff up that you're bringing over to my house and put it into the car?" He suggested. "We'll take it over, I'll show you the house and then we'll come back and go to the party. That will burn the time we need and solve a problem for me. I've got to give something to my mom and dad before they come to the game tomorrow."

Jeremy entered the room and glanced at the other two, cocking his head and shrugging his shoulders as if to agree. "That works for me." He said, rolling a stick of deodorant under his arms, then buttoning the shirt he had hung opened on his body. He turned, walked into his bedroom, pulled out a small athletic bag and began to grab clothes, stuffing them into the bag.

Mike stood from the sofa's arm. "I guess I better do the same thing." He said, shuffling into the bedroom, conceding that Jeremy had made the decision for the entire group.

Eric pulled himself off the couch and opened the door, signaling to Dan to follow him as he informed the other two that he would pick them up in front of the dorm on the way back. It appeared the evening's potential improved with every minute the clock drew closer to nine and he became more excited anticipating his first real college party.

They hurried to Dan's dorm room and quickly packed an athletic bag full of clothes, rushed back to the car and tossed the bag into the trunk. Quickly pulling out of the parking space, they drove through the back of the campus, the roof of the convertible down and the stereo blasting. Stopping in front of the freshmen dormitory where Mike and Jeremy sat waiting on the steps, Eric packed the bags in the trunk as the two boys hopped into the back seat of the car. They were on their way.

They drove out the road and turned onto the highway heading toward Eric's home. The wind rushed through the vehicle and as it entered the narrow valley, the mountains shaded the light of the setting sun and Eric engaged the lights, decreasing the volume of the stereo, sparking an increase in conversation about anything other than himself. He knew his friends were curious about him and though they had constantly accompanied him since his arrival on campus, they knew very little. Eric was a mystery and he intended to keep it that way, at least for a while, as he artfully changed topics when the discussion threatened to focus upon him.

After driving around the open town square and into the countryside, he slowed the car, turned left onto his road then decreased the volume of the stereo even further. For the moment, the vehicle was silent as his friends searched the landscape for a hint of a house until he slowed on the winding road and eased the car into the empty driveway.

As he had been the first time he set eyes on the property, his friends were awed by the size of the complex and they got out of the car looking around surveying the area. They grabbed their bags out of the trunk and followed Eric, who removed two gift-wrapped boxes and closed the trunk's lid before he entered the house through the kitchen door.

It was quiet inside and he reached along the wall next to the door and turned on the light. "Anybody home?" He called, placing the boxes on the table.

He heard a stir from upstairs followed by the thud of someone closing a door. "I'll be down in a second." Carol called as the sound of the back flight of stairs crackled with her descent and she appeared into the kitchen, a sudden smile bursting upon her face as she saw the four boys. "Well hello! I wasn't exactly expecting you tonight, but I'm glad you're here."

A smile broke across Eric's face and he stepped aside not to block Carol's view of his three friends, pointing to each. "Mom, this is Danny, Mike and Jeremy. Fellas, this is my mom," He began, his voice inflection hinting of a question. "But, I don't know where my dad is."

Carol guided the young men inside toward the glass-enclosed sitting room with the fireplace and directed them to sit. "Boys, I am very happy to meet you. Eric talks about you all the time." She warmly stated as she glanced out the window. "As for your father, I believe he just pulled into the driveway."

She quickly stood and opened the door, stepping outside to direct the man to enter through the door she held open. He walked inside the house and set two plastic grocery packages on top of the table in the corner of the room as he greeted Eric and his friends, a broad smile plastered across the face of the tall strapping man.

"Hey buddy, fellas, what brings you out here on a Friday night?" He began. "No wild parties on campus to go to?"

Eric chuckled as the other three quickly glanced at each other. "No pop, they don't start until later. We're just dropping some things off and then heading back." He answered. "By the way, this is Danny, Mike and Jeremy." Don nodded his head. "Nice to meet you gentlemen." He stated. "We're looking forward to having you over this weekend."

"Thank you sir." Dan answered. "We appreciated the invitation."

Don smiled. "Good. Carol, I want you to see something I picked up. Could you follow me into the kitchen?" He asked as he grabbed the packages and carried them into the other room.

Eric wrinkled his forehead as he watched her follow Don out of the room, a twitch of concern rumbling through his body. Was there a problem with his friends being in the house? No, he thought, that might have been the case had he been in Virginia, however that clearly was not the situation here. Maybe it was nothing to be concerned about and the paranoia he dragged with him everyday had over reacted. He turned away from the door to the kitchen, sinking into the chair relaxing for a moment as he continued to talk with his friends.

Carol walked to the center island and began removing groceries from the bag. "What did you want to show me?" She asked.

Don pulled a newspaper out of the bag and placed it face up on the counter. "I got the early edition of tomorrow's Washington Post." He stated. "Read the story on the right hand side under the headlines."

She grabbed the paper and began to read, her eyes widening as she neared completion of the article. When she finished, she folded the paper and let out a deep sigh, looking up at her husband. "We have to tell him." She said. "We promised him we would."

He leaned against the counter and nodded his head in agreement. "I know," He replied. "I'll make some inquiries later because you know he's going to have questions. Do you want to wait until after the weekend is over before we tell him?"

She began to put the groceries away in the cupboards and the refrigerator. "Oh Don, we have to. He was looking forward to this weekend and especially the game tomorrow. Forcing him to play with that on his mind would not be fair to him or his team."

Don pushed himself away from the counter and looked toward the kitchen table, noticing the two gift-wrapped packages sitting on the top. "My only concern would be that he finds out before we tell him." He said, walking to the table and turning toward his wife. "Honey, what are these?"

She peered over the center island and shook her head. "I don't know." She replied, moving to the table, picking up the card of one of the boxes, smiling as she set it down. "I believe these are for us."

"Eric!" Don called into the other room. "Come in here for a minute."

The young man entered the room, quickly stopping when he spotted the two by the table, and he smiled widely. "Those are for you." He said. "They're not much, but I wanted to say thanks."

After pausing for a moment, they carefully opened the packages and removed a dark green Saint Vincent College Soccer sweatshirt from each box, both holding them in front of them for inspection as huge smiles broke onto their faces. "They're just perfect!" Carol exclaimed, turning toward Eric and giving him a strong yet loving hug, a tear running down her cheek. "Thank you very much." She said, whispering in his ear as she held onto him. "From both of us."

Eric grinned and squeezed her in return, seeing Don in the background pulling the shirt over his head. "You're welcome." He replied, and then gently pulled away.

"I know what I'm wearing to the game tomorrow." Don shouted, proudly posing in his shirt as he walked to the opening of the sunroom, stepping inside. "What do you think boys?"

The three of them laughed. "You look good, Mr. Mason." Jeremy replied, standing from his seat and moving toward the man as the others followed. He glanced at his watch and looked out toward the kitchen. "Hey Eric, we've got to get going if we want to make the party."

Eric entered the room and looked at his watch. "Yeah, you're right. Get your stuff and I'll show you where to put it upstairs. Mom and dad, I'll see you tomorrow at the game." He said, giving Carol a quick kiss on the cheek and Don a hug as he rushed out the room, up the stairs and back down out the door.

Carol stared at her husband speechless as they looked out the window watching the boys load into Eric's car, then she grabbed his hand. He knew what she was feeling and inside, he agreed because he felt the same. Now, their job had become more difficult, more personal and he cupped his hand over hers as he pulled her closer into him and wrapped his arm around her.

Eric started the car then put up the top of the convertible before he pulled out of the driveway, sounding his horn and waving as he left. He felt good, not just about what he did for the Mason's but how he felt about them. As he drove up the road away from the house, he thought about his life here. No longer did he feel like an intruder into the Mason's lives or a guest at their house or a burden to their responsibilities, though from the very beginning they treated him like nothing but family. Now, he felt as if he were family and almost as if he were their son, though he did not forget about his family in Virginia or his life there. No that would never happen, not even if he could never return.

He drove closer to the college, his consciousness divided between the conversation he held with his friends and the one he had in his mind. He imagined the fun Greg, Jimmy or especially his brother Kevin would be having with him right now, and he smiled to himself thinking about how, if things were normal, he'd expose his little brother to college life. Hopefully, that opportunity had not passed by.

He turned onto the college driveway and parked his car near the freshmen dormitory. The campus flourished with activity and he climbed out of the vehicle walking toward one of the buildings with his friends, following the blare of music that guided them to its entrance. Pulling a five-dollar bill from his wallet as he approached the door, he entered the building and immersed himself into the body of the party, grabbing a cup and pouring himself a drink.

He took a gulp and looked around, smiling at the few people he knew and working through the crowd, talking with anybody who spoke to him. This is what he imagined a college party to be; music with bass levels so increased that they vibrate everything around sending a second pulse through the body, young women attempting conversations in the hallways or common rooms, some scouting each young man who walked by or entered the room, and hormone-driven guys, some leaning against walls awkwardly gawking at the women while waiting for their liquid courage to assist them in making contact. The rooms were darkened and so warm from body heat that a steam collected on the windows causing several of the men to open their shirts or remove them completely.

He took another swig from his cup and stopped, a girl standing along a wall within a small group catching his eyes. Her light skin and blondish hair accented delicate features that caught the few streams of light in the room. He strolled toward her, politely smiling at the group but contacting her eyes before he took a place along the wall, turned and watched the crowd, intentionally being aloof. As he stood, he sensed the group staring at him, hearing them whisper and he attempted to eavesdrop on their comments, the loudness of the music preventing him. Was the girl interested in him? Should he initiate a conversation or wait?

He nervously thought of words to say to her, quickly composing an icebreaker he hoped would not embarrass him or sound like a pick-up line. Coolly turning toward the group, he again smiled and made eye contact with the young woman. She motioned to him with her hand, calling him closer and he leaned toward her.

"Are you going to ask my name or stand there all night like a grinning idiot?" She inquired, the faint odor of alcohol following her words.

Eric raised his eyebrows. "Excuse me?"

"My name, are you going to ask me my name?" She repeated. "You came into the party, smiled at me and walked across the room. Then you walked over here, smiled at me and turned away. Now you're grinning at me again. Is this going to be an all night event or are you going to muster the courage to ask my name."

Eric stepped back from her and snickered, pausing for a moment. "I think you greatly exaggerate my desire to talk to you at all." He replied, then turned and walked away.

Shuffling past one of the adjoining rooms, he caught a glimpse of the red numbers of a digital clock glowing inside realizing that he spent two hours at a party with nothing to show for it and decided to leave. He searched the larger room and spotted Dan cozied up in a corner with a girl he recognized from one of his classes, catching his friend's attention and signaling his own departure. Exiting into the cool, late night air, he breathed deeply, wiping his head with the bottom of his shirt from the sweat that accumulated in the heat of the party. As he stood on the grass away from the buildings, the quietness of the outside invaded him and the loneliness he fought so hard to forget restored itself in the pit of his stomach.

He turned onto the walkway and shuffled his way back to Dan's dormitory room, turning on the light as he entered. Sitting on the empty bed across from Dan's, he kicked off his sneakers and slipped into a lengthy stare across the room. He saw it and it just sat there while he reviewed all of the instructions given to him over the past weeks until he breathed deeply and stood, knowing he had just lost the battle. He moved to Dan's desk, popped up the screen of the computer and logged on. This was her fault, he thought, the arrogant somewhat intoxicated girl he met at the party. Had she only let him speak first, he wouldn't be sitting here now.

Connecting onto the Internet, he gazed into the monitor as he struck a few keys on the board, stopping suddenly. He sat there, the blank expression of his face reflecting back to him on the screen, and he leaned forward in his chair resting his elbows on his thighs, his head sunk downward staring at the floor. Did he really need to do this now? He thought for a moment, then shook his head and sat up in the seat, deleting his entry before he clicked the icon on the screen to turn the computer off. Blankly he stared onto the darkened monitor angry with himself that he lacked the nerve to contact anyone from home.

Letting out a deep sigh, he slid away from the desk and returned to his bed, sitting in the silence of the room. Hearing the springs of the doorknob turning, he peered toward the door and watched as it slowly opened. It was Dan and he entered the room closing the door behind him.

"You didn't stay long." Dan stated as he sat in his bed across from his friend.

Eric shrugged his shoulders. "We have a game tomorrow." He replied. "I don't want to be hung-over. What's your excuse for coming back so soon?"

"Same reason." Dan replied as he took off his shoes and slid back onto the bed, leaning against the wall. "I take it you didn't have a good time."

"It was a blast." Eric sarcastically responded. "The girls are great."

Dan nodded his head and pressed his lips together simulating a smile, and then he rolled over to the foot of the bed, reaching into a mini refrigerator next to it and removing two cans of soda, flipping one to his friend. "I thought the girls were pretty cool." He replied. "So what's the real story?"

Eric popped open the can and took a drink. "What real story?" He inquired, hanging the soda in his hand as he leaned against the wall.

"With you." Dan answered. "What's the real story why you're here and your girl is somewhere else far away? I mean that is the underlying problem with you tonight isn't it? Your girl."

"No." Eric denied.

"Of course it is." Dan argued. "This girl you've got back in Connecticut, or where ever she is, has you all fucked up doesn't she?"

Eric stared at his friend, raising his eyebrows as he took another sip from the can and remained silent.

Dan stood and moved to the desk, hoisting himself up and sitting on its top. "I thought so." He said, and then leaned forward looking directly into Eric's eyes. "So why are you here? I mean, your talent far exceeds a division three school, you're intelligent and, from what I could see tonight at your house, pretty well off. Y'know?"

Eric cocked his head and squinted his eyes, a cynical grin growing across his face. "I was working at a resort and overheard a conspiracy to kill the President, so I was put here for witness protection." He stated.

Dan shook his head and chuckled. "Nice." He drawled out, assuming that Eric was joking with him. "So really, what was it? Did you get busted for something and your parents made you go to school close to home?" He asked.

Eric hesitated, raising the can into the air and tilting it slightly toward his friend in a simulated toast. "Yeah, something like that." He answered, gulping down the rest of the soda and crushing the can with his hands, tossing it into the garbage. He stood, pulling his shirt over his head and throwing it onto the bed. "Look, there's just a lot I don't talk about."

"Hey that's cool, and I'm sorry if I crossed the line here." He said, sliding down off the desk.

Eric held up his hand in a half wave and shook his head. "You didn't, it's cool. You're my friend, so you can ask me anything." He replied, pausing for a moment as he removed a towel from his bag. "But it doesn't mean I have to answer. So, if the quiz is over, I'm goin' to grab a shower before I go to bed." And he walked out the door closing it behind him.

At least he didn't lie, he thought to himself as he shuffled down the hallway toward the showers. That would have been easy, repeating the story he told the professor. However, he wanted to tell Dan the truth because his friendship was important and he was proud of himself that he did, even though Dan mistook the truth as a joke. But since there was no reason to try to convince him otherwise, he conceded to his friend ending the conversation. Maybe that would put a stop to all the questions.

He got up early the next morning, glancing across the room seeing Dan soundly asleep and figuring there was no use getting him up to go to breakfast. Instead, he decided to drive to the grocery story to pick up something for them to eat before the game. Quietly he pulled on a shirt and his sneakers, quickly brushed his teeth and left the room. It was cool outside, but he slowly walked to his car in his shorts, shirt and shoes with no socks as if it were a warm summer morning.

He drove off the campus to a plaza down the highway and parked, entering the store and grabbing a cart. A plan existed in his mind as to what breakfast would consist of, the perfect pre-game meal designed to enhance an athlete's performance, and he slowly wheeled through the unfamiliar store searching for the items he needed.

As he returned to the front of the market, he passed a small newsstand and he stopped. Should he look for the Washington Post? After all, it wouldn't hurt for him at least keep up on what was happening at home since he couldn't be there. He peered down at the selection of papers at the bottom of the rack, scanning the titles. There was no Washington Post, only an empty space with a sold out sign printed on a single sheet of paper, and he sighed in disappointment as he continued to the checkout line.

Returning to the dormitory, he walked through the stillness of the empty hallway and reached the room, carefully opening the door to not wake his friend. It remained dark inside and he quietly placed the plastic grocery bag on the vacant desk before easing the door shut, turning the knob to avoid the click of the lock grabbing. Then, he walked to the outside wall of the room and pulled the curtain of the left side window opened, letting in the dim morning light.

Glancing at the lump underneath the blanket in the middle of the bed, he shook his head in amazement. How could Dan sleep so soundly with his first college home game only hours away? If only he could be so relaxed.

Eric carefully stepped to the vacant desk and sat in the chair behind it, removing some of his purchases from the bags. Positioning some on the desk, he arranged them in the middle and placed two settings on either side. He was hungry and wanted to eat.

He stood from the desk and sat on his bed, grabbing his watch from the ledge notched into the underside of the desk. It was eight thirty and he looked over toward Dan once again. He was peaceful and if he had his choice would probably prefer to continue to sleep, but that wasn't going to happen.

"Dan." Eric strongly called. "Time to get up."

Waiting briefly and receiving only a disappointing groan from the caverns beneath the blankets, he stood and moved next to his friend's bed, sharply pounding on the side of the wooden desk. "Yo Dan! Eleven thirty!" He yelled.

Popping up quickly apparently startled out of a deep sleep and jumping out of bed, Dan stretched. "Damn Eric, why did you let me sleep so late?" He grumbled, still groggy from the night before. "I only have a half an hour to get ready."

Eric chuckled. "Relax there sleepy, it's only eight thirty. You've got plenty of time."

Dan scowled at him as he scratched the top of his head. "It's what?" He asked.

Eric grinned. "It's eight thirty." He answered.

"You woke me up at eight thirty?" Dan asked, becoming irritated. "Why the hell did you wake me up at eight thirty? I could have slept for at least another hour and a half." He excitedly stated.

Eric shook his head, still grinning. "Not if you want to perform well in this game." He answered. "And since I want us both to kick some ass today, I figured I'd wake you and get some performance food into us before the game."

Dan cocked his head to one side, wrinkling his forehead. "Performance food." He repeated. "What exactly is performance food?"

A smile grew across Eric's face as he prepared to disclose the breakfast menu. "I thought you might not know what performance food was." He answered. "So I took it upon myself to teach you all about it. Now I have to warn you, you might not think of this as a traditional breakfast, but trust me. I eat something like this before every early game and I think the success speaks for itself."

Skeptical, Dan glanced toward the desk and noticed several containers sitting on top and two bags placed close by. "What is it?" He asked.

Eric slid over to the desk. "Ah, so you are interested." He began, his voice adding a teased inflection to his already expressive face. "Well, we start with a fresh fruit salad that I had the people at the store specially make for us consisting of slices of grapefruit, bananas, oranges and pineapple with blueberries. Then, we have enough whole grain bagels, cream cheese, skinless chicken breasts, lettuce and tomato for three sandwiches each. And to top it off, one hundred percent natural white grape juice to drink." He proudly announced, waiting for Dan's response.

Dan surveyed the items on the desk, and then stared at his friend. "Who's going to eat all that?" He asked, overwhelmed at the quantity of food spread out before him.

Eric grinned. "We are, but we don't have to eat it all in ten minutes." He answered. "Let's chill out and take our time. Around ten, we'll walk around campus, play a game of pool then come back to the room to get ready for the game."

"And you do this before every early game?" Dan inquired.

Eric nodded his head. "Every one." He answered.

Dan chuckled then shrugged his shoulders. "You realize it's just a superstition?" He asked, but then conceded that Eric's talent on the field was enough to take his word on game day nutrition, so he reached for a bagel and began to build himself a sandwich.

CHAPTER 12

THE DOOR SWUNG OPEN AND Matt stumbled through the doorway carrying a bag and a large foam cup of coffee in one hand and his briefcase and newspaper in the other. It was breakfast on the go early on another Saturday, one of a series of weekend mornings in which he worked, and he wondered if he'd ever again spend time with his family or even share a quiet breakfast with them in the near future.

Before the night that Eric Lynch came home panicked from work, Matt remembered living a normal life, or as normal as a United States Attorney could have, spending time with his wife or any of his three young children. Now, his contact with them became severely limited, taking a peek at his kids while they slept when he came home late at night or when he left early in the morning for work and barely talking with his wife, let alone sleeping with her. No longer had he been able to get away to see his eight year old son's soccer games, or his six year old daughter's first dance recitals or his four year old son's first day in pre-school. No longer have he and his wife gone out for an evening or shopping or attended one of her school functions. Missing his family's important events now became a habit and it was a habit that he preferred breaking sometime soon. This case consumed all of his time, and though he knew when he accepted the position that occasional working weekends were likely, he didn't count on them occurring so often. But then a case such as this one doesn't occur often either.

He set his briefcase and newspaper on the desk as he sat in his chair, sipping from the cup staring at the pictures of his family that lined the edge. Unfolding a paper napkin on top of the blotter, he removed a bagel and cream cheese from the bag and took a bite, setting it on top of the napkin. Again he stared at the pictures, for now this was the only way he would eat breakfast with his family and he grabbed the newspaper he placed next to the briefcase, unfolded it and began to read.

It was front-page news for the second day, a continuation of the story that Bostic so conveniently leaked to the Washington Post. As he scanned the article, he smiled, proud of himself for the manner in which he answered questions and for the cunning he displayed, giving credit to the Post's reporter for breaking the story, but avoiding confirming the story's accuracy. After all, it was the reporter who connected the shootings in Washington with the death of Kearney and then the German in the motel room, so he should be rewarded with the glory for the discovery.

His plan had the potential to be brilliant, its success dependent upon the reactions of key people to the story being its only flaw, and Matt sat in his chair thinking about them as he scanned the remainder of the article. Would they react the way he thought? How long would he have to wait before they did, if they did? It was just enough to make him more nervous.

He refolded the paper, sliding it to the side of the desk, and then opened the briefcase. From inside, he removed the envelope he mysteriously received several nights before and set it on the desk, opening it and removing the contents. It was the offer and its conditions that worried him, trading a meeting with Eric in exchange for unspecified detailed information from, of all places, the Italian Intelligence Agency. He chuckled at the insanity of the entire situation. How would Italian intelligence know about the events at Saddlewood? Who in the organization would make an offer where the key condition was meeting with Eric? And better yet, why would they? What importance did Eric play in the Italian intelligence community? And then he realized that if he wanted to find out, aside from accepting the offer itself, there existed only one way to answer his questions.

He sat behind the desk and studied the contents of the overstuffed envelope. The information retrieved from Saddlewood exceeded the definition of helpful and he knew that, if what was offered in exchanged for the meeting with Eric actually existed, there was no doubt he wanted it. But was it practical, or better yet, advisable to acquiesce to the very specific terms in order to gain very unspecific information he would have no way of knowing would be helpful until he viewed it? The facts that the unnamed Italian knew something happened at Saddlewood, that he knew Eric was involved and that he knew Matt was responsible for hiding him, caused great concern. Maybe the price of the information was just too great.

He picked up the hand-written letter, reviewing the contents and instructions one additional time. Should he agree to the terms, he was to escort Eric to the Italian Embassy alone on the second Saturday in October at eight o'clock in the evening for a formal private dinner. But it was an offer that made no sense to him. For all of the things that someone could request in trade for this level of intelligence, why a formal private dinner with a seventeen year old high school student? And that's what generated Matt's suspicion.

He returned the information and the letter into the envelope, replacing it into his briefcase until later. Standing from his chair, he moved across the room to the windows, somewhat pacing between them as he looked outside. His impatience grew, waiting for Bostic, and he glanced at the clock on the wall, hoping the man would soon appear at the office with the information on the latest event, the death of yet another one of the eight men from Saddlewood.

Collins thought about his prophecy, predicting the death of the German in the motel room in Winchester as being the first of a series. He hoped he'd been wrong, wanting to detain and question at least one of the men from the villa. But when the first man was killed, he knew questioning one would be unlikely. He sighed deeply as he resumed pacing the room, reviewing his actions over the past week. Did he err when he posted a bulletin to all the enforcement agencies stating the eight men were wanted for questioning? Was that one action the catalyst causing the apparent attempt to eliminate each of the guests of the guesthouse? The logical answer seemed to be yes.

He took another drink of coffee, finishing the cup and crushing the foam in his hand then tossing the remnants into the garbage can. Ending his pacing at the window, he again glanced outside into the early Saturday activity as the door to his office slowly opened and Bostic stepped inside. "Sorry I'm running a little late." He said as he entered, closing the door behind him.

Matt walked toward his desk holding the cup in his hand. "It's a Saturday, so it's not possible to be late." He stated, leaning against the side of the desk and setting the cup down beside him. "So, who was he and where did they find him?"

Bostic stood just inside the door, placing his briefcase along the wall. "It was Motilgin." He answered. "He was found at the bottom of a ravine off of a hiking trail along Skyline Drive."

"How long had he been dead?" Collins asked.

"At least two days." Bostic replied. "The incident had been listed as accidental."

Matt chuckled as he shook his head. "Of course it was. They're all made to look like accidents." He stated, moving behind his desk and sitting in the chair. "Did you have any success with our intelligence agencies?"

Bostic wrinkled his eyebrows. "That depends on your definition of success. I didn't get any help from the CIA." He answered. "They know nothing about it. So where you got the idea that the intelligence community is aware of the situation seems to be erroneous."

"Erroneous." Matt repeated, motioning toward a chair for Bostic to sit. "I doubt it."

Bostic sat in the chair across from Collins' and pulled the briefcase closer to him. "It gets better." He stated as he set the case on his lap and opened it. "Nobody has been able to gather any credible information concerning a threat against the President of the United States." He pulled a legal tablet out of the briefcase, and then continued. "Every one of the men identified as meeting at Saddlewood those nights was cleared through the U.N. as diplomats and other than back and forth to Dulles, they spent virtually no time in this country."

Collins strongly forced air out of his mouth in frustration, then stood from his desk and moved to the window, shaking his head. "I've got people who worked in Saddlewood as well as foreign intelligence agents turning up dead all over Northern Virginia and nobody knows anything." He stated, the anger building in his voice. "Are they not at least suspicious of these mysterious deaths of a German and a Russian operative in their own back yard? What did they say about that?"

Bostic sighed deeply, hesitating an answer. He replaced the legal pad into the briefcase, and then set the case on the floor beside him. "Well, the CIA suggested you look for a local criminal connection."

Matt turned to face the man. "A local criminal connection." He repeated. "Tell me you're kidding Dan. Are they just not interested in any of this?" He asked, waiting for his colleague's response.

Bostic slid forward into his chair and stared at the man. "I have no idea." He replied. "It just doesn't make sense. Eric overheard something secretive for what he believed was an assassination plan, was caught in the process, and now we have an escalating body count of foreign intelligence agents and people he worked with. I would think someone would be very interested."

Collins nodded his head. "Yeah so would I, unless they already know what's going on." He stated as he returned to the desk and removed the envelope he received from the unknown Italian from his briefcase, tossing it to Bostic. "Here's something you might find interesting that adds a new dimension to this whole situation. Take a look at it and tell me what you think."

Bostic picked up the envelope and removed the contents, sorting through the papers before he discovered the hand-written letter. Sinking back into his chair, he lifted the letter to eye level and began to read, reviewing it a second time before he set it aside. Then, he picked up the accompanying pages one at a time and studied each carefully, silently shaking his head as he read some while he flipped through the pages of the others. Completing his review, he arranged the papers into a neat pile, replaced them into the envelope then gently set them on the desk, staying silent as he thought about what he just read.

"Interesting information, don't you think?" Collins asked, interrupting the silence of the moment.

"To say the least." Bostic agreed. "And there's more?"

Matt nodded. "So they claim." He replied. "What obviously concerns me, and I am sure you as well, is the terms for acquiring the additional information."

"The meeting with Eric." Bostic answered. "I agree. It's an odd request. However, what would it hurt?"

"What if it's a trap?" Collins asked, becoming excited. "What if the people responsible for this entire situation sent us the invitation and the information solely to get access to Eric? What then?"

Bostic calmly sat in his chair, and then leaned forward. "Do you really think that whoever sent you this is going to use the Italian Embassy in Washington to set up some kind of trap?"

Collins stayed silent for a moment, sliding back into his seat staring at the papers in front of him. Though in a way he agreed with his colleague, he felt very uncomfortable with the offer. Anything was possible, he thought to himself. Yet, the offer could very well be legitimate. But what if it wasn't? Just because *he* knew that Eric failed to gather damning evidence against whatever went on in that villa at Saddlewood over those couple of months, didn't mean the people who he spied on did. And since Eric's actions those two nights triggered all of this activity, it only made sense that whatever they thought Eric heard, was enough to kill him. So what better way to get rid of the young man than to set him up to a certain place at a certain time, virtually alone, using the offer of undisclosed information as bait? It presented the perfect opportunity.

He shifted in his chair, sitting upright as he rubbed his temples with his one hand. "Then I guess there's only one thing I can do." He stated as he lifted the receiver of his phone and dialed.

CHAPTER 13

MAYBE IT WAS THE ROAR of the crowd on the warm sunny afternoon that incited his drive more than he had ever been driven before. Maybe it was the sudden release of his many frustrations all at one time. Maybe it was the excitement of his first collegiate home game in front of his friends and, in a way, family. Then again, it could have been a combination of all three that caused Eric to score four goals in the first half of the game. Whatever the impetus behind the performance, the significance to Eric was more than the realization that he would excel in this sport at this or a higher level, more than the emergence from obscurity in the school's social structure courtesy of four talent-laden shots into the back of the net and more than any obvious benefit he would receive from dominating play throughout the game while contributing to his teammates' personal successes. No, the significance to him was more personal, more private and far more emotional. The game they weren't supposed to win became a metaphor about his life, destroying an adversary while something or someone came at him from all sides and facing endless battles while keeping his wits about him. With each minute he played, he became stronger, more confident and more focused, feeling that no one could compete with him. And no one could. His first shot penetrated the netting of the back of the goal and he peered into the crowd spotting Carol and Don Mason on the hillside in the shirts he bought for them jumping up and down and cheering. For whatever reason at that moment, he knew that like this game, only he would control his life.

Yet the learning experience was far from over. Eric greatly matured through the course of the game, not in the knowledge of the sport itself, but for the lessons he learned about his own life. Before the game he faced the unknown, masking his nervousness and fear from his friends with a swagger that at times even he failed to understand. Like the game, his life was filled with emotions hidden from everyone around him and like before the game, in life he feigned confidence. Though the first goal taught him that he controlled his own destiny, it was the second that triggered his epiphany of knowing and believing that he possessed the inner-strength to excel in his life, no matter what his life would throw at him. This feeling liberated him and when he walked off the field at the end of the contest, he surrendered all of his insecurities to his past.

He ascended the hillside toward the Masons, the sweat from his body saturating his white shirt, highlighting the green number twenty-nine on the yellow background. He looked at them, seeing the obvious pride they held in their expressions, and he smiled. He saw in them what he remembered in his real parents, an unlimited reservoir of love and support that knew no boundaries, and he walked up to them, a quiet smile quickly growing across his face as he stood in front of them. Without speaking a word, the Masons knew what the smile represented and Carol grabbed the sweaty young man, holding him close while kissing him on the side of the head as Eric wrapped his arms around her. For the moment, the three of them were alone among hundreds of people.

Gently, Eric released his hold on her, cocking his head to one side as the emotion in his voice controlled his speech. "I...I've got to go get a shower." He softly said.

Don grinned at the young man and nodded. "I know, get going." He answered. "We'll see you and the boys at the house in a little bit."

Eric nodded his head, keeping silent though answering with the expression on his face. He slowly turned toward the athletic center and grinned, then jogged to the entrance, disappearing into the building.

As the last player to enter the locker room, he weaved through the mass of teammates on his way to his locker under a showering of used, rolled up athletic tape, compressed paper cups and balls of paper as an expression of congratulations. It was a surreal experience and he sat down on the bench in front of the locker incognizant of the celebration around him, silently staring inside it as what happened to him on the field slowly materialized in his mind. Slowly he stood, undressed, then threw a towel around his waist and walked into the shower.

Already loud inside from the excitement generated by the victory, the room erupted into a boisterous cheer as he entered. Humbled by the reaction, he thanked them, attributing his success more to the play of the team than to himself, then quietly stood under the water soaking his exhausted body. He smiled, as the heat of the water soaked his muscles, pleased with his success and the respect he received from the team.

After he finished dressing, he stepped into the quiet hallway outside of the locker room and walked down the corridor toward the door, graciously accepting congratulations from the people passing by. Relishing the momentary notoriety, he exited the building with a grin on his face and hustled to his car where his three friends waited.

"That was a hell of a performance out there today." Mike stated as Eric unlocked the vehicle with the push of a button on his remote control.

Eric smiled at his friend, shrugging his shoulders in the process. "Thanks." He replied. "I just had a good day."

Dan shook his head. "And there goes the patented Eric Mason modesty." He stated, opening the passenger side door. "Can you just admit one time for us that you know that you're good."

Eric shook his head and he opened his door, climbing inside. "If it'll make you happy, okay... I know I'm pretty damn good." He admitted.

Dan glanced at him, and then turned to Jeremy and Mike sitting in the back seat. "See, I told you he was full of himself." He said, the joking expression on his face causing the other two to laugh.

Eric shook his head and chuckled. "You're an ass." He replied, starting the car, lowering the top and pulling out of the parking space, driving off the campus.

It was a good day, not only because of the outcome of the game but because of everything that seemed to resolve itself, and though the fervor remained from the afternoon, Eric relaxed as he drove toward home with his three friends. They replayed the excitement of nearly every minute of the game, at times embellishing their perspective and adding color to their already colorful accounts. And by the time the four of them shared their versions and disputed the others, they had made it home.

As Eric slowed the vehicle in approach to his house, the lively banter eased and he pulled into the driveway, stopping in front of the garage. It was peaceful outside, the quietness disturbed only by the distant swishing of leaves by the late summer breeze, and they walked toward the house, drawn by the aroma of home cooking.

Eric stepped up to the door, pulled it open and led his friends inside. From the back of the house, they could hear the sounds of a college football game playing on the television and Eric slowly walked toward it, peeking around the corner of the wall.

"Hey!" Don greeted as he looked up from his game and spotted the boys. "We didn't hear you come in."

Eric grinned. "Yeah, I guess not." He joked. "We could have stolen all the food and left."

Don chuckled as he and his wife stood from their seats. "I doubt that you will be able to eat everything your mother cooked for you." He stated, shaking each boy's hand as he walked up to them. "By the way, great game gentlemen."

Carol smiled. "Yes it was." She agreed, leading them back toward the kitchen. "You boys were outstanding."

"Thank you." Dan answered. "And thank you for having us over this weekend." He said, Jeremy and Mike echoing the appreciation.

"It's our pleasure." She replied. "And since I know you boys are hungry, we'll have dinner in about fifteen minutes. Until then, let Eric show you around the house and you can get settled before we eat."

A grin grew across Eric's face. Instead of leading his friends around the house, he insisted they follow him outside and they wondered, of all things, why would he want to show them the inside of a barn? He opened the door and turned on the lights welcoming them to what he called his playroom, a regulation-size indoor soccer field complete with dasher boards, goals and a small electronic scoreboard placed in the upper corner of the building. Flipping a switch next to the lights, he activated two hydraulically operated basketball backboards which, when lowered, created a full-sized basketball court. They stood in stunned silence, awed by the facility.

Since the time he was brought here, this building served as his refuge, a private sanctuary where he could work out his frustrations, relieving the pressure that could surely cause him to break down. Whether practicing soccer on the court or working out in the weight room downstairs, it kept him occupied during the first difficult days when he tormented over leaving his family and friends. Now, instead of serving as a shelter from his fears, it became an illustration of his life and he wanted to show it off.

From the Mason's perspective, this weekend was supposed to create a semblance of normalcy in Eric's life. And to a degree, it appeared to succeed. They continued to strengthen the bond they forged with him and the three young men who spent the weekend seemed to fill the void of friendship that he left back in Virginia. But how successful would the weekend with his friends be? Would it be able to go so far as to solidify the fragile foundation of a life they constructed for him? If it did, only then would he be able to manage the difficulties ahead for him and they knew a test of their work was shortly ahead.

By Sunday evening when all the activity slowed to a calm, quiet evening, the four young men packed their bags with the plan to return to school, hoping to spend at least two hours studying in the library. It was part of a ritual started on the first day the four of them met, a ritual Eric insisted on keeping that resulted in success in the classroom. However, unknown to him, the Mason's had other plans.

As he opened the door of the kitchen, Carol gently pulled him back into the house. "Eric, we need you to come back tonight." She quietly stated.

He tilted his head as he looked at her with a pained expression. "Is there something wrong?" He asked. "Because I thought we agreed when we set up this weekend that I could stay with Dan tonight."

She forced a smile on her face. "I know." She compassionately answered, stroking his arm to ease the tension. "But we just need you to come back tonight."

Eric stared at her for a moment then slowly nodded, sensing the urgency of her request. "I'll think of something to tell them and get back here as soon as I can." And he walked out the door.

Understandably he became concerned. The Masons rarely made specific requests of him, so there was no doubt that whatever caused them to this time was undoubtedly important. And that's what worried him.

Making the excuse with his friends that he forgot his books at home, he left the library early and returned to the house. Stepping through the kitchen door into an eerie almost frightening silence, the nervousness in his stomach intensified. The house was never this quiet, he thought, and he wondered if the morgue-like atmosphere foreshadowed the nature of the information they were about to share with him.

He stepped to the entrance of the glass-enclosed sunroom where they sat waiting for him and stopped. A small fire crackled in the stone hearth that took away the slight chill the clear night produced and he stared at them for a moment. Even in the stillness of reading, they appeared serious and he realized he delayed as much as he could.

"Hey." He softly greeted as he sheepishly entered the room.

They peered up at him and smiled. "Hey." Carol replied. "I hope you enjoyed yourself this weekend." She stated, placing her book on the table to her left.

Eric nodded, his expression reserving any emotion until the small talk concluded. "I did, thank you." He answered, squinting his eyes and taking a deep breath, avoiding starting the discussion of whatever subject that has caused the tension he felt. "How about you?"

Carol stood. "We had a great time." She replied. "We really enjoyed watching your game yesterday. You played brilliantly."

Eric tilted his head in appreciation. "Thank you." He said, taking his shirt off and turning, exposing two large bruises on the side of his torso. "They were pretty physical."

Don stood from his seat and walked toward Eric. "Are you hurt son?" He asked, the genuine concern in his voice comforting to the young man.

Eric shook his head. "No, just a little sore." He answered, pausing briefly while he slid his shirt over his head. He glanced at Don, then quickly at Carol and he sensed their discomfort with the topic of discussion they attempted to put off. He walked over to the fireplace stirring the embers before he turned to face him. "It's bad, isn't it?"

Don retreated to the chairs in front of the fireplace, sat then extended his arm in an invitation for Eric to sit with them. "A while ago you asked us to be straightforward with you if or when we were given information about issues in Virginia. But instead of telling you something second hand, when I can give you the source I will. So I need you to read the articles I highlighted from Friday's and Saturday's Washington Post." He instructed, handing the young man the copies of the two editions.

Reluctantly, Eric took the papers from the man and placed them next to him, lifting the top paper and holding it forward as he leaned over to read. The Masons watched him, his stoic expression causing concern, as it never wavered. The boy inhaled deeply followed by a loud forcing of air out of his mouth as if he were attempting to control himself from breaking down. Then as quickly as he began, he finished the first story and folded the paper neatly, placing it next to him.

Though his head remained tilted downward, the Masons could see his eyes begin to build up with water. And as he lifted the second paper to continue to read, he cupped his right hand over his forehead to shield himself form everything around. But he could not shield the pain from his expression. He set the paper to the side and leaned forward, fixing a mindless gaze to the floor.

Carol watched the young man fight to maintain his composure and she leaned toward him. "Is there anything we can do for you?" She calmly asked.

Eric slowly, almost unnoticeably shook his head. Again he inhaled deeply, strongly forcing the air out of his lungs as he maintained his stare toward the floor. He stayed silent, fighting his urge to break down by continuing to repeat the irregularity of his breathing.

"Do you want to talk about it?" Don inquired, hoping to encourage the boy to speak preventing him from hyperventilating.

Eric cleared his throat and softly spoke. "I don't know what there would be to talk about." He stated, maintaining his downward stare before he slowly lifted his head, making contact with their eyes as he softly continued. "I...I kind of wish you would have kept this to yourself."

Carol sighed. "Would you really have wanted us to do that?" She asked, not expecting an answer from him.

A tear slowly rolled down Eric's cheek and he quickly wiped it away. "No." He whispered as he shook his head.

"Eric, if there's anything we can do to help you through this, just let us know." Don stated.

Eric placed his hands over his face and rubbed his eyes. "I got them killed." He stated, the reality of what he just read becoming clearer in his mind. "Can you undo that?"

Carol moved to the sofa and sat next to him. "You were in no way responsible for their deaths." She replied, placing her arm around his shoulder and holding him close.

He sighed deeply then scoffed at her remark. "I wasn't responsible for their deaths?

That's bullshit! Please tell me how you can possibly spin that in my favor, because as I see it, if I didn't do what I did, we're not sitting here right now having this discussion."

Don stood and walked to the fireplace, setting an additional log on the fire before he turned and leaned on the mantel. "You're right." He agreed

"Don!" Carol interrupted, upset that he would agree with the distraught young man.

"No Carol, he's right." He argued. "If he doesn't act in the manner he did, we would not be having this discussion and there *is* no way to spin that in his favor. But Eric, you did not kill Aaron Butler or Steven Kearney or any of the other people listed in those two articles. Those people were casualties of whatever you heard way before that night ever occurred when someone, other than you, consciously made the decision that protecting those meetings' secrecy included eliminating anyone who had any ties to them."

Eric popped up and shuffled to the window, peering out into the wooded darkness. His eyes began to redden from the tears that built up inside and again he wiped them; fighting for the composure he felt he was close to losing. He thought about Aaron and wondered if he even had known why someone was shooting him. Though he tried, he couldn't imagine how scared Aaron must have been, knowing that he was probably going to die. He couldn't comprehend how lonely Aaron must have felt, dying without being able to see his family that he loved so much for one last time as well as being aware that his girlfriend had already passed away in his arms.

Eric growled in anger, feeling he was the cause of all the pain and destruction his friends were forced to endure. Strongly forcing air out of his mouth, he ran out of the house and into the sports barn, the Masons quickly following behind. As he entered, he picked up a soccer ball and hurled it against the dasher board. It rebounded to his foot and he struck it with such force that when it sailed wide of the net, it cracked a piece of safety glass behind the court. His eyes swelled, filling with tears as he remembered the friend he'd never see again, and he stopped, faced the goal and raised his hands to his face. He knew the Masons were behind him. "Aaron was a great guy." He shouted, laboring with each word.

"If he was anything like you are now, there's no doubt that he was." Don stated as he held Carol from running to the boy's side.

"Thanks." Eric muttered. "And I know you really mean that as well as trying to make me feel better, but now is not the time."

"Do you want us to leave?" Don asked.

Eric turned to face them, his eyes red from the tears that already escaped down his cheeks, and he fell to his knees, broke down and quietly cried.

As Carol held the boy, Don crouched down to the same level with him and placed his hand on the back of his neck, lightly massaging it. "I have no idea what you're feeling right now Eric, but we're both here for you and we always will be." He softly stated as he patted the young man on the back of the head.

Almost unnoticeably, Eric nodded his head. "Thanks." He replied, grabbing the bottom of his shirt to wipe his eyes. "I'm sorry about all of this."

"There's nothing to be sorry for." Carol stated.

He strongly exhaled, and then slowly attempted to compose himself. "What about my family?" He asked.

"Everybody's okay." Don answered. "We checked up on that when we learned of the news about Aaron."

Eric rose from the ground and again lifted the bottom of his shirt, wiping his eyes. He walked to a collection of soccer balls along the boards, but turned and leaned against the board, staring at the Masons for a moment. "So, what do we do now?" He inquired.

"What we have been doing." Don answered. "In fact, had this not occurred, we were going to have you move on campus this week if you wanted to."

"So that's changed." Eric stated.

Carol nodded her head. "I want you to stay around here for a couple of days." She replied. "If you're okay, then there's a room available with a roommate we think you'll like. You can still move in next week."

"Why not right now?" Eric asked.

Don rose from his chair and walked to the table, pouring himself a drink from the pitcher sitting on top. "We can't afford to take any chances. So we need to wait a few days."

Eric gazed at the man, shaking his head. "There's no difference between now and a few days." He said, his voice inflecting the displeasure he felt with the idea.

Don moved close to him and looked directly into eyes. "Eric, you have to understand that we are always just one mistake away from getting you killed. We might have to take what may seem like drastic measures because we don't want anything to happen to you." He stated, the seriousness of his voice emphasizing his sincerity. "And we like going to your games. So think about that for a minute."

Eric stared at him for a moment, glanced at Carol, and then returned his attention to the man. He nodded his head. "Okay." He replied, quickly peering down at the floor then back at Don. "So who's going to be my roommate?"

"Danny will be." Carol answered. "We thought you might like that and we like him."

Eric nodded his head. "Thanks. You made a good choice." He said as he dribbled a ball and shot it into the net. He turned and looked at the two people who he knew cared very deeply about him. He walked away from the dasher board and drifted toward the door. "I've got some work left to do so, if you don't mind, I'm going upstairs for the night."

Carol turned and followed him to the door, stopping him before he left the building. "Are you sure you're all right?" She asked.

He paused, glancing toward the floor quickly before he looked at her and answered. "I'll be okay. I just want to be alone for a little bit." He said. Then he turned and left, walking across the driveway and into the house.

When he reached his room, he flipped on the light and closed the door behind him, tears building in his eyes. Though he told Carol differently, he was not okay or at least didn't feel okay. He was scared and lonely and angry, harboring a full range of emotions that he felt overwhelmed to handle all at once.

He kicked off his shoes and sat on the bed, grabbing the remote control to his stereo. Maybe the music would calm him and he scanned through the compact disks he had stored in his changer until he found what he wanted. Then, he lay back on the bed and stared blankly into the ceiling. So many memories played through his mind, the day he met Aaron, his surprise birthday party on the mall in Washington with all of his friends and his time with Maria. They were good. No, they were great and he sorely missed everyone, worried that he'd never see any of them again, let alone wondering if they were safe.

He pounded his fist on the bed, got up and shuffled to the desk, sitting in front of the computer and pressing the button to watch the monitor light up. He could wait no longer. There was so many things he needed to find out, so many questions he needed answered, that the choice became simple. Sure, the Masons told him his family was okay, but they never mentioned the other people who were important to him. And that he had to know.

CHAPTER 14

SIR CHARLES MAY HAVE COME to the United States Attorney's office voluntarily, but Collins did not want to take that chance or wait that long. The news coverage of the deaths related to the United Nations Consulate at Saddlewood generated more than just local interest. In a matter of days after the story broke in the Washington Post, it was picked up by every major news service in the United States as well as North America, followed by Europe and the rest of the world. Murder was not supposed to happen here. In all of its good intentions, Saddlewood was created as an area free of conflict, where people from every nation could gather to solve world problems, not produce them.

But after the release of the article, questions arose from all corners of the world, not just the United States. There were calls to the State Department concerning the events and the security of the consulate, to the Justice Department for reports on progress of the investigation and to the United Nations for a myriad of subjects. Pressure built on the United States Attorney to solve the mystery and it became clear to him that his slow and conservative approach to the investigation would no longer suffice.

His first contact with the Consul was very ordinary; a phone call from one office to the other requesting a meeting, and Collins fully expected nothing but cooperation. But he failed in his attempt, and the fact that the Consul hesitated to cooperate confounded him. Why would he refuse? Was it because Saddlewood was conducting its own private investigation and did not want any outside influences, as he claimed? At first, it somewhat made sense. But when Collins' request to share information failed, he knew it was far more than the mere possibility that an outside influence could taint an internal investigation. And he wanted to know what it was.

So Collins drove to Saddlewood, and though he was granted entrance, Sir Charles was strangely unavailable to receive him. That may have been expected had he appeared unannounced. But through a third party, Collins had the Consulate called so he could learn of the events that Sir Charles would be attending, hoping to gain an audience with the respected diplomat. Now, when Matt stood within the borders to attend at least one of those functions, Sir Charles inexplicably cancelled his appearances. It was more than a coincidence and more than Matt's imagination. The cancellation was intentional and it became clear that Sir Charles was avoiding him.

Collins left countless messages, numerous personal requests and expended many diplomatic efforts to speak with Sir Charles Hawksworth. The messages were ignored, the personal requests rebuked and the diplomatic efforts unproductive, though the

Consul promised he would clear time for a meeting with the United States Attorney. For a while, there was hope, but days became weeks and it appeared that any sharing of information between Saddlewood and the United States Attorney's Office would never materialize. So it almost had to be expected that Collins, who was one never to give up easily, would not give up now. What was not expected were his actions.

Like most attractions, Saddlewood posted important events on its website. In among them was the listing of times that Sir Charles would be available for photo opportunities and events he would be attending. But within that listing was an announcement that the Consul would be attending a conference in Geneva, Switzerland and it gave Matt an idea, as well as an opportunity.

Saddlewood sat within the jurisdiction of Captain Porter's troop of the Virginia Highway Patrol and Collins decided to call on his captain for a favor. Why not? Porter wanted informed of the happenings at Saddlewood and was very insistent about contributing to the investigation of the two murders that occurred under his watch. So Matt contacted him and the rest became history, as well as an international incident.

Sir Charles Hawksworth enjoyed diplomatic immunity as the Consul of Saddlewood, which meant that he could not be prosecuted for most, if not all, criminal acts. But Dan Bostic found a loophole and three days before Sir Charles was to leave for Geneva, Collins lodged a material witness warrant against the man. Normally, issuing that warrant would have made the front page of every major newspaper. However, Collins gave the responsibility for executing the warrant exclusively to Captain

Porter with the time and location Sir Charles would be available. But available held a different connotation for Matt than it did for Sir Charles, and that presented the problem.

On the first Thursday of October at seven thirty in the morning, Sir Charles Hawksworth, departed the United Nations Embassy at Saddlewood for Dulles International Airport and his morning flight to Geneva. As his limousine left the borders of Saddlewood, a Virginia Highway Patrol Vehicle casually pulled behind the car and followed is for less than a minute before it flipped on its emergency lights. Almost immediately, three additional Virginia Highway Patrol cars joined the first, boxing in the limousine, requesting it pull over. With weapons drawn, the State Trooper approached the car and ordered all occupants out of the vehicle with their hands raised. Everyone complied, but a heated Sir Charles exited spouting phrases that no proper Englishman had ever been taught at Oxford or Cambridge. And as he pointed to the diplomatic plates on the limousine questioning the troopers' intelligence, Captain Porter approached the man, handed him the warrant an instructed him to come peacefully because today, he really didn't feel like throwing handcuffs on a man knighted by the Queen of Great Britain, but he would if he had to. Sir Charles graciously entered the back of the Virginia Highway Patrol car and was escorted to the office of the United States Attorney for the Eastern District of Virginia peacefully. Almost.

"You cannot treat me in this manner." Sir Charles ranted as he burst into the office. "You know that I will have your job when I am done with you."

Matt peered up from his desk and glared at the man. "I really don't think that you will." He replied, standing from his chair and directing the man to a seating area. "But should you decide that is the course of action that you would really prefer to take, please let me thank you first because this entire situation has really been a pain in my ass. And quite frankly, so have you."

The Consul froze in his seat, unaccustomed to being spoken so tersely. "I read that you are an alumnus of Duke University as well as the University of Virginia's School of Law. Obviously from your boorish and petulant behavior those schools failed to teach any of the graces we so treasure in the United Kingdom."

Collins arrogantly chuckled. "Really?" He stated, a sardonic grin spreading across his face. "Should I queue the video tape of your behavior earlier this morning when the fine gentlemen of the Virginia Highway Patrol safely escorted you to my office and compare our educational experiences? Where did you attend? Oxford, wasn't it?"

The Consul glared at the man. "I was being kidnapped." He retorted. "You have no legal authority to detain me."

Collins shook his head, the grin transforming into a full-fledged smile. "I have three young children at home, Sir Charles, the oldest of which is eight. And as a parent I have learned so many techniques that I thought useless with normal people, because as I am sure you know, children aren't normal people. They test your patience every moment they are able, they ignore you at every opportunity and sometimes they make you feel as though you've suffered a stroke because you know you told them to do something and they failed to respond. So I learned to control that behavior in them through a very simple method. First, I ask them nicely to perform whatever task I want them to perform. After they agree to perform that task, they don't do it and I ask myself why, because I spoke to them in English. What could I have done wrong? Then I become more insistent, telling them that I really need to have them perform this particular task now. Again they ignore me and now it becomes personal. So instead of going through all this banter for nothing at all, I grab them up, take them to the task that I nicely asked them to perform some fifteen minutes ago, and angrily make them do it. Do you know they possess the audacity to say to me that all I had to do was ask them and that I didn't have to get mad? Please tell me, Sir Charles, that you are far more intelligent than my children by not telling me that all I had to do was ask."

The Consul squirmed in his chair, pouting for a moment while he digested Matt's story. "So what do you want that it became necessary to intercept my vehicle and drag me to your office?"

"A hint of cooperation," Collins began. "I like that. And since you asked, let's start with Une Maison de Campagne."

Sir Charles interrupted. "Mr. Collins, you know that I will not divulge any information about guests or staff. And since no crime was committed on the grounds, I am not obligated in any way to do so. Therefore, unless you want a floor plan of the villa, there is nothing I can do for you." He stated.

Collins sat in a chair directly across from the man and looked the man directly in his eyes. "Have you at least conducted an internal investigation into the events of that villa?"

The Consul paused, slowly shaking his head. "Again Mr. Collins, there was no crime committed within the borders of Saddlewood, so therefore no need for any investigation."

"So," Collins began, momentarily hesitating to work his next phrase correctly. "What you are telling me is that if there was a crime committed within Saddlewood's borders, you would have conducted an investigation?" He inquired.

"Absolutely." Sir Charles replied.

"Do you consider a guest shooting at an employee something worth looking into?" Collins asked.

Sir Charles coolly sat back in his chair. "Yes I would, but I never received such a report. If you possess such information, please share it with me so I may interview the employee who claims he or she was assaulted in such a manner."

Collins softly snickered, a feigned smile forced across his face, as he knew the Consul was well aware of the incident to which he was referring. "Unfortunately, Sir Charles, that is not going to be possible at this time."

The Consul stood. "Then it appears there is nothing more to discuss." He said. "May I leave?"

"Not so fast." Collins replied. "What about the two employees and two guests of that villa who were murdered? Is there not some sort of an inquiry for those incidents?"

Sir Charles arrogantly grinned. "Now Mr. Collins, though all of us at Saddlewood are deeply saddened by the events, those events did not occur on Saddlewood property so they are out of our jurisdiction. We have interviewed all surviving employees, except for one, about any irregularities at that guesthouse and found none. So far as an investigation, we have no right to conduct one, nor will we incur the responsibility for doing so. That would be for you to do. Now if you think that the one remaining employee we have not yet been able to locate would offer us information that would cause us to want to launch an investigation, then help us find him. Until then, there is nothing I can assist you in."

Matt stared at the man momentarily, and then rose from his chair. "Then there is no reason to keep you any longer. Please have a safe trip to Geneva." He stated, ushering Sir Charles to the door. "Oh by the way, once in a while, we have a decent collection of reporters hanging around downstairs. Though they weren't there when you arrived, don't be surprised if they're standing there now."

Sir Charles sneered at Collins. The last thing he wanted to have to deal with were reporters seeing him leave the office of the United States Attorney. There would be questions that he did not want to answer nor knew how to answer and he stormed out the door as angry as he came in.

Collins sat behind his desk satisfied, knowing that the meeting served its purpose. He knew ahead of time that Sir Charles would refuse to release any information about Saddlewood or ay of its employees or guests. What he wanted from the meeting was for the press to assume that Sir Charles, though forced to, cooperated with the United States Attorney in his investigation. And to accomplish that, five minutes before Sir Charles was scheduled to arrive, Matt had Bostic inform the press. They swarmed to the office almost immediately.

When the Consul exited the office, Collins figured he'd be presented with two options, either make no comment at all or tell the reporters that he was forcibly detained and escorted to the office. So Collins bet that Sir Charles would make no comment, because should he divulge the circumstances of his arrival to the office, it would only spawn additional questions,

questions that Sir Charles would have to avoid and in doing so, would make him appear as if he were hiding something. And when he reached the reporters, Sir Charles said nothing.

After Sir Charles negotiated his way through the swarm of reporters leaving the building, a peacefulness settled throughout the office and Collins sat studying information, but thinking more about the trouble that lie ahead for him when the Consul asserts his influence. A knock on the door interrupted his thoughts and he peered up from his desk, shouting for the person to enter.

"I have something for you." Jason Taylor began as he walked through the door. "But if you make anything of it, I'll be surprised."

"What are you talking about? Eric?" Matt asked. "Did he finally make a move?"

"You could say that." Taylor excitedly replied. "He finally used the Internet to send a message to someone, but it wasn't to any of the e-mail addresses you thought he'd contact."

"It wasn't?" Collins answered, puzzled by the development. "Who did he contact?"

Taylor tilted his head, a pained expression shooting across his face. "Well, we're not exactly sure who he contacted." Taylor replied. "But we did trace the server address to somewhere in North Central Italy."

"Italy!" Collins exclaimed. "He contacted someone in Italy? Are you absolutely sure it was someone in Italy?"

Taylor nodded. "We are quite certain." He answered. "Do you know of a reason why he would contact someone in Italy?"

Matt grinned and slowly shook his head in disbelief. "No, I don't. However, once I find out, it will answer a whole lot of questions. Did he send any other messages?"

Taylor shook his head. "No sir, that's it. He's sent no e-mails nor did he make any phone calls." He reported. "He's doing what he was told to do."

Collins smiled. "Yes he is and in a way, that's unfortunate for us." He said as the man turned toward the door. "Thank you Jason."

Matt watched the man close the door, and then he stood and shuffled toward the window chuckling to himself as he peered outside. Of all of the seventeen-year-old kids in the world, he would have to be hiding the one kid who actually does what he's instructed to do. Normally, that would have been a good thing. But Collins counted on this seventeen year old to act like most others would have. He expected him to make mistakes and surely expected him to contact his girlfriend or his best friend. And in preparation of those events occurring, he enacted a plan to take advantage of them. First, he systematically withdrew money from Eric's bank account along a pre-planned route leading south. Next, he re-routed all of Eric's calls and Internet activities from the safe house in Pennsylvania through a decoy house set up in south Florida. Finally, he planted a person inside that house who was made up to look like Eric with the hope of luring the people responsible for the Saddlewood killings into a trap. It was a well-thought and well-conceived ruse. And it failed.

Collins turned away from the window and returned to his desk, worried that the plan's failure may have sealed Eric's fate or greatly delayed his return to his family. Now he was forced to concede to the realization that he would not be able to lure anyone to the house in Florida and he knew that resolving this entire situation would now depend, not on trickery or planning, but on a little luck and more knowledge. Fortunately he knew where he could acquire additional information and he thought it funny that a combination of what Eric did and didn't do, left him with his only choice.

He opened the center drawer and removed the envelope he received from the unknown Italian, placing it into the secured section of his briefcase. It would now go with him. After removing his suit jacket from a hanger and putting it on, he lifted the briefcase and walked out the door of the office. The press was waiting for him and he stopped in the middle of the corridor and smiled. The press was waiting for him and just maybe he could use them again.

CHAPTER 15

ERIC STOOD, CAREFUL NOT TO hit his head on the bottom of the wooden loft above his desk, one of the two lofts that he and Dan had built in their room, which added to their living space. Though still saddened by the report of Aaron's death, he showed no emotion and moved in as Dan's roommate on the following Monday after practice had ended, finally experiencing the independence that most other college students experience. It felt good and, in a way, relaxing, many of the pressures that complicated his life easing from his mind. He settled into this creation of someone else's imagination, but established a personality of his own, or at least that of Eric Mason. Yet in spite of the subsiding pressures and the settling into a recognizable life, there remained his past and it continuously haunted his thoughts.

He quietly sat behind his desk on this Saturday morning, a morning in which he wished he could sleep longer, but did not. It was not that he chose to rise so early. No, it was frustration and anxiety that woke him, the frustration of waiting for something to happen that hasn't and the anxiety of wondering why. Maybe they didn't care anymore, he thought, or maybe they knew some bit of information that was being withheld from him and they chose to move on with their lives. Could it be that? Or, was it something far worse? He stopped imagining the scenarios and shook his head, confident that neither was the case. There had to be some other logical explanation.

It was cool outside, normal for the first Saturday in October, and he left the room casually walking in the morning sunshine along the sidewalk of his dormitory building headed for his car. This weekend morning before a game would be no different than the others, breakfast in the room with Dan followed by light exercise and a billiards challenge. It became a pre-game ritual between the two, one that undoubtedly worked as the two experienced unparalleled success during games, and one that would continue until it proved useless.

He drove to the same grocery store he always patronized; bought the same groceries he always bought before a weekend game and followed the same path past the newsstand. This time, when he peered downward toward the rack, he noticed the Washington Post and a picture of Sir Charles plastered across the front page. He stopped, bent over and peered at the caption underneath the photograph, then lifted the newspaper and tossed it into his cart. Maybe there was a clue inside the article as to why he hasn't heard from home. Maybe there was information he could use to find out if he soon would be returning back to Virginia. No matter what, the article was sure to be interesting.

He returned to the school and parked the car. It was quiet around campus, many of the students recovering from a party-filled Friday night and he stopped for a moment to enjoy the silence. In a matter of hours, the hillside below the dorm along the soccer field would be jammed with spectators, many cheering him on. They liked him here, not only because of his outstanding athletic performances but also for the manner in which he conducted himself and he smiled as he turned to continue to his room.

Expecting his roommate to be asleep, Eric quietly opened the door and peered inside, careful not to crackle the plastic grocery bags he held in his opposite hand. "Hey Eric!" Dan greeted, standing with a towel wrapped around his waist and running a comb through his wet hair. "I thought I'd get up and save you the trouble."

Eric grinned, setting the packages on his desk. "I see that." He replied as he began to remove the groceries from the bags. "I guess I'm starting to rub off on you."

Dan tossed the comb on his desk and moved under his loft into a closet, grabbing a shirt and sweat pants. "If I get anything to rub off from you, I hope it's your luck." He replied, sliding the sweat pants over his boxer shorts.

Eric cocked his head, a confused expression forming on his face. "You hope you get my luck." He repeated. "What luck are you talking about?"

"You're luck at scoring!" Dan teased. "Nobody scores goals like you do, off the post and in, off the crossbar and in, off the defender and in. It's damned disgusting after a while." He stated, the grin on his face blossoming into full-fledged smile.

Eric slowly nodded his head. "That's all skill there brother." He jokingly replied. "It takes a lot of practice to be able to score off all those different angles."

"All skill my ass." He chuckled as he picked up a balled up piece of paper and threw it at his friend. "You can't tell me that the goal you scored Wednesday, where your shot hit off their sweeper, then hit the inside of the right post and went in, was all skill."

Eric wriggled his eyebrows, a cocky grin covering his face. "Okay, that one was a little lucky. But if the dude doesn't get in the way, it's a perfect pass to you." He replied, a wide smile extending across his face as he stretched out his arm and pointed. "And that, my brother, is pure talent."

Shaking his head, Dan laughed. There was no doubt in his mind that Eric was joking as he would have been the last person on the team to boast about his abilities, so he moved toward Eric and pounded fists as a show that he appreciated the humor, then he sat down and started to eat. It was time to get ready.

As it had been all season, the game became a show dominated by the two freshman roommates and now, Jeremy and Mike as well. The four of them did everything together, including taking extra practice sessions at the Mason's indoor facility and following a weight training program, all of which Eric instructed. So it made perfect sense that, with Eric as the leader, the group experienced the success it did. And as he walked off the field toward the Mason's like he did after every game, he shook his head thinking how great it would have been if his real family could have shared this success with him.

After talking with the Mason's after the game and walking them to their car, Eric entered the locker room. There were no extra celebrations by the team, only what had become the usual congratulatory remarks after games as he walked through the crowd and he squeezed through his teammates until he reached his corner locker where he sat waiting to take a shower. He leaned against the wall closing his eyes, tired from the game, the remnants of perspiration and dirt covering his body.

"Hey Eric." Jeremy called, poking his friend to wake him. "There's a girl outside who I think is waiting for you."

Eric slightly opened his eyes and stretched. "What did she say?" He asked, not seeming interested.

Jeremy shook his head. "Not much." He answered. "All she asked was if number twenty-nine was in here."

Eric motioned with his hands, asking for more information. "And?" He said, queuing his friend to continue.

"And, I told her you were taking a shower so wait here with the rest of your groupies." He answered. "What the hell did you expect me to say to her?"

Eric stood from the bench and looked toward the locker room door. "You didn't really say that to her, did you?"

Jeremy smiled. "You know me better than that." He replied.

"So you *did* say that to her." Eric stated, moving toward the door.

Jeremy grabbed his arm. "Nah, I didn't." He answered. "I told her you'd be out in about fifteen minutes, so I guess she's going to wait for you outside."

Eric smiled. "Cool. What'd she look like Jay?" He asked.

Jeremy grinned, his eyes widening as he nodded slightly. "She was pretty hot dude. I'd do her."

Eric shook his head, grabbed his towel and turned to go into the shower. "I'm not exactly sure I like the sound of that. I've seen some of your girls." He replied and he disappeared into the shower room.

There were always girls waiting for him after the games, not that he minded of course. That was one of the benefits he really enjoyed about being one of the premier athletes in the school. But unlike so many, he always found time to politely speak with every one of them, whether he was interested or not.

He walked out of the athletic center with his equipment bag over his shoulder and scanned the area searching for the hot-looking girl Jeremy said was waiting for him. Though there were people waiting by the door, no one approached him. He shrugged his shoulders then turned toward his dorm and began walking slowly to it along the path between the athletic fields, his mind focused only on meeting the Masons for dinner.

"Hey! Number twenty nine!" A voice shouted from an unidentified spot among the trees.

Eric stopped on the walkway and quickly scanned the area by the large evergreens along the path. There was no one around. Maybe he only thought he heard someone call his number and he discontinued the search, turned and resumed his trek toward the dormitory.

"You wouldn't happen to be looking for us?" Greg asked as he and Beth popped from behind a tree along the baseball field.

Eric froze in his tracks, his mouth agape and the startled expression on his face that most would expect to see in a haunted house, quickly transformed into an enormous smile. He dropped the equipment bag on the ground and jumped toward his friend, almost tackling him with the bear-like hug, holding him tightly. "I missed you bro." He softly said.

Greg hugged him for a moment. "I missed you too buddy. Now let go because there's someone here who would like a little of this love too." He replied, gently breaking away from his friend.

Eric turned toward Beth, her cheeks wet from the tears that escaped her water-filled eyes and he gazed at her, his heart pounding strongly as he gently took her hands in his. He took a deep breath and grinned. "Hey." He bashfully greeted, the softness of his voice and brooding look causing tears to again run down her face.

Through the tears, she smiled at him. "Hey." She muttered, pausing for a moment then choking out a laugh. "You would think we would have a little more to say to each other." She softly stated, wiping the tears off her face.

Eric glanced toward the ground then cocked his head as he looked into her eyes, wet his lips then moved closer to her, passionately kissing her. When he gently broke away, he stared at her and smiled, again quickly glancing toward the ground before his eyes contacted hers. "Yeah, you'd think we would." He replied, gently grasping her hand and leading her and Greg further along the path. "I didn't think you were ever coming."

"Well," Greg began. "When I received the letter from this school with the return address as the soccer office, I didn't actually get all excited enough to open it right away." He replied.

"But when I opened it and saw it was from you, I got hold of Beth and we planned our trip here. Sorry we couldn't make it sooner."

Eric shook his head. "Don't be." He stated, then stopped and turned toward the two. "But, we've kind of got a problem."

"What's that?" Greg Asked.

"I'm supposed to have dinner with my, a…damn this is weird saying this to you. I got a new set of parents when I was put here. I'm supposed to have dinner with them in about a half an hour." He answered. "In fact, they're due here any minute and if they see you, I'm in deep shit."

Greg shrugged his shoulders. "They won't……"

Eric interrupted him. "Yes they will." He said. "They'll know who you are and how you knew to come here and the next thing you know, they'll send me off to God knows where and I'll never see you again."

Beth wrapped her arm around his waist and leaned into him. "What do you want us to do?" She asked. "We can't go home because we are supposed to be in Charlottesville this whole weekend and it would be suspicious if we went back home tonight."

Eric stared at his dorm ahead of him, and then looked at Greg. "Did you get a hotel room somewhere?" He asked.

Greg nodded. "Of course, it's just up the road a little." He stated.

Eric smiled as he reached into his equipment bag removing a notebook and pen, ripping a sheet of paper from the notebook and handing it to Greg. "Good. Write the name of the motel and room number on this. Give me about an hour and a half and I'll meet you there." He directed. "I'll fill you in on everything then."

Greg scribbled the name and room number on the paper and folded it, returning it to Eric. "Okay, I guess we should get out of here before your, you know, new parents get here." He stated. "See you in a little bit."

Eric grinned, nodding his head. "Definitely." He replied. "I'll see you in a little bit." He quickly kissed Beth and pump-hugged Greg, and then he turned and jogged toward his dormitory.

For the first time since that night in Saddlewood, he felt completely happy and when the Masons picked him up at his dormitory room only a few minutes later, a large smile filled his face. They were happy to see him that way and didn't bother asking the cause. Whether the result of the game or the hope that Eric was actually enjoying his life now, the reason for his contentment was irrelevant to the Masons. Throughout dinner they relished his mood, his joke telling and domination of the conversation far different from most of the dinners he shared with them. And for over an hour and a half, they treasured Eric more as a son than they ever had before.

He returned to his dormitory and quickly changed out of his suit, already late for his rendezvous with Beth and Greg. Swinging open the door, he ran out the room and jogged to his car, quickly driving to the hotel. He was understandably nervous and he knocked on the door, his heart again strongly pounding from the excitement.

Greg opened the door and grinned, stepping aside letting his friend into the room. "I was beginning to think you weren't coming." He said, closing the door behind them.

"Nothing could have kept me away from this." Eric answered, taking off his jacket and lying next to Beth on the bed. "Y'know, I thought about what we can do tonight during dinner and I figured maybe you would want to hang out with some of my friends at a party they're having. Then, we could come back here and, y'know, talk a little bit."

Greg glanced at Beth and raised his eyebrows, a pout of disapproval crossing his face. "That would be cool but," He began pausing for a moment, again glancing at Beth and shaking his head. "That's not exactly what we had in mind." He replied. "Is your roommate pretty cool about things?"

Eric wrinkled his eyebrows. "Danny? Yeah, why?" He inquired.

Greg grinned. "Well, I thought after the party, I'd crash with him and the two of you could spend some personal time together here." He replied.

A smile grew across Eric's face and he glanced at Beth. "Seriously?" He asked.

"Seriously." She repeated, nodding her head.

Eric stared at her for a moment then quickly glanced at Greg before returning his attention toward her. "Okay." He repeated. "But first, I better clue you in on a couple of things and give you a cover for being here."

He briefly explained to them his new life courtesy of witness protection and that he hoped it remained a temporary situation. But there was no need to explain why he was here. Greg knew what Eric had overheard at the villa that night and when the Saddlewood killings became public, he told Beth, swearing her to secrecy. They knew that they could not admit to any knowledge of Eric's whereabouts, not only for his safety but also for theirs. They understood the necessity of the precautions Eric was taking with them and after he created their different identities, he delayed no longer asking the questions that had been rumbling through his mind for so long about his family.

Greg saw the concern in Eric's expression, understanding the torment he must have been going through and he attempted to comfort his friend by telling him how well his family was handling his absence now, though there were difficulties at the beginning with rumors spreading as to the actual reason why Eric was gone. There had been many theories, ranging from a problem at home to getting into some type of legal trouble. But when his family announced that he had simply accepted an opportunity to attend a private prep school, the questions immediately subsided. It made perfect sense; a talented athlete with an outstanding academic record would be a prime candidate for such an opportunity. So the mystery ended, until Jimmy entered the picture.

Jimmy never believed that Eric accepted a placement in a private prep school. His belief rose from the fact that he was confident Eric would have informed him about such an opportunity, but never did. So in spite of what everyone told him, including Greg, he set out on his own on a mission to find his friend, being quite resourceful in the process. Remembering the bank where Eric held his account, he hopped onto the Internet and broke into Eric's account information using the passwords he knew Eric used. Within minutes, he was able to trace every bit of activity, including the automated teller withdrawals that Matt Collins had set up as a trap. After mapping each transaction, he determined Eric was living south of Tampa. When he reported his findings to Greg, the two of them argued with Jimmy storming away vowing to find his friend. He was within hours of leaving for Florida when Kevin Lynch saw him and showed Eric's new team picture with the accompanying letter, all of which had been manufactured courtesy of Matt Collins. But, it stopped Jimmy from leaving, accomplishing its goal. So when it was time to plan to go to Latrobe, it was that incident which caused Greg not to tell him, citing his actions as being too risky to Eric's safety. It was a decision that Eric respected and agreed with, but he understood Jimmy's actions and felt honored that his friend would go through so much just to help him.

After all the stories ended, Eric stood, announcing it was time to return to campus, and the three of them departed the hotel, Eric and Beth driving in his car, while Greg followed in the other. Using both cars was another safety measure, a measure that prevented Eric's vehicle from being seen in a motel parking lot because he suspected his actions were monitored. They arrived at the college and walked through campus, first stopping at the dorm and introducing Beth and Greg to his roommate. Pleased to be meeting someone from what he thought was Eric Mason's past, Dan paid special attention to them. He figured Beth was the girl Eric tried to call the first night they met and, without anyone telling him, knew visiting Eric was not where she was supposed to be this weekend. So after they went to all the parties they planned, Dan agreed to let Greg stay in the dorm while Eric and Beth returned to the hotel.

The door to the hotel room opened and Eric, a small duffel bag strapped over his shoulder, led Beth inside; his shirt unbuttoned exposing his skin. He tossed the bag onto the floor, closing the door behind them, then kicked off his sneakers and took off his shirt before he sat on the bed. It was still early by college standards, nearly midnight, and Beth sat behind him, gently running her fingers through his hair as she massaged his shoulders. " So how are you, really?"

He cocked his head to one side, slightly shrugging the one shoulder. "Now that I know that my friends and family are safe, I'm a whole lot better." He answered. "But I want you to promise me that if there is something I should know, you would tell me."

She slid to the top of the bed and pulled him next to her, gently rubbing his chest and stomach. "Do you know about Aaron?" She asked.

Eric hesitated, bringing his hands up to his face, rubbing his forehead to conceal his eyes. "Yeah, I do." He muttered, strongly exhaling before he continued. "I'm really going to miss him."

Beth held him close and he wrapped his arms around her. "I know you will." She replied, pausing as she gently kissed his head. "But what's important now is that we keep you safe however we have to."

Eric rose, sitting on the edge of the bed. "I worry about that sometimes." He admitted. "Just like I worry about if any of this is ever going to end and I get to go home."

Beth moved next to him, sitting silent as she thought about what she should say next. "Is that a possibility? I mean, not coming home."

Eric stood, slowly pacing in front of her. "I'm sure it is and it's frustrating because I don't really want to be Eric Mason for the rest of my life." He answered.

Beth stood and silently approached him, stopping his pacing. Looking into his slightly tear-swollen eyes, she held him, caressing the sides of his chest. "I don't know what to say to you because I cannot imagine being in this situation. But no matter who you turn out to be for the rest of your life, I will always love you."

"I will always love you too." Eric replied, holding her tightly as he rested his head on her shoulder.

There was nothing more to say, no words left to express how he felt and he slowly moved closer toward her until their lips met, kissing her passionately. Then, slowly they began undressing each other, collapsing into each other's arms and gently falling onto the bed.

CHAPTER 16

ERIC SAT ON THE KNOLL of the grassy hillside, the setting sun, which warmed the fall day to summer-like temperatures, at his back. The brightness of the light illuminated the autumn hues of the leaves surrounding him accenting the deepening blue sky with a golden glow. He turned and stared toward the mountains, the intense reflection of orange, gold and red appearing painted on the gentle sloping landscape by a delicate stroke of an artist's brush. A slight breeze shimmered through the leaves creating a tranquil chord interrupting total silence. He looked back toward the sunset, seemingly unaware of the world around him, watching the cars driving along a distant highway wondering their destinations. The world, however, was aware of him.

He stood, peered at his watch realizing that he had been gone for an hour, then moved to return to his car at the bottom of the hill, but stopping and crouching behind a tree. A figure appeared noticeable through the trees, standing at the rear of the vehicle, and he kneeled on the ground to attempt a better view to identify the person. He quietly sneaked closer, careful not to signal the individual of his approach, becoming more tense the nearer he crept. As he positioned himself to approach the person from behind, he thought. Had this situation occurred only six months ago, he would have carelessly lumbered down the hill to greet whoever it was next to the car. That was six months ago. To react in such a casual manner now could surely get him killed.

He maneuvered behind the cover of another large tree as twilight helped to make him even less noticeable. He surveyed the area and after a lengthy study, decided the person was alone at this time. He moved closer, still cautiously attempting to remain undetected. He could see that the figure was a man, but because of the darkness beginning to surround them, the man was unrecognizable.

Slowly, Eric advanced to the car, approaching the rear noticing the man seemingly oblivious to his imminence. The simple tenseness transformed to uneasiness as he realized he would need to speak or stand a car's length away from the man for the rest of the night. He peered down at the ground, quietly picking up a large rock and standing, moving around the vehicle. "Can I help you with something?" He asked.

The man turned and smiled, revealing a gun. "I knew you'd turn up sometime. I was wondering how long you would make me wait."

Eric dropped the rock on the ground, realizing its uselessness, and stepped toward the man. "You scared the hell out of me." He said.

Collins leaned on the car's fender and chuckled. "Well I certainly didn't mean to do that." He replied. "Are you all right?"

The young man peered past the attorney along the road. "Yeah, I'm okay." He answered. "So, why are you here? Am I going home?"

Matt smiled, tilting his head to one side. "Not exactly." He stated. "But I think we need to have a little talk."

Eric ruffled his eyebrows as he stared at the man. "And you came all the way out here to do that?" He curiously asked. "I thought that's what Dr. Miles was for."

"Normally, that's exactly how this is supposed to work but this isn't a normal situation and you're the one who caused it." Matt stated.

Puzzled, Eric leaned against the car next to the man. "So, what do we need to talk about that's so important you came here yourself?"

Matt stood from the fender, pressing the boy's shoulder to guide him along the road to walk. "I would say we need to talk about who you've been e-mailing in Italy." He stated.

Eric stopped and turned toward the man, hesitating to speak as he stared at him. "What are you talking about?" He asked.

Collins smiled. "You couldn't have thought that I would just place you here without taking some kind of precaution, could you?" He asked. "I have an obligation to keep you safe."

"And knowing where I e-mail falls into that category in what way?" Eric inquired.

"In the way you weren't supposed to be contacting anyone at all." Collins replied, the tone of his voice showing his displeasure. "I thought we made that perfectly clear to you. You were not supposed to contact anyone from your former life."

Eric turned around, walking toward his car. "So how do you know the person I e-mailed in Italy is from my former life? What if I told you I met someone over the Internet and we exchanged e-mail addresses?" He asked.

Collins chuckled. "I would have believed you had one very strange incident not occurred a couple of weeks ago." He answered. "I received an anonymous package form the Italian Embassy with information about Saddlewood that cannot be obtained through public channels no matter what is attempted. Then I was offered more for a very unusual price. Would you happen to know what that price is?"

Eric shook his head and shrugged. "No sir I do not, but I have a feeling that you're going to tell me." He replied.

Matt nodded. "Good guess." He sarcastically responded. "The price for this additional information this party claims is very relevant to this case, is that I am to bring you to the Italian Embassy tomorrow night for a private dinner. Now before you made contact with someone in Italy, I thought the request was entirely suspicious. But after you sent your e-mail, there was no question in my mind that you knew someone in Italy who you met at Saddlewood. I want to know who that person is."

Eric stopped and glanced toward the ground, remaining silent for a moment. He looked up at the man and strongly exhaled, knowing he had been caught. "Her name is Maria Alberini." He answered. "And before you ask, she was Sir Charles' personal assistant."

Collins nodded, pleased that the young man admitted to making contact with someone he knew from before. "I appreciate your honesty." He stated, his tilting head accentuating the pensive expression on his face. "Now, did she say anything unusual to you during your e-mail exchanges? For example, did she ever mention seeing you at the Italian Embassy?"

Eric shook his head. "No sir, she didn't." He replied. "In fact, she didn't say much at all except that she hoped to see me soon, if I was smart and worked everything out. I thought she was referring to my current situation, but maybe she wasn't because I never really told her what my current situation was."

Matt hesitated, scanning the trees beyond the two of them. "You're right." He acknowledged. "Maybe she wasn't referring to your current situation. Maybe she already knows." He said, pausing for a moment. "I'm going to guess she's very intelligent. Is that correct?"

Eric widened his eyes and nodded. "Very correct." He emphasized. "She's brilliant."

Matt smiled. "Then assuming she knows what happened, maybe she sent you a clue to accept the invitation and, figuring that all of your transmissions would be monitored, also knew that I would eventually ask you about it." He stated.

Eric wrinkled his eyebrows in disagreement. "Don't you think that is just a little bit too cloak and dagger?" He inquired.

"This whole invitation to the Italian Embassy is nothing but cloak and dagger. And since you probably don't know all that much about her, you wouldn't know what her or her family might be involved in." Matt countered. "I mean, other than knowing she's from Italy and quite attractive, you know nothing much about her, do you?"

Eric shook his head. "Not really, though I do know that she's not from Italy." He replied, leaning against the fender of his car. "She's from San Marino, which is a little country surrounded by Italy."

Collins sarcastically smiled. "I know where it is." He smartly answered. "But other than that, what else do you know about her?"

Eric shrugged his shoulders. "Her father was one of the head of the government and still serves it in some capacity. She's intelligent, as you said, beautiful and, I don't know, real cool to be around." He said. "We were just really getting to know each other."

Collins smiled. "So you were becoming friends." He stated.

Eric gritted his teeth, widening his eyes. "Well not exactly." He began, cocking his head to one side. "We kind of dated."

"You dated." Matt repeated. "Who at Saddlewood knew you dated?"

He shook his head slightly. "As far as I know, only Aaron and Mr. Kearney knew we were dating." He answered, and then continued. "Sir Charles also might have known, but as far as anyone else, I'm not sure."

Collins nodded his head, yet remained silent as he thought. The fact that Eric dated a young woman who eventually returned to Europe cleared the mystery of whom he contacted. However that fact failed to make Matt's decision any easier. Knowing that Italy represents the tiny country of San Marino in many of its foreign affairs, he thought it entirely possible that the requested meeting was a father's attempt to satisfy a daughter's wish and help the young man she became enamored with while living in the United States. But he also knew that the possibility existed for this invitation to be nothing more than a trap, and that is what concerned him. What if someone involved in this scheme knew about the romance between the two, then decided to use it in an attempt to get at Eric as well as the man conducting the investigation? No matter which way he chose, the risk would be great and maybe that was the problem. Maybe it shouldn't be his choice. He glanced at the teenager and quickly attempted to guess how the young man would respond if the decision was left to him. Would he consider the risks involved to himself, or would the possibility of seeing Miss Alberini cloud his judgment on the choice of whether or not to accept the invitation? And he thought that this decision should wait until tomorrow after his game, so they left and Eric returned to the campus.

Keeping away from the sight of the majority of the crowd, Collins watched Eric's game from the obscurity of the trees above the goal at the end of the field. It wasn't Eric best performance of the year, nor was it the best performance Matt had seen him play over the span of his short career, and Collins concluded that the possibility of visiting the Italian Embassy this evening occupied Eric's mind more than the game itself. Was he nervous about seeing Maria again, or was the possibility of the invitation being a trap a haunting thought that refused to go away? And as the time wound down in the second half of the contest, Eric scored his second goal and Matt began his walk toward the door to the athletic center.

After the whistle sounded ending the game, Eric ascended the hillside toward the Masons, talking with them as he did after every game. Though he walked toward the locker room smiling as friends congratulated him on the team's win and his play, from his behavior he appeared displeased with his performance on the field as well as preoccupied with events off of it. It was a forced, almost fake happiness masking his true feeling and when he glanced toward the athletic center seeing Collins from the corner of his eye, he quickly returned his attention to the people around him, obviously wanting to avoid speaking with the man. But Collins would wait no longer.

He quietly approached the group on the walkway and interrupted their conversation. "Don, Carol, it's nice to see you." Collins stated. "How is everyone?"

Startled by his unexpected appearance, the Masons turned, their expressions changing from happiness to concern. "Matt." Carol greeted. "What brings you up here?"

Collins grinned as he glanced toward Eric and sarcastically chuckled. "Well, I'm not at all surprised that he didn't tell you." He began as he placed his arm around the young man's shoulder and pulled him closer while the happiness drained from Eric's face. "I need to borrow him for the evening."

Don glanced at Carol, then returned his focus toward the United States Attorney. "You're the boss Matt. Is everything okay?"

Collins quickly nodded. "For the moment, yes it is. We have an appointment to keep at the Italian Embassy this evening." He replied. "So Eric, go take a shower. We've got a plane waiting at the airport with a pretty tight schedule to keep."

Silently, Eric acknowledged the man and jogged away from the group to the locker room as the Masons slowly walked with the attorney. "I know it's not my place to get involved in your decisions," Don Mason began. "But I thought the whole idea of placing him in the program was to protect him from exposure, especially in Washington. For whatever reason you are going to the Italian Embassy, are you not taking a grave risk returning Eric to Washington even if it is just for one evening?"

Matt slowly nodded. "Yes I am and I understand your concern. In fact, I held some of those same feelings until I spoke with him yesterday. But as it turns out, Eric had been e-mailing a young lady who apparently has some connection to the Italian Embassy." He reported. "I was contacted by someone from there to accompany Eric tonight for a private dinner in exchange for information about our investigation and after some lengthy reflection, I do not believe that he is in danger from anyone at the Embassy."

The three of them stopped at the hillside next to the athletic center and Carol Mason turned, facing Collins. "I am confident that you considered every potential problem for this evening and want to assure you that we are only concerned about Eric's safety." She stated. "He's a fine young man to whom we've both become quite attached, whether we were supposed to or not."

Collins smiled slightly. "I certainly understand." He replied. "So please let me assure you that Eric's safety and preservation is of paramount importance. I will not risk him in any way for anything. And in the unlikely event that this meeting we have been invited to becomes something other than what we were led to believe, precautions have been taken to protect him and return him safely here."

Don extended his hand to the man, grasping it strongly. "We know, and we do appreciate the effort you've put forth." He replied. "I apologize because I guess we actually sound like parents."

Matt chuckled and he smiled widely. "I would hope you do because right now, you are exactly that. And I wouldn't have it any other way."

Eric walked out the door of the athletic center, his equipment bag over his shoulder, and he approached the three standing alone at the hillside under the trees. He was unusually quiet, ostensibly uneasy as he handed Carol his small equipment bag, quickly kissing her on the cheek before shaking Don's hand and announcing to Collins he was ready to go, walking to the car a few yards away. As he entered the car, he re-examined his anxiety in attending the function at the Embassy. Was it from the potential danger his return to Washington could cause him? No not really, he thought. Strangely enough, he found the prospect of danger somewhat exciting, even stimulating to a point. So what was it? What was the reason he felt so unsettled about going to the Italian Embassy tonight? Could it be the possibility of again seeing Maria?

When he first met Maria at Saddlewood, he saw innocence, beauty and poise, a classic of a woman who every man should experience once in his lifetime at an age when he could appreciate the perfection she emitted, not at seventeen when his judgment becomes clouded by the rampant hormones rushing through his body. Now, he feared that his original feelings toward her could be soiled by discovery of who she really might be.

Remaining silent for the short trip to the airport, the constant thought about the awkwardness of the evening played in his mind. Would the spark that set his wildfire of passion this past summer rekindle at the first sight of her? Did the emotion from the summer stay with her until now, feeling the same for him as he obviously still felt for her? Then he realized that his nervousness was not at all caused by the potential danger of returning to Washington or of this meeting being a trap to catch him. It was caused by the potential of seeing Maria and the regeneration of the intense feelings he held for her, feelings that exposed the weakness in his character he never admitted to existing.

The car slowed and Matt directed that he pull the car into the exact hanger Eric walked into his first day in protection. In a way, his life had become science fiction every time he walked into a government building, a space he likened to a porthole into another dimension, magically transforming him from Eric Lynch to Eric Mason and back to Eric Lynch at the whim of some government agent and he exited the car, standing for a moment in the emptiness almost expecting some supernatural event to occur. It was eerily quiet and he was silently directed to enter the aircraft while Collins used a cellular phone to make a call before he joined him.

Eric stepped onto the jet, choosing one of the seats next to a window while Collins sat across form him. "If you haven't noticed, I'm not exactly dressed for a reception at an Embassy." He stated.

Matt smiled. "If we're both correct about the actual purpose of your visit tonight, I don't think what you wear will really matter." He replied, the humor in his voice generating a smile on Eric's face. "But if you're worried about it, we did come prepared. There's an appropriate selection of clothing in the storage compartment as well as cosmetics. You can properly prepare yourself when we land."

Eric nodded, then turned his head to glance out the window, seeing the buildings slowly pass by as the jet prepared for departure. His stomach still fluttered from the nervousness and he strongly exhaled to try to relax. Yet as the aircraft rumbled down the runway and smoothly lifted into the air, the fluttering in his stomach intensified from the anticipation of once again seeing Maria.

When the plane leveled off, he unbuckled his seat belt and stood, walking to the small galley in the rear, pouring himself a soft drink. He returned to his seat and glanced toward Collins who was reading a newspaper. "How do they know we're coming?" He asked.

Matt lowered the paper from his face and peered up. "I'm sorry?" He replied, inferring to Eric to repeat the question.

"How do they know we accepted the invitation?" He repeated. "You never mentioned how they would know if I was coming."

Collins folded the paper and placed it next to him. "I called them before we stepped on the plane." He answered.

Eric wrinkled his eyebrows. "You called them before we took off." He repeated. "From the hangar?"

Matt nodded his head. "Yes from the hangar. Oddly enough, they seemed to be as concerned with your safety as I am and insisted, for security reasons, that we accept the invitation only between six and seven o'clock today." He reported.

"Then they know we're on our way." Eric softly stated, quickly glancing out the window, the strained expression on his face suggesting a discomfort with the meeting.

Matt stared at him for a moment, studying the young man's reaction, before he responded. "Yes they do know." He replied. "Are you nervous?"

Eric shook his head, then turned toward the man and smiled. "No." He answered, pausing before he continued. "Well, I guess I am a little nervous."

"About?" Matt inquired.

Eric widened his eyes, shrugging his shoulders as he gritted his teeth in a smile. "About Maria and seeing her again." He answered as he rubbed his hand across his chin.

"So you're excited." Matt restated.

Eric tilted his head, the expression on his face indicating a slight disagreement. "I don't know if I would say that I'm excited." He responded. "It's more like, I don't know....scared."

A wide smile broke across Matt's face and he leaned back into his seat. "You know, when I began dating my wife, before every date this intense fear would come over me and I would think to myself, what does this incredible woman see in me? And whatever she sees in me, what am I going to do wrong to screw this up?" He stated. "Do you kind of feel that way right now?"

A puzzled expression formed on Eric's face. "That's almost exactly what I feel, except I was wondering if she still feels the way she did this past summer." He replied.

Matt shook his head and snickered. "You're worried about that as we sit on a jet taking you to a dinner that she flew half way around the world just to have with you? A dinner that she secured with information she probably stole?" He stated, the broad smile on his face transforming into chuckle. "Think about what I just said and tell me how you think she feels."

A grin grew on Eric's face and he adjusted his seat to be more upright. "Yeah I guess I know." He admitted.

The jet landed at the Air Force base and as it taxied down the runway, he peered out the window seeing a large black limousine with darkly tinted widows sitting to the side of the hangar he remembered leaving from the night he ran from Saddlewood. Slowly the small aircraft pulled into the hangar, the doors closing behind it, then stopped. As complete silence replaced the whine of the engines, the door to the jet opened and the two stood from their seats, stretching for a moment before they moved out into the aisle.

"In that storage closet," Matt began as he pointed toward the back of the plane. "are your clothes for this evening. Even though I said what you would wear probably wouldn't matter, it's still an embassy affair. Therefore, you have a tailored traditional black suit and tie with the appropriate accompaniments. Also you will find a selection of your favorite colognes and styling products in the overnight kit on the floor. Bring all of that with you to the back room and get dressed. I have some of my own preparation to finish." He directed.

Eric shuffled to the rear of the aircraft and opened the storage compartment, removing a garment bag hanging on a rod and the small suitcase placed on the floor. Slinging the garment bag over his shoulder while carrying the suitcase in his opposite hand, he carefully descended the stairs of the jet and walked to the room to the rear of the hangar.

The room appeared far different from the last time he remembered. Instead of a dark and dreary prison-like area, it was brighter, sporting a fresh coat of paint on the walls and more lighting than the singular bulb that he remembered hung down from the middle of the ceiling. He hung the garment bag on a clothing rack and placed the small suitcase on a table, opening both. Removing the clothes from inside, he carefully examined each piece before placing them on the rack, then opened the suitcase and removed the articles he needed. Slowly, he undressed then meticulously prepared himself for the evening, styling his hair with the precision of a professional and cautiously dressing himself to perfection.

He opened the door to the room, exiting into the hangar, and moved to the awaiting car where Collins stood. Matt studied the young man for a moment and smiled. "You look very handsome Eric. Your mom and dad would be proud of you." He stated.

Eric nodded once and smiled. "Thanks Mr. Collins, I appreciate that." He replied. "You clean up pretty well yourself."

Matt grinned. "Thank you. Are you ready to go?"

"As ready as I'll ever be." Eric answered and he climbed in the opened door of the black sedan.

Under the cover of darkness, the vehicle pulled out of the Air Force base and circled Washington on the beltway toward the northwest part of the city. Eric stared out the window as the limousine passed through areas not far from his real home and he hoped to be able to catch a glimpse of someone he knew just by chance. But as the vehicle crossed into Maryland, he knew that any chance meeting was unlikely.

Eric never toured through the area of Washington that hosted the majority of the embassies and as the car weaved its way through the stately complexes, he marveled at the diversity of people and cultures all gathered in the same area. Just seeing the embassies generated an excitement within him and as the vehicle made its last turn onto Fuller Street and the Italian Embassy stood in front of him, his heart began to race.

After registering at a security gate, the vehicle was waved through to a reception area of the complex where it stopped and discharged its occupants. Eric stood in the small plaza staring toward the doors. As he was escorted toward the doors, his excitement heightened to such a rate that the pounding in his chest from his heart beating became so pronounced it could be felt from anyone who touched him.

The doors swung open and the two men entered the building to a reception hall where two formally-dressed men stood behind another man who stepped to the side. "Mr. Matthew Collins, United States Attorney from the Eastern District of Virginia and Mr. Eric Lynch." The man who stepped to the side softly announced. "Gentleman, may I present to you His Excellency Carlo Dettore, Ambassador to the United States and his guest Senor Guisseppe Alberini, Member of the Grand and General Council, La Serenissima Repubblica di San Marino."

The four men stepped toward one another, shaking hands as the ambassador directed them to a small reception room down a hallway. The door closed behind the four of them and Eric became nervous wondering about Maria. Where was she, he thought? Was there a secondary purpose for this dinner? He quickly scanned the room until Ambassador Dettore invited the men to sit, offering a drink which no one accepted.

With a strong Italian accent, but in perfect English, Senor Alberini began speaking. "Mr. Collins, I am very pleased you accepted our invitation for this evening." The man stated. "I apologize for the circumstances of that invitation, though I am sure you understand the necessity of taking precautions with the safety of our young people."

Collins smiled. "No apology is necessary Senor Alberini." He replied. "I quite agree that the safety of our young people is of the greatest importance."

Alberini tilted his head in acknowledgment. "Thank you." He responded. "I do owe you an apology though, Mr. Collins, for the extortive nature of this meeting. But, I naturally must consider my daughter's needs above all else when making such decisions. Ambassador Dettore and I brought you here on the promise of information, information that was obtained through the resources of my country as well as that of Maria's uncle who is the minister of the Italian Intelligence Agency. So with your permission, may I address Mr. Lynch directly, and then we can discuss the business afterward?"

Collins nodded. "That would be fine Senor Alberini."

Alberini grinned, nodding in appreciation. "Mr. Lynch, I am very happy to see that you are well, as will my daughter once she joins us and I assure you, to calm your apparent uneasiness, she will be joining us in a few moments." The man stated. "But I wanted to speak with you before so because, you see, it is of her fondness for you that we meet this evening."

"I am very fond of her as well sir." Eric respectfully answered.

Alberini smiled. "I am quite sure you are." He said, then leaned forward in his chair. "Not to become boastful, but my daughter possesses many excellent qualities, two of which are her intelligence and perceptiveness, and I am very proud of her because her decisions were normally well reasoned and deliberate. That was, until she met you."

Eric bent his head forward, glancing down at the floor briefly breaking eye contact with the man. "I'm sorry Senor Alberini," He began, returning his attention to the man. "But that's not exactly an endorsement for a continuation of my relationship with your daughter."

Alberini interrupted. "No, no Eric, it is very much, as you say, an endorsement for you to continue a relationship with my daughter." The man began, his thick accent now more pronounced as his hand gestures became more exaggerated. "A beautiful woman such as my daughter must be full of life and must think so much not with her mind but sometimes with her heart. Maria used to never think with her heart and now, because of you, my beautiful daughter now thinks with her heart. You bring great joy to her life and that gives me joy."

Eric grinned, bashfully tilting his head downward. "Thank you Senor Alberini. I don't know exactly what to say."

"You do not have to say anything Eric. Your actions speak very well of your character and I see that my daughter has very good taste on her choice of people who she calls friends." The man stated. "Now, with Mr. Collins' permission, I would like you to excuse us and go into the parlor where Maria is waiting for you while we have business to discuss."

Collins smiled, nodding his head. "By all means."

Eric stood from his seat and shook the hands of Senor Alberini and Ambassador Dettore then exited the room, slowly walking to the parlor to which he was directed. The nervousness built inside from the anticipation of finally seeing Maria and he stood at the opening of the door, staring inside the room. She turned in her chair as a smile gradually formed across her face, then she slowly rose, a soft tear sliding down her cheek. Eric stepped into the room, awed by her beauty and he reached for her hands, gently grasping both of hers in his. They stood in silence but only for a moment until he tenderly pulled her close to him and kissed her.

CHAPTER 17

THE DORMITORY WAS QUIET FOR once and Eric stood from the desk walking over to the window. It was warm and sunny outside, unusual for this time of year with Thanksgiving only a week-and-a-half away, and he thought to himself, why did he decide to stay in to study? It's not like he actually needed to study, especially with the success he achieved in the classroom. He peered outside watching the few birds flying from tree to tree, somewhat depressed with the fact that for the time between his visit with Maria at the Italian Embassy and now, he had done nothing but go to practice and study. Did he bury himself in his class work to hide from facing the loneliness that re-established itself within him? Or was its something else? Whatever the case, for some reason this day got him to realize that he could hide no longer.

Maybe, in a way, he had been hiding from choosing one of the women in his life as, for the past weeks, almost every thought was about them. He felt guilty about not making a decision and the problem was, he could not. Beth was his first love, the girl who, for so many years, unknowingly became the object of his secret affections. But Maria, well Maria swept him off his feet and there was no comparison to that. She was the woman who made his heart flutter. She was the woman who challenged him every opportunity she could. And she was the woman who made his life more difficult, because she was never in his plans.

He turned from the window and shuffled to his desk, slamming the book closed. There was no reason to study, no reason to torture himself any longer with trying to determine which girl was best for him. He was seventeen for God's sake, and neither girl was within sight or reach. Why would he ponder about making a choice that doesn't need to be made? And he shook his head as he chuckled to himself for being so stupid as to waste nearly three weeks of his life laboring over two women who he could not even date and may never see again.

He grabbed a pair of sneakers then sat on one of the arm chairs he and Dan added to the room making it more like a den, deciding it was time he circulated back into the school's social circles. Why shouldn't he? After all, there was no reason for him to abstain from dating. It wasn't like he was actually involved with either Beth or Maria at the moment and he convinced himself that going out was definitely his best option.

After he finished tying the last sneaker, he stood and scanned the room for his jacket. He missed the activity this past weekend, dedicating most of his time to spending quiet nights in the library until it closed, lifting weights or some form of exercise in the fitness center until it closed, watching as countless students walked by. Not once did he attend a party and not once did he do anything that other students do on a weekend and it occurred to him that he didn't do any of these things not just for this weekend, but for the entire time after seeing Maria. Maybe now, he could find something to do, something fun or exciting to change the pace of things even though it was a Monday and he grabbed his jacket, quickly throwing it on his body as he exited the room locking the door behind him.

"Where are you going?" Dan asked as he walked up the hallway, looking surprised to see his friend.

Eric smiled. "I don't know yet." He replied, the lilt in his voice marking a change in his mood from the past several weeks. "If you have any suggestions, I'm pretty much up for it."

A grin grew across Dan's face and he glanced at his watch before he stepped in front of his friend and unlocked the door, slowly opening it. "Well, it's only three o'clock but if you can hold this mood for the rest of the night, I'm sure we can come up with something." He answered as he stepped inside, setting his books in his desk.

Eric shook his head, following him into the room. "I haven't exactly been the life of the party around here, have I?" He said.

Dan shrugged his shoulders. "Well, I just figured you had a lot on your mind. In fact, we all have had a lot on our minds." He stated, turning toward his friend with a wide smile on his face. "This is why I think we should partake in a little mindless activity tonight."

Eric leaned back on his desk, his eyes widening. "What mindless activity were you thinking of exactly?" He asked.

A thoughtful expression formed on Dan's face and he moved to one of the arm chairs, falling into it. "Something involving alcohol to chill out, followed by some yet-to-be-determined steam-blowing activity." He stated.

Eric slowly nodded his head, contemplating the suggestion. "What? Like beer and bowling?" He asked.

Dan quickly hopped up from his chair and turned to his friend. "I haven't exactly figured out the details, but beer and bowling isn't bad." He said, his expressive gesturing causing Eric to snicker at his friend. "I'll work on it. I know we can do better than beer and bowling."

Eric grinned. "You do that." He replied as he turned to leave. "And whatever you come up with, I'm in."

As he walked down the hallway to the door leading outside, he grinned thinking about Dan working out the entertainment plans for the evening. With Daniel doing better than beer and bowling could mean absolutely anything and he decided that no matter what, it was exactly what he needed. The truth was, Dan was correct. He did have a lot on his mind, though there could be no way his friend could ever develop a guess close to what it was.

It was not so much being torn between two women that currently he could not see. No, he surrendered himself to the fact that problem would not resolve itself any time soon, if it did at all. The real issue was that in a week and a half, it would be Thanksgiving and he was no closer to seeing his family than what he was on that day in August when he left. It would be this time of year when his house would become more alive with family activity than any other time and he missed that. It would be now that he and his brother would be arguing with his father about bringing down the Christmas lights and stringing them outside. It would be now that his mother would begin preparing for the elaborate family dinner she would serve as well as the scores of relatives who regularly ventured from different parts of the country just to be with them. He thought about all of the time he and Kevin would try to avoid being around so many people at the same time and how he would give anything just to be in that position right now. And then it struck him that there existed yet another issue, one that he failed to consider until right at this moment and it angered him that all this time he had been so selfish.

Ever since he left Virginia, he had been feeling sorry for himself without ever considering how the situation affected his family, especially during the holidays. How were his parents going to explain his absence to the rest of the family? What possible excuse could they give for him not being home for the holidays as he had been for every holiday season he had been alive? And he concluded that no matter how badly he felt right now about his absence from his family, there were four people at home who felt just as bad if not worse.

It was good then that Dan thought of hosting a small alcoholic event because maybe, Eric thought, he could drink himself silly or at least drink until he forgot all about home. And that was it, this event was far from about blowing off steam, at least for him it wasn't. No, this event was all about forgetting, forgetting about home, forgetting about what happened at Saddlewood and mostly forgetting about his responsibility for the whole mess.

When he finally returned to the room, he swung opened the door, and stopped suddenly in his tracks, staring at his waiting friends, all who were dressed in dark clothing and black-knit ski hats. It was like a flashback to his night he taped the meeting at Saddlewood and he stood there speechless as his insides suddenly liquefied wondering, if by some unbelievable circumstance, they found out about him. Hopefully this was just one weird coincidence.

"Well hello." Jeremy greeted, sitting underneath Dan's loft. "We were beginning to think you that you weren't going to show up."

Eric grasped a hold of his composure and grinned. "And miss a night out with you three thugs." He joked, referring to their clothing. "I couldn't do that. So what did you plan for tonight, a robbery?"

Mike nodded his head and began to smile. "You're close." He said as he stood. "Very close."

The grin on Eric's face disappeared and he stared at his friends for a moment before he spoke. "What do you mean very close?" He asked.

Dan moved past his friend and closed the door. "Don't get all bent out of shape. We're not going to commit a robbery." He replied. "But we are going to go on a little mission that will provide a service for everyone who comes into this room and hopefully brighten up your sorry ass."

The grin returned to Eric's face and he leaned against the post of his loft glancing at each of his friends quickly. "A mission that will provide a service and brighten up my sorry ass." He repeated. "This ought to be good. So, what are we doing?"

Mike walked over and placed his arm around Eric's shoulder. "Now take into consideration that this plan was all Jay's idea, so we're all probably going to jail." He stated.

"We're not all going to jail." Jeremy interrupted as he stood and moved to the center of the room. "I figured that you just might be missing being back in Connecticut around the holidays, so I thought that tonight, we'd bring the holidays to you."

Eric wrinkled his forehead and tilted his head. "You're going to bring the holidays to me." He repeated. "How are you going to bring the holidays to me?"

Mike chuckled. "Well originally, we were going to bring them to you as a surprise because we all noticed that you were in a little funk." He began. "But since you appeared to be in a better mood, we figured we should just bring you along."

Eric shook his head. "You still haven't answered my question." He stated. "How exactly are you bringing the holidays to me?"

Jeremy spread his arms wide in the center of the room. "We asked ourselves, what does this room need to cheer you up and become more festive?" He stated. "And after a not-so-lengthy discussion, we decided that since your birthday isn't until late January, we couldn't decorate it for that. So we decided that the Christmas season always brightens up people's lives and that this room... needs a Christmas tree."

Eric laughed. "A Christmas tree!" He repeated. "And where are we going to get a Christmas tree?'

Dan joined Jeremy in the middle of the room and turned, facing Eric. "And that's where the little mission comes into play." He replied. "You need to get dressed in some dark clothes, because after we go kill off a couple beers down by the lake, we're going to cut us down a Christmas tree and put it in this room."

"A Christmas tree. You want to go cut down a Christmas tree and put it in this room." Eric repeated, shaking his head in disbelief.

Dan nodded his head. "You got it. And you're in, right?" He asked. "Because if I remember correctly, before you left earlier you said that whatever I came up with, you were in for."

Eric again shook his head. "I kind of wanted to exclude some type of criminal activity." He stated, pausing before he continued. "So, how did you plan to cut down then drag a Christmas tree to this room?"

Jeremy smiled. "We have a saw, some beer and you have a car." He replied. "I think you can put it together from there."

Eric moved away from the loft and circled the center of the room, in his head sizing the space before he looked toward his friends who stood patiently awaiting for his approval. "You know what? I think you're all nuts." He said as a smile broke across his face. "But I also think that we can't get anything larger than a six-footer and the three of you have to clean out my car when we're done."

The three of them smiled widely, happy that Eric decided to participate. "That's a deal." Dan replied. "Do you have some black clothes? Because it's already dark outside and we can jet as soon as you get ready."

Though this night's activities retained the appearance of an eerie replay of the events at Saddlewood, Eric quickly changed into dark clothing and followed his friends out the door despite the uneasiness he felt about participating. It wasn't that he thought the four of them would get caught and land themselves in trouble, though admittedly he felt a twinge of concern somewhere within him about drinking, stealing a tree and driving it back to his dorm room. No, it was the similarities to the night at Saddlewood that disquieted him, recalling memories he attempted to extinguish from his mind, not because the night itself was so traumatic, but because his actions of the entire day caused him to be here now. He became angry with himself every time he thought of it, wishing that he would have just minded his own business. If he had, he thought, he would be living a regular life working toward the goals set for him so long ago, not living this life at this time.

The car slowed as it approached a bridge and Eric turned the steering wheel, guiding his vehicle onto the old access road that wound through the brush and trees and ended in a turn-around area between the old grist mill and the lake. From the road's termination point, a footpath cut through the foliage to the lake and Eric stopped the car, the four of them getting out then walking to the water's edge. They found two long, hollow logs, dragged them across the somewhat sandy earth and placed them opposite each other, setting the case of beer between them, then began to drink.

It was quiet along the lake, the type of relaxing silence where the muffled sounds of cars passing by on nearby roads and the occasional ripple of water caused by a soft breeze or jumping fish blended into the night. There was no intent to spoil the solitude and the four young men sat on the logs cracking open their cans, softly breaking the stillness of the world around them.

"So what's been up your ass here lately?" Jeremy asked, lowering his can to his side as he directed his attention toward Eric. "You've been pretty much anti-social the past couple of weeks."

Eric quickly took another drink, swallowed then exhaled. "I don't know if I would call it anti-social." He replied, tilting his head in disagreement. "I think I was just more focused on some things that I usually am."

Mike chuckled. "Yeah right! The only thing you were focused on the past couple of weeks was your girlfriend who sneaked here to see you." He stated, a huge grin forming on his face. "I can't say I blame you because she is hot."

Eric grinned. "She is hot. But she was not my sole focus for the past couple of weeks." He sarcastically replied, grabbing another can from the case and pulling open the top.

Dan stood and reached over to the case, lifting a can but not opening it. "If you say so." He said, sitting back on the log next to Eric. "But ever since Beth came to see you, you've been in another world."

Eric shook his head as he took another sip. "Well, I don't know about that." He stated. "But you know, I do worry about other things in my life."

"One of which should have been me." A fifth voice interrupted from the path to the old mill. "A little beer party? Oh, I'm very disappointed in you. Don't you remember I told you it dulls the senses?" The man stated as he moved into the clearing, revealing a gun in his hand.

Eric choked, an intense fear surging through his body. "Mr. Hamilton." He muttered.

"Eric, who is this guy?" Dan asked in a low and very concerned tone.

Hamilton drew closer to the four young men and motioned for Jeremy and Mike to move to the other log as he waited for Eric to respond to the question. Silently, he stood for a moment becoming inpatient. "Eric, I believe your friend asked you a question." The man stated. "Are you not going to answer him?"

Eric glared at him, the anger seething from his eyes burning into the man. "He is one of the men who used to stay at this resort I worked at last summer." He calmly replied, his eyes fixed on the man. "What do you want?"

Hamilton smiled. "Obviously I need the four of you to come with me." He stated. "I think we need to do some talking."

Eric shook his head. "Then you can talk to us right here, because we're not going anywhere with you." He defiantly replied.

Hamilton scowled at him. "You always have to make such a simple operation so much more difficult." The man stated and he paused, contemplating Eric's response as he moved to the empty log and sat. "Well, have it your way."

Boldly Eric stared down the man. "You've got the gun, what do you want to talk about?" Eric asked, the tone of his voice revealing his anger but no longer showing fear.

Dan leaned over, softly speaking in his ear. "Eric, I don't think it would be a good idea to piss the man off right now."

"The hell with him." Eric spouted loudly. "If he were going to kill us, he would have done it by now."

"Kill us!" Mike exclaimed. "What the hell did you do that he came here to kill us?"

Hamilton laughed. "Another good question Mr. Lynch." The man stated. " Would you like to field this one also or may I have the pleasure?"

Eric shook his head. "I really don't think it matters, but if you feel the need to tell a story, then go ahead." He replied.

Hamilton chuckled. "Of course it matters." He stated. "Or don't you believe they have the right to know why you have put their lives in jeopardy tonight?"

Feeling anger unknown to him before this moment, Eric quickly glanced at his friends hoping their composure held for a few more minutes. He saw fear in them as they sat in stunned silence, their eyes fixed on the man with the gun sitting on the log opposite from them and he knew he would have to cooperate in some way in the hope of saving them. Lowering his head to stare at the ground, he realized that he needed more time so why not let the man answer the question? His sure to be pompous response would, at the least, buy him a few extra moments. As he focused his eyes to the left, he noticed the full can of beer Dan held in his hand and he lifted his head to stare at the man. "You know Mr. Hamilton, you're absolutely correct, they do deserve an explanation." He stated. "But I believe that you should have the honor of giving it to them."

Outwardly pleased with the hint of cooperation, Hamilton's face brightened, his eyes almost twinkling at the suggestion from the young man and he smiled, directing his attention toward the end of the log where Mike and Jeremy sat. While the man looked away from him, Eric slowly and slightly moved his hand closer to the unopened can his friend held. Dan glanced downward, then peered out the corner of his eye toward Eric and inched the beer closer to his hand though, he didn't know why. Concealed by the man's focus on the other two young men, the can quickly, yet unnoticeably exchanged hands then they returned their attention to Hamilton.

"I met this young man in the spring of this past year." Hamilton began. "And I found him to be a very intelligent and well-bred young man who I grew to like as well as respect."

Mike interrupted. "We feel that same way about him."

Hamilton turned, directing his full attention to the young man who commented, and sneered at him. "I am quite sure you do."

Jeremy gently elbowed Mike in the side as he motioned with his head toward the gun. "Please excuse the interruption sir, sometimes he doesn't think." He said.

Hamilton smiled, tilting his head in acknowledgement. "As I was saying, I met him this past spring as I conducted various meetings for my boss," He began, then directed his attention to Eric. "Who by the way, Eric, doesn't know quite yet that I have found you, but will be pleased when I tell him. I hope the night with your girlfriend was worth it." He arrogantly stated, returning his focus to the others. "Anyway, if there are no more interruptions…"

Suddenly, Eric jumped up from the log and whipped the unopened can of beer at Hamilton, impacting the man on the side of the head with such force that the can exploded on contact, knocking the man backward over the log. Almost simultaneously, Eric bolted from his position with tiger-like agility, pounced on the stunned man and grabbed for the gun that had been drawn close to the man's chest. Instantly the firearm discharged, the shot muffled by the clothing and bodies of the two men, as the other three quickly stood, stunned by the speed at which Eric attacked. Two additional shots sounded followed by a haunting stillness.

Cautiously, the three young men peered over the log. It was a sight never before witnessed by any of the three, two bodies lying motionless in the dirt with puddles of blood forming to the sides of them, and it frightened them. Seeing Eric lie completely still on top of the unknown man who moments ago threatened their lives etched itself into their minds. Yet, defying instinct, they crept closer out of curiosity instead of running as their senses told them to.

Slowly, Eric pushed himself off to the side, the gun now in his possession, and he exposed the motionless, blooded body of the man on the ground. The young man's dark clothing dripped from the blood that splattered and as he stood, he stared at the lifeless body below him. The wounds were extensive. Two shots ripped open jagged gaping holes in the man's chest as a third shot severed the lower part of his jaw, the sight transforming from frightening to gruesome. Dazed and sickened by the sight, Eric stumbled nearly ten yards from the scene before he stopped, bent over and threw up.

Though paralyzed by the fear of the event, Dan peered toward his friend, calling him. "Eric, are you okay?" He asked.

The sound of a second strong heave interrupted the silence before Eric stood, turned and staggered over to his friends who stayed staring at the young man. "He's dead, right?" He asked, his face dripping with perspiration and his normally styled hair ruffled.

Mike slowly nodded his head as he stared at the young man in the blood-drenched clothing. "Oh yeah, he's dead." He answered.

Clearly panicked, Jeremy shook his head then turned. "Damn Eric, you killed him! This has got to be some kind of a bad dream." He yelled. "I can't believe that you were the one who was worried about our little trip into some minor criminal activity and then you go and do this!" He excitedly stated. "Where exactly does murder fit into your scale of illegality?"

"That's not funny Jay." Dan answered.

"That's good Dan, because I'm not laughing." He strongly replied. "What the hell do we do now? We can't just leave him here."

Eric glanced at the body, then stepped across the log away from the scene. "I know we can't." He nervously stated. "Let me think."

Jeremy backed away from the body and sat on the log, sliding himself to face the lake. "I have to give you credit Eric, you've made this an exciting evening with something I've never done before." He sarcastically stated.

Dan joined him on the log and scowled. "Again, not funny Jay."

"And again, I'm not laughing." He replied, becoming irritated. "He just killed this guy, damn it. How can someone be so composed when he just killed a guy?"

"Did you not just see me throw up?" Eric replied, shaking his head. "Believe me Jay, I'm not as composed as you think I am right now." Eric nervously stated as he began to pace between the logs and flail his arms in the air. "I didn't want to kill him, it just happened. The gun went off and it happened and I didn't have a choice. This guy was getting ready to kill us, so I had to do something."

"Why?" Mike asked as he stepped in front of Eric and guided him to sit down on a log, realizing that his friend was more upset than he led on to be. "That's what I have to ask you. Why was he getting ready to kill us? What happened between the two of you?"

Eric inhaled deeply to collect himself, then shook his head. "Look, that's a real long story that I'll probably have to tell you later." He said, standing from the log and carefully removing a small cellular phone from the inside of his coat pocket. "But right now, everybody stay here while I call my dad. And don't go up to the car. Hamilton may have booby-trapped it."

The three of them looked at each other in disbelief. What was going on here? And Eric, well it was as if he almost expected a situation like this to happen, so if that was the case, who was he really? Now they knew that Eric was far more than just your typical college student attempting to cross into adulthood. Clearly there were parts of his life they knew nothing about and one of them just tried to kill them all.

Eric stepped away from his three friends and opened the small cellular phone, pressing the number two on the keyboard and calling Don Mason's emergency line. Immediately the man answered and Eric, as quietly as possible, described the situation to him, though there was no question the young man was frightened. As he spoke to Don he thought to himself, how did Hamilton find him here? How did he know about his night with Beth, unless he followed her here? It didn't matter because now, he had other problems.

He listened carefully to the instructions he received from Don Mason then turned, walking toward his friends. He began to shiver, not only from the coolness of the night, but from being so nervous and scared, anticipating a flurry of questions he didn't want to answer as well as questions of his own he would have to face. What was going to happen to him now? Would they make him leave? It was only a matter of time before he found out.

He returned to the logs and found his three friends sitting facing the lake and away from the body. He could see an entire range of emotions from their expressions as they stared at him and he knew that his next question seemed silly, but he cared about them and had to ask. "Is everyone okay?"

"Compared to the dude over there, I'm fuckin' incredible." Jeremy excitedly stated. "I mean, I'm okay as far as I'm not dead, but hell no, I'm not okay."

Eric exhaled deeply as he ignored Jay's anger, understanding that sarcasm was his way to cope with the pressures of the incident and he glanced at the other two, looking for an indication of a response. But there was none, just stunned silence and it was evident there were no words to describe how his friends felt. In spite of his desire to talk to them about what happened, he knew he could not and it was now his responsibility to keep them calm as well as keep them together because within minutes, everything would be out of their hands. He briefly glanced down at the ground before looking at Jeremy. "I know you're not okay buddy, I'm sorry about all this." He calmly replied. "I never wanted any of this to happen, especially not to you guys."

Dan stared at his friend for a moment, wondering from where he mustered the ability to keep calm in this situation. "Eric, are you all right?" He asked, unclear if his friend truly understood the gravity of what just happened.

Eric nodded. "Yeah, I'm fine other than being covered in someone else's blood." He replied. "Thanks."

Dan shook his head. "Are you sure, because you just killed a man and I know if I was in your position right now, I don't think I'd be as composed as you are." He stated.

Eric tilted his head forward and widened his eyes. "If you're asking whether or not I'm comprehending what just happened, believe me I understand." He responded and glanced toward the ground. "But acting any other way at this time wouldn't solve anything and our current problem will be under control in a couple of minutes."

"In a couple of minutes." Mike repeated. "And what are we supposed to do until then?"

Eric hesitated, preparing a response to their obvious question once he gave them the instructions. He raised his head and stared at them. " We are supposed to wait until Doctor Miles arrives and then I promise you everything will be okay."

Dan glanced at his friend, his pensive look queuing a question. "What does Doctor Miles have to do with all this?" He asked.

"I honestly can't answer that right now." Eric stated. "And it may not be fair to you, but you'll understand why I can't give you an answer a little later."

CHAPTER 18

THE TWINKLING COLORED BULBS OF the Christmas tree left lighted from the night before illuminated the family room as Matt walked down the stairs. It was the Saturday morning before Christmas and the first stirrings of life in the Collins' home became the sluggish steps of the attorney sleepily negotiating his way to the kitchen. He was tired and though this was the first day in which he could rest since the night Hamilton was killed, he woke from a restless sleep thinking about the case that, now more than ever, continuously haunted him. It should have ended with Hamilton's death on a lake shore in Pennsylvania. However, it seemed to begin there and that is what disturbed him.

He shuffled to the coffee maker and removed the glass pot, pouring some of the freshly-brewed drink into a cup that sat next to it, being thankful automatic appliances had been invented. If the rest of his life were only this easy, he thought, he could actually sit down to enjoy drinking this cup and maybe spend a day with his family. Instead, on this Saturday before Christmas, he would again go to work after taking his son to practice because Hamilton's death did nothing but complicate his life.

How easy it would have been if the gun Hamilton used that night in his attempt to kill Eric would have matched the type responsible for the shootings in Washington at the hotel. How easy it would have been if they were able to place Hamilton near the motel in Winchester or the road near Front Royal or even the ravine off of Skyline Drive. But when Doctor Miles searched the man by the lake and found his rental car keys, which then led to his hotel key and his room, any hope of Hamilton being connected to just one of those other incidents died with him when they found receipts and records that helped to trace his steps from Saddlewood in August to the night of his death in Pennsylvania. Unquestionably, Hamilton had been busy, but his business landed him in Europe during those months and he stayed there until two weeks before his death. So it became painfully clear that someone else ordered, then carried out the deaths related to Saddlewood and that someone appeared to be the unknown ninth man.

Quietly Matt walked down the hallway to the front door to retrieve the morning paper, the pressures of the day yet to begin. As he lifted the paper off the front porch, he wondered what they would report today about the events at Saddlewood and his related actions which reached worldwide exposure. It was no longer about the mystery of the killings that occurred in Northern Virginia, because all eight of the registered participants in the meetings at Une Maison de Campagne had died some way or another. Now the mystery to the press became why were they killed? What was going on in that guesthouse at Saddlewood that, if it were exposed, would warrant each guest and several employees to lose their lives? The press demanded answers while Collins, who found himself in the hot seat day after day, could not yet provide any and he realized that his plan of using the press to help solve the case had backfired. Sure he possessed a wealth of information given to him courtesy of the Italians and Senor Alberini, but that knowledge was detailed and it overwhelmed Collins' small staff as they spent hour after hour putting it all together. So as pressure increased from the press as well as from the Justice Department itself, Matt and his staff extended their hours at work, and that intensified pressure at home.

It was bad enough that Matt rarely made it home or that when he was at home, all of his time was consumed by work and none of it spent with his family or his wife. But the greatest cause of conflict between he and his wife was the fact that he carried a weapon. It was not the weapon itself that was so alarming, though his wife objected to its existence. No, it was the necessity of arming himself that generated the most conflict. The gun became a symbol of his admission to what the case now represented, an additional danger to him and a new danger to his family, a danger which produced argument after argument. Therefore, in order to keep a temporary peace between he and his wife, he agreed to a compromise, an understanding that if at any time the family became threatened, he would resign from his job and begin his own firm.

He sat at the kitchen table with the newspaper and began to read as he sipped from the cup. For a third day in a row, he did not see a scathing article concerning his investigation or any articles at all about Saddlewood. Could it be that the press finally tired of the subject? No, he thought, that surely was not the case and he set the paper down on the table as he heard footsteps coming down the stairs.

"Good morning." His wife greeted as she entered the kitchen and poured herself a mug of coffee. "You're up a little early today."

Matt smiled as he leaned back in his chair. "I know. I couldn't sleep any longer." He replied, gazing at the woman. "So how are you this morning? I hope I didn't wake you."

She took a sip from the mug and sat across from him at the table. "You didn't." Jean tersely replied. "I didn't sleep all that well last night."

Matt stared at her for a moment, knowing the reason for her restlessness, and exhaled deeply. "I thought we were done with all that." He stated.

"We may be, but it doesn't mean that it stops bothering me once you end the discussion." She strongly responded as she looked through the newspaper. "Just remember you have to take Tyler to practice this morning, because I have to drive over the campus and enter my grades for my night class then pick up my rosters for next semester."

He nodded his head. "Yeah, I remember. Just remember you have to pick him up." Matt snidely replied.

Jean sighed and shook her head, placing the paper on the table as the phone rang. "I know." She replied as she lifted up the receiver and answered, listening for a moment, then thanking the person on the other side. She replaced the receiver and turned toward her husband. "Shawn forgot part of the paper, so Jimmy is bringing it over."

Matt nodded his head, then gently grabbed her arm as he softly kissed the back of her hand. She stopped, tilted her head downward and smiled, the tension between them, though still apparent, seemingly subsiding. She walked to the counter, removing several plates from the cupboard, then moved to the refrigerator opening the door. Suddenly, the stillness of the morning erupted into a rumble of thunderous blasts, crashes and sounds that resembled rocks being thrown through the windows. Matt quickly popped up from his seat and after glancing at his wife, bolted toward the front of the house as his wife followed. He quickly scanned the living room, finding it intact other than the blown out window, then swung open the door, freezing in his steps as he stared at his car engulfed in flames sitting in the driveway. Jean stood next to him, the horror in her face preventing her from speaking until she looked to her right in the yard and screamed.

Matt quickly turned his head and spotted Jimmy Thomas sprawled face up on the lawn. He ripped open the door to the closet, quickly grabbing several coats then rushing to the teenager's side as he yelled at his wife to call nine one one and check on their children. The boy lay motionless on the grass, most of his clothing blown completely off his body, exposing the badly bleeding wounds from the glass and other pieces of the car that embedded into his skin. Matt covered the young man to keep him warm, checking the pulse in his neck to make sure he was still alive. After finding a pulse, the man leaned closer to the boy and began talking to him, hoping to get some kind of a response as the burned in the background. Tears began flowing down Matt's face as he stayed with the boy, holding his hand while telling him that help was on the way and that everything would be all right, whether Matt believed it or not.

Nearly as quickly as Matt rushed to the front yard, neighbors ran to the house offering assistance, shocked at the devastation and dismayed by the sight of the seriously injured young man on the lawn. Within seconds of the first neighbor's offer to help, Matt heard a scream from the edge of the driveway and he need not look up to know that Charlene Thomas had entered the yard. He jumped to his feet and intercepted her as she attempted to rush to her son's side, though there was nothing she could do for him. Instead Matt briefly held her, trying to comfort her as he knew he could not calm her, then he let her go to her son as he fought with his own composure.

Jean emerged from within the house, tears freely flowing from her eyes as she walked up to her husband. "Help will be here in a couple of minutes." She reported as she began to sob. "How is Jimmy?"

Matt lowered his head and tightly held his wife. "He's bad honey. He's real bad." He whispered in her ear, choking on his own tears. "How are the kids?"

"They're scared, but they don't know what happened." She replied as emergency vehicles began to pull into the driveway. "I told Tyler to keep them in the family room."

Matt gently released his wife as he watched a team of paramedics rush to Jimmy's side and begin treating the young man. The reality of the dangers of his job hit home and it may have cost a young man his life. He surveyed the area, scanning the yard, the house and the horrified neighbors who came to his family's aid. This should have never happened and he stopped there in shock as he watched firefighters battle the inferno that used to be his car and paramedics treat the broken body of his neighbor's son.

He spotted his wife at the edge of the lawn, helping a sobbing Charlene Thomas into a car as a helicopter landed and the paramedics hurriedly loaded Jimmy onto the aircraft. He walked over to her, pulling her aside and hugging her as he spoke into her ear. "I want you to pack the kids and yourself up and go to your parent's. Ask your father if his offer to give us the property in Charlotte is still good and if it is, buy it from him as soon as you get there. Then get him to find us a builder, because as soon as this case ends, I'm resigning."

Jean softly broke her hold of her husband and stared into his eyes. "I'm sorry." She said as tears rolled down her cheek. "And not because..."

Matt interrupted her by placing his finger on her lips. "You don't need to explain." He softly replied. "I know." And he kissed her.

After the last emergency crew left the Collins' home and Matt answered the final question from the ATF investigator, he walked around his house not only surveying the damage, but also hunting for clues of his own. The home had now become a crime scene related to Saddlewood and his personal involvement aside, his professional duty required him to conduct an investigation. But for once, he did not have to ask any questions, he did not have to search for answers nor did he need to find time to visit the crime scene. It was all in front of him for his own disposal at any time and that angered him.

He walked inside and checked on his terrified family. By now, telephone calls from concerned friends and family poured into the house interrupting any attempt to quickly pack. As Jean placed the phone down on the table, she unplugged it then glanced at her husband. "I don't feel like talking to anyone right now." She mournfully stated.

Matt nodded slightly. "Neither do I." He dejectedly replied as he leaned against the wall. "Did you call your parents?"

She wiped the few remaining tears from her face. "They wanted to fly up here today." She replied as a forced smile formed across her face. "I convinced them to stay there because I was leaving as soon as we get some things packed. But Matt, I want to stop by the hospital first."

"So do I." Matt stated. "First though, let's get you packed and loaded in your vehicle, because I want you leaving here today."

She closed up the suitcase and looked at him, the concern in her face showing an additional fear. "What about my car?" She asked.

Matt nodded, understanding her fear considering the events that just occurred. "I had it thoroughly checked and it's perfectly safe." He calmly answered.

She slowly nodded then moved toward her husband, holding him tightly. He wrapped his arms around her as he gently kissed her on the side of the head. Through all of the chaos of the morning, she held her strength when she could have completely fallen apart. Matt felt lucky, not just for the fact that he married her, but for the fact that she stayed standing beside him through all of the difficulties associated with this case when she could have walked away. It was a test of the resiliency of their marriage and he understood that the foundation it was built upon was as strong as ever.

The Collins family rushed through the emergency room entrance of the hospital, walking to the nurse's desk for information where they were directed to the surgical waiting room. Charlene turned and sadly smiled, hugging the woman as she approached. Again the door to the waiting room opened, the Bostic and remainder of the Lynch family entering, and Matt stepped aside as Dan Bostic eased next to him.

"How is he?" Dan softly asked.

Matt shook his head. "I haven't actually asked yet." He somberly replied. "I'm letting Jean ask the questions. I uh, don't really know what to say to anyone right now."

Dan moved his head closer to Matt's ear. "You're not responsible for this." He said.

Matt tilted his head and shrugged. "Maybe not directly." He stated. "But it happened in my front yard and ..." He paused as he inhaled sharply, then slowly exhaled in an attempt to compose himself. "The sight of that kid will be something I'll never get out of my mind." He peered toward the ceiling as tears swelled in his eyes and he attempted to control his escaping emotions. "Then, as I knelt next to him telling him what a good kid he was and how proud I was to know him, I slowly realized that had this been an hour later, Tyler and I would have gotten in the car."

Bostic gently tugged on Matt's arm and led him out of the room. "Maybe you should take some time off." Dan suggested. "Just until you get yourself together and take care of your family."

Matt shook his head in disagreement. "That won't be necessary, I'm fine." He strongly replied. "And as far as Jean and the kids, well they're moving down to Charlotte with her parents and as soon as this case if over, I'm resigning and moving down with them. So taking some time off will only delay things, but thank you all the same."

Bostic stared at him for a moment, shocked by the announcement, and quickly glanced toward the floor before returning his attention to the man. "I understand, but I really do wish you would reconsider and I am very sure you will receive the same reaction form the Attorney General." He stated.

Matt smiled with the statement. "I appreciate that and will take it under consideration." He replied.

Bostic nodded, then wrinkled his eyebrows. "Where's Ray?" He asked. "I didn't see him in the waiting room."

Matt opened his hands and shook his head. "I don't know. Charlene told me he had been spending a lot of time out of town lately. He may not even know yet." He replied as he opened the door to the waiting room and walked inside.

Charlene Thomas sat in a chair by the door leading into the operating rooms while a doctor spoke with her, the other three women sitting close by for support and Matt could see from the expression on their face that the news was far from encouraging. As the doctor left the waiting room, Jean stood and walked to her husband.

"You don't have to say anything, I could tell from your faces." Matt softly stated.

"It's not good." Jean confirmed. "But they stopped the internal bleeding for right now and he's a strong boy, so there's at least a chance."

Matt glanced past his wife, quickly scanning the room then looked at her. "How much of a chance?" He softly asked.

Jean grabbed his hand. "Only about thirty percent in his favor at best." She reported, holding him as support knowing how personally he had taken this case with Eric first and now Jimmy. And with Greg as part of them, she knew how much Matt enjoyed watching the three boys grow up together, their strong friendship setting an example on how friendships should be, and she not only wondered if the three boys could survive this disaster, but also if her husband could. Sure he was a strong man, but one of the qualities that attracted her to him was his compassion for people, especially children who were disadvantaged or in trouble and that, she believed, is what made him such an exceptional father. And she held him tightly, more for his fears than her own.

Suddenly, the door swung open and Ray Thomas bolted inside the room, running to his wife who began to sob with the sight of him. He held her tightly, tears flowing down his face as she explained to him the extent of their son's injuries. Matt watched them, the sorrow and pain he felt from the pit in his stomach becoming stronger and more unbearable with each moment that passed. It did not matter anymore what Dan Bostic had told him, he felt responsible for the Thomas' pain and he wished he could do something to relieve them from it, yet he knew he could not.

He walked over to Ray, an uneasiness he never felt before when around the man taking hold, and he sharply inhaled as he prepared to speak. "Ray, if there's anything we can do..."

Ray turned, the look on his face not expressing grief or concern, but that of anger. "You know Matt, Jimmy and I spent the past couple of years fighting with each other because I believed he was constantly heading for disaster. And I regret each day we were at odds as well as the fact that I prepared myself to one day receive this exact call. However, I expected to get this call for a far different reason, either because he got into an accident or did some other stupid thing. Never could I imagine you being responsible for that call."

"Ray!" Charlene yelled, her displeasure with her husband's words clearly evident with her tone and expression.

"No Charlene, let me finish." Ray angrily insisted and he returned his attention to his stunned neighbor. "All you had to do was stop this stupid investigation that should have ended a couple of weeks ago anyway and none of this would have happened. But you kept mouthing off in the newspaper and on television that you would not quit until you solved what nobody seems to care about anymore. Now someone obviously took exception to your arrogance and it could very well have cost my son his life. I hope the hell you can live with that, because I'm having a little difficulty with it myself." He yelled.

Matt exhaled sharply, glaring at the man as total silence filled the room. There was nothing for him to say and though everyone in the room sat staring at the attorney waiting for some kind of response, he said nothing, shaking his head as he glanced down at the floor. Instead, he quietly stepped away from Ray Thomas, turned and walked out of the waiting room.

Jean grabbed their three children and followed him out of the room, trying to catch up with him as he walked down the hallway. "Matt!" She called, drawing even with him until she pulled on his arm and stopped him. "Matt, he didn't mean any of that. He's hurting and you were convenient to lash out at."

Matt gazed at her, pressing his lips together as he thought. Slowly he began to shake his head, then squinted as he looked into her eyes. "No Jean, he meant every word of that." He replied, the stoic tone of his voice cluing his wife that instead of being upset, he was angry and she thought she understood why.

She grabbed his arm and looked into his eyes. "Okay, maybe he did mean every word. Just let it go." She requested.

Matt arrogantly smiled. "I already have." He said as he wrapped his arm around his older son and held the boy close to him. "In fact, I'm still going to work. What I want you to do now is take the kids and leave for Charlotte. Call me a couple of times along the way on my cell phone, then when you get to your parents, call me at home." He ordered, then he kissed his wife and three kids before he walked down the hallway and left the hospital.

CHAPTER 19

THE HOUSE WAS TOO QUIET and maybe that was the problem, there was just not enough noise, not that noise was something he needed in order to get some sleep. No, most of the time he liked the quiet, the calmness he had not been used to for such a long time, and for all the days he thought to himself how great it would be if he could just have some quiet, he now wished he would have never thought about it because this kind of quiet meant loneliness, and he never wanted that.

Matt rolled over in his bed one last time before he reached for the lamp on the nightstand and turned on the light. Slowly he slid out from under the covers and sat on the side of the bed, rubbing his face as he glanced at the clock. It was three o'clock in the morning and he remained wide awake. The cause of his insomnia was more than the house being too quiet from his family leaving. No, that became only part of the problem. Instead, something lingered on his mind and that prevented him from sleeping, yet what agitated him remained unidentified. Was it something he read or did he hear it? Was it something that just didn't make sense, or was it a piece of information he could fit into his investigation? And for days upon days he scoured his memory trying to recall where he was when it crossed his mind.

Matt slid on a pair of sweat pants and walked downstairs to his den, remembering in his mind the different aspects of the investigation. Whatever the bit of information, he knew that it was far from obvious and he most likely failed to recognize its importance when he read it or heard it, if in fact it was important at all. It could have been just a loose end that he forgot to tie up. But what if it wasn't? What if it was a fact that would put an end to some of his speculations? Therefore because of this last possibility, he knew that this empty thought which irritated him so much had to be important, so he continued his search.

He walked downstairs to the den, sat behind the desk and opened the box that contained his copy of all of the information concerning Saddlewood that his staff collected. It was a vast amount of paper and he wondered how many details, if any, might have been missed in the race to get through it all. Inside the box were ten bulging files, one each for the eight known guests of Saddlewood, one filled with intelligence covering TNR and the final thinner folder for the unknown ninth man. Attached to each folder in a protective plastic cover was a summary of the file and a newspaper clipping with the newspaper article reporting the date and circumstances of that guest's death. Matt removed one of the summaries with the clipping and shook his head, smiling with a snicker to himself as to the reason for including the article. He placed the summary and the article to the side and peered further into the box. In addition to the folders were several computer disks that his staff prepared, one of which was marked as a cross-referencing of each guest with the movements of the others. He lifted the disks out of the box and flipped on the switch to his computer, curious to their contents. Inserting the first disk into the slot, he waited for the information to appear on his screen

As he scanned the file index, he began to think. Why exactly were he and his staff having so much difficulty with this case? They received various levels of cooperation from every agency from which they asked assistance. They received intelligence from unexpected sources. They had witnesses. But participants in whatever was being planned were eliminated one by one until there remained a single person still alive left from the meetings at Saddlewood, and Matt didn't know who he was.

Again, the subject of the meetings were in question, as the press emphasized in many articles. What could have been so secretive that the price to prevent exposure was death? In addition, who determined that penalty? If he could answer the first of the questions, Matt thought, he might be able to figure out the rest. Deciding as he opened the first file on the list that he would concentrate on discovering the subject matter being discusses in the villa, he reviewed the facts from the beginning of this case.

Eric overheard a meeting in the villa's pool house that he was sure outlined plans to assassinate the President of the United States and Matt thought about that statement. There were two significant parts to it, an assassination and the President of the United States. Yet no security agency in the country could confirm any threat against the President and there had been no attempt on his life. So logically there existed a flaw in Eric's statement, though the entire statement could not possibly be in error. So what was in error, the assassination attempt or the target? With the collection of people attending the meetings, all foreign intelligence agents, it only made sense that the target was in error. So then, who was the target?

Matt reviewed the backgrounds of the eight identified men of Saddlewood and realized that there was not an American among them. The group consisted of one German, one Russian, one Frenchman, one Brit, one Saudi, one Indonesian, one Bosnian and one Pakistani. It was an odd combination of people, he thought, and it piqued his curiosity as to what their connection was to each other, let alone this case. What did these men all have in common? What brought them to the United Nations Embassy at Saddlewood?

For a moment, he leaned back into this chair staring into the screen, the stillness within the house breaking his concentration and he realized that he wanted to answer at least one of his questions before he drove to the airport for his flight to Charlotte on Christmas Eve. He pulled himself up from his chair, sliding it away from him as he walked to the stereo where he pushed the button to turn it on. As Christmas music played softly in the background, he exited the room, continuing into the kitchen to make as small pot of coffee and rummage through the refrigerator for something to eat while he thought about the questions. Finding a whole grain bagel and cream cheese, then spreading the soft white cheese on the dark brown bread, he took a bite, then watched as the glass pot slowly filled with the golden brown liquid, but didn't really see it. Instead, he remained deep in thought about the eight men. Where, other than at the villa, did they cross paths or at least visit a common location?

He poured himself a cup of coffee, carrying it and the remaining half of bagel into the den, returning to his seat. Quickly, he removed the disk from the drive, inserted the one marked cross-reference and began scanning the file that was built with information given to him by Senor Alberini. It was obvious from the detail of the intelligence, that the Italians were far more interested in the meetings at Saddlewood than any other country, tracking the eight agents before Eric's incident even occurred. Yet they didn't seem to be involved. So if that was the case, why were they so interested? What did the Italians know that they kept from him? And he sat for a minute wondering, if Senor Alberini and Ambassador Dettore went so far as to give him information, why then would they hold things back, unless they were restricted for some reason from giving him everything. Maybe they gave him enough to put it all together, releasing them from some violation of an agreement, and he began to concentrate on the files appearing on the screen in front of him.

He continued closely studying each file and disk from the box when he discovered a program hidden inside a sub file, becoming curious as to why it was there. Several times, he attempted to run the program but failed, entering some wrong code until on his forth attempt, it opened for no apparent reason. He peered up to the screen, watching a map of Europe and the Middle East materialize before him and then a series of letters, A through H, appearing next to the dots marking the cities. It wasn't hard to figure out, each letter represented one of the guests and Matt placed the cursor over one of the dots then pressed the button on his mouse. Immediately, a map of the country enlarged and dates appeared next to the letters. There was no question that the dates represented a visit to that particular city by that guest. It worked like a puzzle, leaving the person reading the map with the responsibility of figuring out what letter represented which guest.

Knowing the nationalities of each of the guests, Matt carefully examined the maps of each country and noted the letter which appeared on that map the most, figuring the agent from that country would visit it the most. It was the correct path to take, yet he noticed one strange detail on one of the maps, one of the countries hosted each of the guests equally, yet never at the same time. They weren't conducting a meeting and he noticed that each date was followed by a trip to the United States. Could it be that they were planning the assassination of that country's president? Was that what Eric heard when he reported the one man saying that they would have to conduct an assassination and he thought they were referring to the President of the United States? It was a possibility. No, in fact it actually made sense, so much so that it explained why these same agents died after Eric overheard part of the discussion. It explained why Aaron Butler was shot and why Stephen Kearney's Porsche had a remote control device controlling it, forcing him to run into a tree at over eighty miles an hour. It explained why James Hamilton searched for Eric and tried to kill him and why the ninth man still would.

He sat back in his chair and reviewed the wording of the information on his screen. Again the oddity caught his eye and he studied it a little longer, looking for some clue to pop out at him to help decipher this riddle. Why did the person creating this file always refer to Saddlewood only as the United Nations Consulate and each of the men as the Russian member or the British member and not by name? Without moving, he stared into the screen looking at the words that bothered him so much. What was the connection? He wrinkled the skin of his forehead as he thought, suddenly widening his eyes as an idea crossed his mind.

Quickly he exited the program and the disk, then typed into his keyboard to log onto the internet. This could be the first major piece of the puzzle if his hunch were correct and he could feel a twinge of excitement rush through him as he scanned through the United Nations' website searching for information. When he found the section concerning the United Nations Counsel on Human Rights, he stopped, clicked the button and quickly read. All eight countries the agents represented were listed as members of the counsel. Matt knew that in no way was it a coincidence. Was the United Nations responsible for running a covert operation to remove a head of state? Could it be possible that the very same organization that promoted world peace was planning an assassination? If this were true, it could never become public without the possibility of triggering a war or the end of the United Nations and maybe that is what necessitated the killings.

The ninth man knowing Eric was the most puzzling aspect of the entire case and Matt sat in the chair staring at the monitor as questions rambled through his mind. Who could Eric know that would have any ties to this kind of operation? Obviously he wouldn't know the man's profession, especially with the man involved in something like this, so where did Eric know him from?

Matt turned away from the computer and again looked into the box, removing each of the files of the guests of the villa. Opening the plastic covers of each folder, he took out the summaries and the newspaper clippings then began to read. Though Mueller's summary and news release were very similar, the news release listed his death as suspicious and not a murder despite the fact that he was electrocuted in a bathtub with no signs of an electrical device anywhere near him. Of course it was suspicious, Matt thought to himself, there was no question it was a murder.

As he shook his head replacing the first clipping into the packet, he lifted a second folder and removed the summary. He scanned the report then carefully read the newspaper clipping, not knowing exactly what he was looking for, if he was looking for something specific. If anything, it served as a good way to review the case and the players in it. What about the eight men from Saddlewood were the same and what about them were different?

Matt continued the process with the remaining six folders, but when he came to the last one, Hamilton's, and removed the summary form the packet, he could find no newspaper clipping and he thought it odd that Dan Bostic would have placed an article in each of the first seven folders but not in the last one. He opened the folder and searched inside. Maybe in his haste, Bostic forgot to insert the clipping into the packet and it was placed in the folder by mistake. But when no clipping surfaced from within the folder, Matt wanted to know why. He picked up the telephone, called Bostic and asked him to meet him at the house. Not only did he want to ask him a few questions, but he could share with him his discovery and get a little assistance. Then, maybe he could spend Christmas in Charlotte with his family and not have so much on his mind.

Bostic entered the house and Matt led him to the folder-ridden den where the endless hours of work seemed to have exploded into mounds of paper. "You've been kind of busy." Bostic said as he stepped over a box then sat in a chair by the desk.

Matt nodded his head and smiled. "And I don't really want to be this busy because I'm supposed to catch a flight to Charlotte tonight."

"Then take the holiday off." Bostic replied as he shrugged his shoulders. "You need to spend this time with them. Everything will still be here when you get back."

Matt grinned. "I know that, but I would like to have something resolved so I can actually enjoy the holiday." He stated, moving to his desk and sitting in the chair. "I've already ruined Thanksgiving for the family because of this case. I don't want to be responsible for ruining Christmas too."

Bostic grabbed a stack of papers and brought them closer to him. "So what do you need me to do?" He asked as he began to read.

Matt lifted a folder from the edge of the desk, holding it up beside him. "Answer a question for me." He replied. "You included a newspaper clipping in every pouch with the summary with the exception of Hamilton's folder. Why? Did you just forget to put in inside?"

Bostic shook his head. "No, I didn't forget. There never was a news article reporting Hamilton's death." He answered. "You told me because of the circumstances surrounding his death you did not want it publicly released. Did you change your mind?"

Matt stared at his friend for a moment while he thought, before he reclined in his chair, quickly glanced at the ceiling then gestured as he spoke. "So did we ever release any information about his death at any time?" He asked.

Bostic shook his head and shrugged. "No." He replied. "We thought about reporting that he had died, but decided to keep the information as to the date or cause of his death a secret. As far as the world knows, Hamilton's whereabouts are still a mystery."

"Except that it isn't." Matt began as he squinted his eyes, staring down at the floor beyond his associate. "So therefore the only people who should know that Hamilton is dead would be the few people associated with his death." He slowly stated. "And you're sure that nothing ever slipped out?"

"I know it didn't." Bostic insisted.

Matt leaned forward onto his desk, resting his elbows on the top and burying his head in his cupped hands, the slight movement of his head disclosing his discomfort. There was no way, he thought, no way that he could be correct and for a moment, he prayed that he wasn't. But what had bothered him for days finally resurfaced from his memory and he realized that what he thought was the only way it could be.

CHAPTER 20

IT WAS A COLD AND barren February morning, the kind of morning where the wind, no matter how softly it blows, drives a frozen twinge through the thickest of clothing and the bright sunlight fools the senses into thinking that it is warmer than it really is. Yet, Matt chose to meet outdoors and he ascended the marble steps of the Jefferson Memorial by himself, hoping the man would show. He walked into the Rotunda and gazed at the inside. This building, more than any other, was his favorite in Washington. The beauty of the circular structure that from one side looked across the Tidal Basin toward the Washington Monument and on the other towered over the southern end of the park on the banks of the Potomac, sent chills through his spine every time he walked inside. For whatever reason, he gained an inner strength from this building, a strength from what it represented and he slowly strolled through the emptiness of the structure waiting for the man to show.

From his gut, Matt felt he would not be meeting today the mystery man who attended the meetings at Saddlewood, the man he figured engineered the elimination of every possible witness except one and the man he figured tried to eliminate him. There would be no way the man would meet with him face to face and it angered Matt that there was nothing he could do about bringing the man to justice for the killing of innocent people.

He walked to the edge of the steps and peered out over the Tidal Basin. There was a peacefulness to the day, interrupted only by the occasional whine of engines from jets departing Reagan National Airport or from a horn blowing in the distance from one of the many freeways and he watched as a lone figure strolled up the walkway, then climbed the steps toward him.

"He didn't show, did he?" Bostic asked as he reached the top step and stood next to the man.

Matt slowly shook his head. "No and I didn't really expect him to." He impassively stated. "I figured that when I contacted him from Charlotte last month and we set up this meeting, he concluded that I finally put it all together and decided it was time for him to leave town."

Bostic scanned the surroundings, then turned to look out toward the water. "But he left his family here."

Matt raised his eyebrows as he turned his head to make eye contact. "I've seen people leave their families for far less." He replied. "But in this case, I don't think he was given much of a choice."

Bostic paused as he considered Matt's statement. "So what do you plan to do?" He inquired.

Matt stepped down, beginning his descent toward the walkway, as Bostic followed. "I informed the people keeping Eric and they have been preparing him, as well as taking the necessary precautions." He reported. "It's a different ball game for us now, but for Eric it is something even we could have never imagined."

As the two reached the walkway along the basin, Bostic hesitated while he thought, then tilted his head toward Collins and responded. "So where do you think he went?" He asked.

Collins peered across the Potomac River as a jet took off in the distance and it seemed clear to him what the man would do next. "He's got one loose end that he needs to clean up." Matt replied. "I think he's going to look for Eric."

Bostic stared at him, an astounded expression forming upon his face. "Why? He has to know by now that Eric couldn't identify him or we would have picked him up months ago." He stated. "And even if Eric recognized the voice, he couldn't identify it as his, so why go after the boy?"

Matt squinted his eyes in the sunlight, pausing before he answered. "Apparently there is still something Eric can connect him to and I don't think that even matters anymore. It's now a matter of survival." He began to explain. "Let's assume that after Eric ran from the pool house, the men tore it apart and found the tape recorder. At that time, they knew he taped the meeting and took the tape with him, therefore the content of the meetings had been exposed and its secrecy compromised. So under the set rules that clandestine operations function, the sterilization process begins and one by one, the people who could expose the players are eliminated, all of them except for Eric that is. They can't find him and properly assume he's being protected by whatever authority he ran to. Because he hasn't been found, the people actually running the operation have no choice but to begin getting rid of everyone involved with it, until either Eric is found and eliminated or the others are. And now, it's come down to two people on opposite sides and the death of either one of them ends it all."

Bostic stood speechless in the small parking lot as everything he just heard fit perfectly and he turned to Collins. "Does Eric know this?" He asked.

Matt nodded his head. "I think he knew it before. Otherwise, there would have been no e-mail to Italy." He stated.

Bostic glanced toward the ground, then returned his attention to the man. "You may be right." He said, pausing for a moment. "So, what do we do now, go to the Thomas home?"

Matt nodded his head, knowing the difficulty facing him, a difficulty that transcended his professional responsibilities into his personal life. There was a family who faced further damage if the details of the investigation are disclosed and that is what Matt wanted to guard against. He refused to contribute to the family's destruction.

For a moment, he thought about going alone because of the sensitivity of it all, but after careful consideration, there was no question he wanted Bostic there with him. After all, Dan was a friend of the family as well and an integral part of the investigation. He prepared all the press releases and was present when Ray Thomas erred in his speech at the hospital, letting it slip that entire case should have been closed three weeks earlier. It was that speech that had taken residence so covertly in Matt's memory, but hid in its deep recesses. Hamilton's death had never been detailed, there was no mention of a date, a location or cause. Yet Thomas knew with Hamilton's death, the case could have closed and it could have closed three weeks prior to Matt's car exploding in his driveway. So when it all finally registered in Matt's mind, he was left with no choice but to investigate the Thomas family, people he had known and liked for years and having Bostic there with him as he asked questions would not only make sense, but also would be a comfort.

As they drove toward the Thomas home, Matt thought to himself how well Ray Thomas covered his tracks and how connecting him with Hamilton would still prove to be difficult. Yet the key in doing so rested within Thomas's personality. He loved his family, not something unusual by any means, but he required them to live by certain standards and Jimmy rebelled from most of them. Ray Thomas engaged in a continuous struggle with his eldest son and it was a situation that failed to be as hidden as the family wished it to be. In fact, the physical confrontations between Ray and his son became somewhat well-know within a small circle of people. So because of his demand for his son to conform to his wishes, Ray Thomas monitored the boy's actions not only from home, but when the man stayed out of town and probably at Saddlewood. It was that action that seemed to connect Thomas with the people at Saddlewood. The man's cellular phone records indicated his presence in the area during many of the meeting times, all of which supported the theory of his involvement as a major player in the operation, but it wasn't enough by itself. There was something that undoubtedly connected him to Saddlewood and Matt wondered if his dominance over his son actually caused his own downfall? Did something happen between Jimmy and his father the night that Eric recorded the meeting that ended up on the tape and would have given Ray away? It would make sense and account for Ray's interest in finding the boy.

CharleneThomas smiled as she opened the door to let him in. It was a genuine smile, not forced or purposely feigned to put on a front and she seemed to be at peace with herself despite the fact that her family had literally been blown apart. Matt walked inside, uncomfortable with the fact he could be the person responsible for causing the family additional pain, and he quickly thought how he could avoid doing it.

"Matt, Dan I'm very happy the two of you stopped by." Charlene stated. "How are Jean and the kids, Matt?"

Collins feigned a smiled as the two men walked into a sitting room off of the entrance hall. "They're just fine, thank you Charlene." He replied. "How are you?"

With a motion of her hand, she invited them to sit as she eased herself into a wing chair. "I'm doing well." She replied, the positive tone of her voice showing the woman's inner strength. "So, what can I help you two with? You look as if you are here on business and not a social call."

Matt hesitated, then responded. "Well, I've wanted to speak to Ray for the past couple of days, but have not been able to reach him." He stated. "Is he out of town?"

The smile on her face faded as her head sunk slightly forward. "I don't know where he is Matt. Ray and I separated a little after Jimmy's accident. He just couldn't handle what happened to Jimmy." She softly said. "I think in some way he felt responsible."

Collins glanced at Bostic then slowly returned his attention to the woman. "I'm very sorry Charlene. I didn't know." He replied. "Do you keep in contact with him at all?"

She slowly shook her head. "No. I haven't heard from him in about a month when we filed for a divorce." She answered, glancing past the men as she paused for a moment collecting her thoughts. "Is there something you came to tell him?"

Matt sat in his seat, silent as he thought while Bostic and Charlene Thomas stared at him. Was there even a purpose in telling her? Was there a way to spare her and the rest of the family the pain of knowing that their husband and father caused so much destruction to other people as well as to themselves? He glanced at Bostic, then shook his head. "No, I just wanted to see how everyone was doing." He answered, standing from his seat and hinting Bostic to follow toward the door. "I know it's been rough so if you need anything, please don't hesitate to call me. I'll talk to Ray some other time." He stated and he headed for the door.

Again, Charlene smiled. "Thank you very much, I really do appreciate it." She replied as the two men exited the house. "And if I do hear form Ray, I will tell him you would like to speak with him. I am sure he would appreciate hearing from you."

Matt smiled and nodded his head in acknowledgement, then turned to walk across the street while Bostic followed.

"That was good of you, but I think you should have told her." Dan began as the two entered Matt's driveway. "All you did was delay the inevitable pain of finding out the facts about her husband when you release the information at a press conference you know will eventually have to conduct? Had you told her, she could have had time to prepare."

Matt stopped in front of his door and turned toward the man. "Who said I have to release that information?" He replied. "What exactly can we connect Ray to, so far as the killings are concerned?"

Bostic glanced past the man before returning his attention to Collins. "So you don't think he was at all responsible for at least the deaths of the workers?" He heatedly inquired.

Matt shook his head. "No, I think he was entirely responsible for them." He strongly replied. "But, I don't have actual proof so what good would it do now to report it? We have an out for that. And remember this, when he found out about Hamilton's death, Ray knew he became a marked man because he knew Hamilton located Eric, yet failed to take him out. Now he possesses only one chance to save himself, and that is to find Eric before someone finds him. And you know someone is going to get to him before he gets to Eric."

Bostic stared at the man, knowing he was correct and it pained him to realize that officially this case would remain unsolved. There would be no arrests, no trials and certainly no press conferences aside from the one announcing Matt's resignation, sacrificing his career for whatever good was left. Now, it would be the responsibility of the United Nations to explain what occurred in Saddlewood, though they would in no way take responsibility for the event. No, they could never admit to planning an assassination of anyone and instead would blame some radical group who leased the villa under false pretenses. They would provide counterfeited supporting documents and announce administrative changes to ensure the incident would never be repeated, all in the effort to dupe the public. It would work, brilliantly taking the United Nations and the countries that participated in the action off the hook for any contribution to such a plan. But a select few knew the truth and they weren't talking about it. For most of them, the case was over.

CHAPTER 21

THE WARM BREEZE OF THE early afternoon feathered through his hair as he sat with his back to the tower, staring off into the distant land below him. He had been here for what seemed to be a lifetime, but what amounted to only seven difficult months and he thought about all that had happened to him in this year since his last birthday, knowing where it all went wrong. It was useless to dwell upon it now, senseless to think about anything in the past because the past was just a faded memory, even though the past was all he could think about.

He had been torn away from his life not once, but now twice and he wondered if he would ever live a life that even resembled what he had planned for himself, because this surely failed to fit any plan he constructed. Yet, he knew that his actions were solely responsible for his life now and what it transformed into these past few months. He could have gone through life easily as Eric Mason and actually began to enjoy himself in it. But instead, that identity died the night that he killed Hamilton and the conception of yet a new identity arose.

His life as Eric Mason ended shortly after Don Mason and Doctor Miles rescued him and his three friends that night along the lake. There was no warning, no closure and no consideration to the possibility that Eric could not handle moving again, but then that was not the greatest worry Matt Collins dealt with that night. His interest lay solely in Eric's protection as he knew that if Hamilton found the boy, there were others just as close. So instead of taking the risk, he contacted the only people he knew he could trust and the identity of Eric Hunter was conceived.

Still, the night of Hamilton's death remained horribly lodged in Eric's mind, not for the terror he experienced when his friends' lives were one shot away from ending, but for the swiftness in which he lost everything for a second time and that is what finally broke him. In less than an hour from when he was returned to the Mason home, he was whisked away onto an awaiting jet at Latrobe Airport. There were no pleasant good-byes, no explanations or discussions about what would happen next as a dozen or so Federal Agents closely monitored his every move while they guarded Danny, Jay and Mike as if the boys had just committed a series of heinous crimes. He hated that his last memory of his friends was them sitting handcuffed on the couch in the Mason living room and it angered him that it all happened that way.

Now he sat with his back to the tower on the mountainside, the walls which once protected the ancient community from invading hordes now protecting him. This tower was his favorite place to sit and ponder all of the issues that his life forced him to face when he first arrived here, but today it served as a refuge from his fears and anxieties. He hurt more on this day than he ever had in his life, so much that even the comfort of the old stone tower or the picturesque surroundings could not make things better for him. Still, he held on to the hope that he was one step closer to returning home someday, a fact that came to light with the latest news even though the latest news was what triggered his sorrow and he continued to sit, staring down onto the land below.

"It is beautiful, isn't it." Maria said as she sat down next to him, placing her arm around his shoulder.

Eric nodded his head as he looked at her, the glimmer in his eyes caused by the yet unfallen tears that had collected on the sides. "I was just sitting here thinking about how much Jimmy would have liked seeing this place." He answered, he eyes swelling slightly as a tear escaped down his cheek that he caught with a swipe of his forearm.

Maria stood and pulled Eric up with her. "Maybe he's looking down on us right now, seeing my country with us, happy that you are well on your birthday." She said, holding onto his hand as they strolled around the tower and toward the winding cobble-stoned streets of the city.

"Yeah," He smiled. "That would be really nice if he was, but it doesn't make this any easier even if it were true."

"I know it doesn't." Maria replied. "I don't believe that there is anything I could do or say that would make this easier on you, though I wish there was."

There was no answer though Eric's silence served as one. She was right, nothing existed that she could say to him that would allow him to feel better and he thought to himself how he also wished there was. He just couldn't grasp the madness of it all. Ray killing Jimmy, whether accidental or not, would have never crossed Eric's mind as a possibility even though he witnessed Ray's physical battles with his friend on several previous occasions. And maybe that was the key to understanding it all, the fist fights and Ray's continuous treatment of Jimmy for as long as Eric could remember. It bordered abusive, all the while Jimmy remaining a strong and loyal friend, one who showed his compassion and love for his friends without regard for himself. He would have done anything for Eric and Eric for him. Yet as he thought about how he wished he could have said good-bye to Jimmy that one last time, it occurred to him that Ray saw that love and loyalty as a weakness and Ray Thomas never tolerated weakness, unless he could use it against someone. So maybe Jimmy's death was no accident. Maybe it was meant to bring Eric home one final time.

Eric stopped in the middle of the street and turned to Maria. "So do you really think he's going to try to find me?" He asked, his mood no longer reflecting a sullen and saddened young man, but that of a young man with a rekindled anger.

Maria squeezed his hand tighter. "You are safe here." She answered. "He will never find you in San Marino."

Eric squinted his eyes in the bright sunlight as a grin formed across his face. "That's kind of unfortunate." He answered. "I want him to find me."

"Why?" She asked, the puzzled expression on her face begging him for an answer.

Eric smiled at her. "Because we have something to settle and I'm not going to rest until we settle it." He answered as he turned, held her hand and disappeared down the street.

Printed in the United States
62101LVS00005B/55-60